FIRE AND DESIRE

BRENDA JACKSON

FIRE AND DESIRE

ARABESQUE®

Recycling programs
for this product may
not exist in your area.

FIRE AND DESIRE

An Arabesque novel published by Kimani Press/January 2009

First published by BET Publications, LLC in 1999.

ISBN-13: 978-0-373-83054-1
ISBN-10:   0-373-83054-8

© 1999 by Brenda Streater Jackson

www.kimanipress.com

Printed in U.S.A.

This book is dedicated to the memory
of my baby sister,

LISA L. HAWK

January 14, 1967–October 8, 1998

Thanks for all those special moments
that I will cherish forever.

Acknowledgments

To my husband, Gerald Jackson, Sr.
You are my hero.

To my family and friends. Thanks for all
the special things that you do.

To Brenda Arnette Simmons. Thanks. Once again
your helpful feedback on the finished product
kept me on track.

Thanks to my coworkers, who made
my extended business trips to Minnesota
and Illinois such enjoyable ones. And yes...
they are finally out of the jungle.

To Raymond and Marsher Boyd, parents of the real
Trevor Maurice. Thanks for being special people.

To Fabio Fasanelli. Thanks for sharing information
with me about your homeland of Brazil.

And most importantly, thanks to my
Heavenly Father, who gave me the gift of writing.

THE MADARIS FAMILY AND FRIENDS SERIES

Dear Reader,

I love writing family sagas, and I am so happy that Harlequin is reissuing my very first family series, the Madaris family. It's been twelve years and fifty books since I first introduced the Madaris clan, and in that time this special family—along with their friends—have won their way into readers' hearts. I am ecstatic to be able to share these award-winning stories with everyone all over again—especially those who have never met this family—up close and personal—in this special-edition collectors' series.

I never dreamed when I penned my first novel, *Tonight and Forever,* and introduced the Madaris family, that I was taking readers on a journey where heartfelt romance, sizzling passion and true love awaited them at every turn. I had no idea that the Madarises and their friends would become characters that readers would come to know and care so much about. I invite you to relax, unwind and see what all the hoopla is about. Let Justin, Dex, Clayton, Uncle Jake and their many friends transport you with love stories that are so passionate and sizzling they will take your breath away. There is nothing better than falling in love with these Madaris men and their many friends.

For a complete list of all the books in this series, as well as the dates they will be available in a bookstore near you, please visit my Web site at www.brendajackson.net.

If you would like to receive my monthly newsletter, please visit and sign up at www.brendajackson.net/page/newsletter.htm.

I also invite you to drop me an e-mail at WriterBJackson@aol.com. I love hearing from my readers.

All the best,

Brenda Jackson

THE MADARIS FAMILY

Milton Madaris, Sr. and Felicia Laverne Lee Madaris

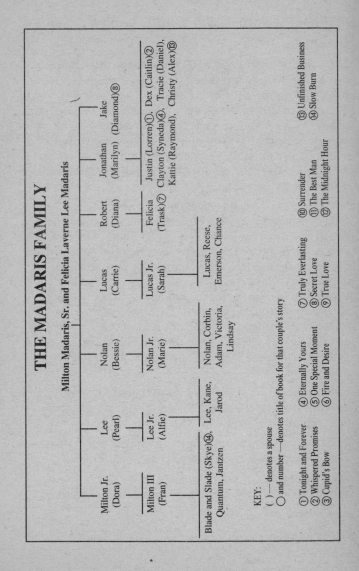

KEY:

( ) — denotes a spouse

◯ and number —denotes title of book for that couple's story

① Tonight and Forever	④ One Special Moment	⑦ Truly Everlasting	⑩ Surrender	⑬ Unfinished Business
② Whispered Promises	⑤ One Special Moment	⑧ Secret Love	⑪ The Best Man	⑭ Slow Burn
③ Cupid's Bow	⑥ Fire and Desire	⑨ True Love	⑫ The Midnight Hour	

THE MADARIS FRIENDS

Angelique Hamilton Chenault

Kyle Garwood (Kimara) ③

Sterling Hamilton (Colby) ⑤,
Nicholas Chenault (Shayla) ⑨

Maurice and Stella Grant

Trevor (Corinthians) ⑥,
Regina (Mitch) ⑪

Drake Warren
(Tori) ⑫

Trent Jordache
(Brenna) ⑨

Nedwyn Lansing
(Diana) ⑭

Ashton Sinclair
(Netherland) ⑩

KEY:
( ) — denotes a spouse
◯ and number —denotes title of book for that couple's story

① Tonight and Forever   ④ Eternally Yours   ⑦ Truly Everlasting   ⑩ Surrender   ⑬ Unfinished Business
② Whispered Promises   ⑤ One Special Moment   ⑧ Secret Love   ⑪ The Best Man   ⑭ Slow Burn
③ Cupid's Bow   ⑥ Fire and Desire   ⑨ True Love   ⑫ The Midnight Hour

Above all else, guard your affections.
For they influence everything in your life.
—*Proverbs* 4:23

Prologue

"Who the hell are you?"

The sound of the unfamiliar voice made Corinthians Avery turn around quickly. Her eyes locked first on the stranger's dark, handsome face, then drifted down to his bare, wet chest, before moving downward to the white towel covering his middle…barely. Her gaze flew back up to his.

Her throat suddenly became dry, but somehow she was able to conjure up a voice. She cleared her throat. "You're not Dex." She quickly snatched her robe off the chair, shielding herself from him.

The man merely stared at her without comment. The only sign he gave that he'd heard her was the sudden lift of his brow. When seconds ticked by he finally spoke. "I know who I am, but who the hell are you?"

The man's rudeness, as far as Corinthians was concerned, was totally uncalled for. And it didn't help matters that he'd seen her outfit. How embarrassing! Could she have made a mistake and entered the wrong room? No, that could not be possible. Dex was to arrive for a two-day business meeting with her employer. She had made the reservations with the hotel herself, making sure they were given connecting rooms. So who was this man?

"I'm a friend of Dex's. Where is he?" she asked, suddenly feeling light-headed.

Trevor Grant's gaze took in the woman standing before him who'd been dressed in what he thought was the sexiest getup he'd ever seen on a woman. Too bad she had put her robe on. She had to be the most gorgeous woman he'd ever laid eyes on. He couldn't help wondering who she was. Was this some sort of joke Clayton Madaris was playing on his brother Dex? It wouldn't have been the first time Clayton had gone a little overboard by sending one of his numerous female friends to liven up what he considered as Dex's dull and boring life.

"Did Clayton put you up to this?" he asked the woman.

Corinthians frowned. "What?"

"I asked if Dex's brother Clayton put you up to this. If he did, you're out of luck. He forgot to cancel you out."

"What are you talking about?" Corinthians straightened her shoulders and met the stranger's gaze head-on. She tried putting out of her mind just how handsome he looked.

"You're looking for Dex Madaris, right?"

She nodded. "Yes. Where is he?"

The man continued to stare at her, seemingly totally nonchalant with *his* state of half-nakedness, but definitely not with hers. His gaze moved over her from head to toe, occasionally lingering in certain places. He acted as if he had X-ray vision and could actually see through her robe.

"Dex's home with his wife," he said bluntly.

His statement came as such a shock that Corinthians had to lean against the bedpost. "You're lying. Dex isn't married."

Trevor frowned. Not too many people called him a liar and got away with it. "Look. I don't know who you are or what you're doing in my room, but you're going to tell me, or you'll have a lot of explaining to do to Security. You have no right to be in my room."

Corinthians could feel her head spinning. This couldn't be happening to her. Everything was going wrong, and this man claimed Dex was married.

"I know Dex got married a few years ago. But he got a divorce a short while later. Are you saying he got married again?" she asked him dazedly.

Trevor saw the bleakness in her face. It was obvious that whomever she was, she wasn't taking the news of Dex's marriage very well. He began having doubts she was someone Clayton had sent, but was someone who knew Dex personally. He came to stand before her.

"Dex and his wife were separated, but they never got a divorce. Now they're back together. All three of them," he said.

"All three of them?" she asked softly.

"Yes, all three of them. Dex, his wife and daughter."

The next thing Trevor knew, the woman had fallen in a dead faint at his feet.

Chapter 1

Two years later

Trevor Grant knew the exact moment Corinthians Avery entered the huge conference room. A tremor of heated desire shot through his entire body. It hadn't taken the alluring scent of her perfume to alert him of her presence. The primitive, male part of him had immediately set off his internal radar, warning him that she was within close range.

He shifted uneasily in his seat. The sensation he felt was not a new one, just an unwelcomed one. He'd been attuned to her since that night two years ago when they had met. The woman he held within his sight looked as she always did in his dreams, only today she was wearing more clothing.

A lot more clothing.

Last night, in the deep recesses of his sleep-induced mind, she was dressed in the outfit she had worn the first time he had laid eyes on her. It had been a skimpy black negligee that had barely covered her body. Even now, he could recall seeing her in it. Another slow tremor began in his stomach and spread down his body at the steamy memory. He shifted in his seat again.

It didn't take much to envision her as he had seen her that night. And it didn't take much to remember the shocked look on her face when he had been the one to walk out of the shower instead of the man she had planned to seduce.

Trevor allowed himself a small grin when he thought of her fainting at his feet after he'd informed her Dex Madaris was married. It had been his supreme pleasure to pick her up off the floor and place her on the bed, then watch her expression when she had come to and realized her carefully laid plans of seduction had backfired. Unfortunately the embarrassment of her folly had not curtailed her biting tongue or her fiery spirit. She had lashed out at him as if it had been his fault she had made a complete fool of herself.

Now here they were two years later, still bitter adversaries. She disliked him because he knew too much about that night, and he disliked her equally as much because he had seen too much that night. Way too much. And he hadn't gotten a decent night's sleep since without her and that skimpy black outfit invading his dreams.

Since she was head geologist for Remington Oil, and he was head foreman for Madaris Explorations, their paths had crossed a few times since that night. A little over a year ago, their companies had worked together on a major project, and she had gone out of her way to avoid him. At the time, her actions had suited him just fine because each time he had seen her, he had been reminded of a night he could not forget.

He watched her move around the conference room, greeting various business associates. She had not seen him yet so he continued to just sit and watch her, patiently waiting for the moment she would become aware of him.

Trevor leaned back in his chair and appreciated how her body moved with an unconscious gracefulness that he couldn't help finding seductive. The conservative navy blue suit she wore should have downplayed her beauty. Instead it fueled the fire within him because he knew just how sexy the body was underneath the tailored skirt and jacket.

His gaze continued its survey of her trim, five-foot-eight-inch curvy figure before zeroing in on her face, a perfect oval shape. It was the color of rich, creamy chocolate, and was a face any man would take a second look at. Her hair was a rich glossy black, and was a lot longer than it had been that night. The stylish cut framed her face and made her features more profound and even more radiant. He wondered how one woman could convey such an aura of total professionalism in a boardroom and be such a sensuous temptress in a hotel room.

"Ladies and gentlemen, if you'll take your seats, we can get our meeting underway," Adam Flynn, senior exploration manager for Remington Oil, was saying.

Trevor watched as Corinthians glanced around the room, looking for an available place at the huge table. The smiling glint in her dark eyes immediately disappeared when she saw him. Flashing her a dimpled smile, he nodded. She frowned. Just as he had known, the gesture had teed her off. He enjoyed getting a rise out of her.

He saw sparks of anger leap into her eyes. His smile widened when he noticed the only available chair was the one across from him, and he knew she had realized that fact. His gaze held hers as she took her seat. With satisfied amusement in his eyes and without missing a beat, he said, "Good morning, Miss Avery. It's so good seeing you again."

Knowing she was in earshot of others, he watched as she pasted a phony smile on her face and replied, "Likewise, Mr. Grant."

He let out a deep, throaty chuckle. She could lie so well. He was the last person she would have wanted to see. The last time their paths had crossed had been at a wedding last month when his friend Clayton Madaris had married Syntel Remington's daughter, Syneda. Even then, the daggered looks Corinthians had given him would have sent most men running. But not him. He had accepted it as a challenge.

By the time the meeting was underway, Trevor relaxed in his chair. It was business as usual.

The look in Trevor Grant's eyes was hot, nearly burning her with its intensity, Corinthians thought. Each and every time he looked at her, his gaze was like a fire that heated her in some places and torched her to flames in others. She sat stiffly rigid in her chair as she tried to control the fiery emotions that flowed through her. How could the one man she despised arouse such feelings within her?

She tried getting comfortable in her seat, knowing his gaze was still on her. Her frown deepened. She would ignore him. At least she would try. She knew it would not be easy putting him out of her mind. She hadn't had any success in doing that since meeting him.

Corinthians had to grudgingly admit there was something totally sexy about the ruggedly built man with dark, piercing eyes. There was no way she could deny he was handsome. His black, curly, close-cropped hair was trimmed neat on his head. And his dark, coffee-colored face encompassed high cheekbones, a straight nose, full lips and a strong jawline that made any expression he wore serious, almost lethal. She knew he stood well over six feet four inches tall, and her memory of him that night with only a towel wrapped around his waist reminded her of wide shoulders, a broad hairy chest and long muscular legs. That image of him was still vivid in her mind.

Every time she saw him, his presence reminded her of the night she had made a total fool of herself. For years, she had thought herself in love with Dex Madaris and had finally made up her mind to do something about it. She had put her carefully laid plans of seduction into action, going so far as to get connecting hotel rooms and then sneaking into his room when she had heard him in the shower. But it had not been Dex who had emerged from the bathroom wearing nothing but a towel wrapped around his waist. It hadn't been Dex whose virile, near-naked body had rendered her speechless…at least almost speechless. Nor was it Dex who now continuously haunted her endless sleepless nights. To her utter misfortune, the man responsible for her nightly tortures was sitting across from her. His full attention was centered on her, and she knew he was doing it to deliberately rattle her.

And it was working.

"Corinthians, are you still available to fly to South America to represent Remington Oil at the oil research summit?"

Corinthians gave Adam Flynn her full attention and replied with a smile. "Yes, I'm available to go and looking forward to the trip."

"Good. And we'll look forward to hearing your report at our next meeting," Adam Flynn replied. He then turned his attention to Trevor. "Do you know if Dex Madaris is still going?"

Trevor smiled at Corinthians before turning his attention to Adam. "Due to family obligations, Dex has relinquished all travel plans abroad for a while. I'll be the one representing Madaris Explorations at the meeting in South America."

He turned and met Corinthians's shocked gaze. His smile deepened. "And I'm looking forward to the trip, as well."

When the meeting ended, Corinthians tossed Trevor a chilling glare before quickly leaving the conference room. A smile of satisfaction curved his lips. The gauntlet had been thrown down and the battle lines were officially drawn. The bout was on and it would be a fight to the finish; a fray he didn't intend to lose. He wouldn't accept anything but Corinthians Avery's complete, unconditional surrender.

Her days of avoiding him were over.

Chapter 2

"Welcome to Rio de Janeiro, *senhorita*."

Corinthians Avery smiled at the irony of the man's greeting as she signed the hotel register. She hadn't felt welcomed a few hours ago when she'd been detained at the Brazilian airport by a customs inspector who thought her luggage appeared a little too full.

"Thanks," she responded in English, momentarily forgetting to use some Portuguese words she'd learned over the past couple of weeks.

"Would the *senhorita* like a cup of *cafezinko* delivered to your room later?"

Corinthians smiled. A cup of coffee, even strong, Brazilian coffee, sounded pretty good right now. *"Sim obrigada,"* she answered in Portuguese. She was awarded a smile from the hotel clerk for her effort.

"*Senhorita,* you have a message," he said, handing her the key to her room along with a sealed envelope.

She opened the letter and scanned its contents. *Call me when you arrive. I'm in room 301. Trevor.*

A deep frown appeared on Corinthians's face. She crushed the paper in her hand and tossed it in a nearby wastepaper basket, feeling angry that she had wasted even a second of her time reading Trevor Grant's note.

"When did Mr. Grant arrive?"

"Yesterday, *senhorita.*"

She nodded. "Under no circumstances do I want my room number given out. And the only calls I'll accept are those from Remington Oil or from Reverend and Mrs. Avery. All others take down as messages."

The hotel clerk nodded in understanding.

For the moment Corinthians felt a sense of relief in knowing she wouldn't be bothered by the likes of Trevor Grant…at least not for a little while. She would see him soon enough when the research summit began in a few days. As far as she was concerned, the less she saw of him, the better.

"Don't you think it's time you stopped avoiding me?"

Corinthians looked up from her meal and momentarily paused, startled by the beauty of Trevor Grant's dark eyes. She hated admitting it, but his glare made him appear even more handsome. But she also conceded that at the moment, standing next to her table in a menacing stance with hands on his hips, he looked downright threatening. Her eyes narrowed as she looked him over, noticing the casual way he was dressed, wearing a pair of khaki pants and a dark shirt with the sleeves rolled up to the elbows. She wondered if there was any type of clothing he didn't look good in.

"I asked you a question, Corinthians."

His sharp tone brought her gaze back to his face. "Trying to avoid you, Mr. Grant, would take too much effort, and I wouldn't waste my time on such a task." She resumed eating, knowing in all actuality, she *had* been avoiding him since arriving yesterday.

"Then you shouldn't have a problem if I joined you for dinner," he said, taking a chair across from her.

She frowned. "I do have a problem with it. It was my intent to sit here and enjoy a quiet meal."

Trevor's face melted in a buttery smile, showing beautiful white teeth. "A quiet meal? I see no reason why you won't have one." He glanced down at her plate. "I doubt that food will make any noise. Trust me, I'll be the first to leave if it does."

Corinthians didn't find his words the least amusing. "Look, Mr. Grant, I—"

"I'm Trevor, remember."

"You're whatever I see fit to call you. Just be glad it's not something a lot worse."

Trevor leaned toward her. His eyes turned cold as he met her glare. "I'm not worried about you calling me anything but my given name. You're too much of a *lady* to do anything else."

Color flamed Corinthians's cheeks as she reacted to his statement, not liking the emphasis he had placed on the word *lady*. He had insultingly reminded her of that night she had stood before him looking like anything but a lady.

Her facial muscles tensed and her glare hardened. No true gentleman would deliberately remind a woman of one of her most humiliating experiences. She sighed. If she was no lady, then he certainly wasn't a true gentleman. She was spared from telling him that fact when the waitress came to take his order.

"You look nice today, Corinthians," he said after the waitress had left.

She lifted her head. The look she gave him indicated his compliment didn't faze her. However, since she'd been brought up with the belief that displaying good manners was essential, even to someone like Trevor Grant, she answered stiffly. "Thank you."

"You're welcome. And you smell nice, too."

Corinthians stared into Trevor's eyes. "Why all the compliments? Let's be honest with ourselves, shall we? I don't like you. You don't like me. For reasons that I'd rather not get into, we don't get along. However, since our jobs occasionally bring us in contact with each other, I believe we can handle the situation like two professional adults."

Trevor eyed her thoughtfully. "If you believe that, then why are you always avoiding me?"

"I don't always avoid you."

"Then why haven't you responded to my messages?"

"I had a rather taxing flight yesterday from Austin to Miami. And to top it off, when I arrived at the airport I was stopped. Brazilian customs officials who went through every piece of luggage I brought with me detained me. By the time I checked into the hotel, I was too tired to be bothered by anyone."

Corinthians sighed. That much of what she had just told him had been the truth.

Trevor raised a surprised brow. South America was known to be lax when it came to airport security. More drugs and contraband were smuggled in and out of this continent than any other place that he knew of, and usually under the airport officials' indifferent eyes. He wondered why she had been stopped. "Brazilian officials actually stopped you?"

Corinthians met his stare. "Yes. I was detained for more than two hours. It probably would have been longer had I not made a scene and threatened to contact someone at the American Embassy."

At that moment the waitress returned with Trevor's meal. He had ordered *churrasco,* an array of different kinds of meats grilled on skewers. In addition to his glass of Brazilian brandy, the waitress also left him a small bottle of *mala-*

gueta, a spicy sauce made from crushed, hot red peppers. When he uncapped the bottle, the spicy-hot aroma nearly took Corinthians's breath away.

"I can't believe you're putting that stuff on your food," she said, watching him pour the sauce all over his meat.

He didn't look up when he replied. "Believe it." But he did lift his gaze to meet hers when he added, "I happen to like hot stuff. Nothing stirs my blood more. The hotter, the better."

The look he gave her, as far as she was concerned, was just like the sauce he had poured over his food: red-hot. She felt her insides sizzle from the heat. He was staring at her with those dark eyes of his, hard and intense. She took a shaky breath. "Then enjoy yourself."

He smiled. "I will." He lifted a skewer and with his teeth pulled a piece of sauce-covered meat into his mouth without flinching. He smiled a slow, seductive smile.

Corinthians tried hard not to stare, but watching him chew his food was having an arousing effect on her. An involuntary shudder of simmering heat ripped through her. Her gaze followed every contoured movement of his mouth. Its motion was slow, provocative and alluring. She could just imagine his mouth working those same slow, steady and measured movements on hers, smothering her lips with demanding intensity. She tinted a darker shade, mortified because she'd had such thoughts.

"Want some?"

The sound of Trevor's voice, deep and husky, startled Corinthians. She tinted at having been caught staring. She ran her tongue over her lips to moisten them before asking. "Want some what?"

Trevor leaned over toward her and whispered, "Some of my food, what else?"

Corinthians took a deep breath. He was back to being arrogant again. She frowned at him. "No, I don't want any of your food. Mine suits me just fine," she snapped irritably, annoyed for letting him have such an effect on her. She had to get away from him to retain her sanity.

"I hope you enjoy the rest of your meal," she said brusquely, motioning to the waitress to bring her check.

"Where are you going?" Trevor asked, looking at her curiously.

"Not that it's any of your business, but I'm going to my room. I plan on doing some sightseeing in São Paulo all day tomorrow and want to get a good night's sleep."

"Can I tag along tomorrow?"

Corinthians was startled. "I prefer that you didn't."

Trevor didn't look up as he poured more sauce on his meat. "Why not? Like you said earlier, we're two professional adults." He lifted his gaze to hers and grinned. "Surely we can put our dislike for each other aside for at least one day."

"I don't think us spending time together is a good idea."

"Why do you feel that way?"

"Because I do."

Trevor pushed his plate aside. "Then let's discuss why you feel that way and really get to the crux of the problem. Don't you think two years is a long time for you to carry a chip on your shoulder?"

"I'm not carrying a chip on my shoulder. And I prefer not talking about that night. I don't even like thinking about it."

"Then don't."

"That's easy for you to say."

"Not talking about it won't make it go away. That night happened, Corinthians. Get over it. However, I think it will make you feel better if we got it out in the open and discussed it."

Corinthians doubted that. Her embarrassment and humiliation that night were too great. There was no way she could discuss how she felt, especially with Trevor of all people. He had seen her in a way no other man ever had. "What's there to say?"

"Whatever you want." A part of Trevor hoped she would

say her feelings for Dex were a thing of the past and that she had accepted his marriage. He hoped she wasn't like the woman who had become obsessed with his father and had destroyed his parents' marriage. The thought that she could very well be that sort of woman—scheming, conniving and manipulating—angered him.

"Get over Dex, Corinthians. He's a married man who loves his wife very much. You don't stand a chance."

Corinthians's angered flared. Why was he telling her that? She knew Dex loved Caitlin. Anyone with eyes could see that. At the time that she had decided to make her move on Dex, she had not seen him in more than four years and had not known his marital state. When she had first gotten hired at Remington Oil right out of college at Grambling, Dex had been her trainer. They had worked together for a couple of years before he was sent to work in Australia. Although she had wanted him to notice her, he had only treated her fondly, like a sister. After the fiasco that night two years ago with Trevor in the hotel room, she had reevaluated her feelings for Dex. She had come to the conclusion that whatever feelings she'd thought she'd had for Dex hadn't been love, but an oversized amount of infatuation she'd harbored for him over the years. Even Dex's wife, Caitlin, knew she once thought herself in love with Dex. After meeting Caitlin and seeing what a beautiful person she was, both inside and out, Corinthians had felt that in order for her and Caitlin to have a true friendship, she needed to let her know what her feelings had been for Dex at one time. She had also made it clear to Caitlin that Dex was unaware she had harbored such affections. He considered her a good friend and nothing more. Caitlin had appreciated her honesty and forthrightness, and she knew Caitlin considered her a friend.

What bothered her now more than anything was not any feelings of love she still harbored for Dex, since she knew for certain there weren't any, but the unexplained feelings she'd begun to feel for Trevor Grant. He was the last person she wanted to feel anything for. The man had her pegged as some two-bit home-wrecker, for Pete's sake! That meant he didn't think a whole lot of her character. That angered her more.

"You don't know what I stand a chance of doing," she said finally. "I've discovered when it comes to love, most men are fickle. Otherwise they wouldn't have mistresses, now would they?" she added, knowing her words would fuel his anger.

It did. Trevor's gaze showed his seething rage. When the waitress came to collect Corinthians's money, she turned her attention away from Trevor. After taking a calming breath, she decided to thank the waitress for her meal in the woman's native tongue.

The waitress's face suddenly turned a hot crimson and tears appeared in her eyes. She whirled and ran from the room.

"Why did you say something like that to her?" Trevor snapped.

Corinthians flinched at the harsh tone of Trevor's voice. She noticed the sudden quietness in the hotel's restaurant and that other patrons were openly staring at her. "What's wrong? I don't understand," she said in alarm. "I merely told her I had enjoyed my meal."

"No, you did not! You didn't even come close."

Corinthians swallowed slowly, afraid to ask but knowing she had to. "Then what did I say to her?"

Trevor's glare deepened. "You told her she had the face of a dead horse."

Shocked denial appeared on Corinthians's face. "I did not!"

"You did, too! I strongly suggest you brush up on your Portuguese before spurting off your mouth." He then motioned for the attention of the restaurant manager, which wasn't hard to do since all eyes were on them anyway. When the man arrived at their table, Trevor spoke to him in rapid, fluent Portuguese.

Corinthians's mouth dropped in surprise. When the man rushed off in the same direction the waitress had gone earlier, Corinthians found her voice to ask, "Where did you learn to speak Portuguese?"

Trevor glared at her. "While in the Marines I learned to speak several different languages."

Corinthians's face showed another shock. "You were in the Marines?"

"Yes. I was in the Marines for more than fifteen years."

At that moment the manager returned with the distressed waitress in tow. Corinthians felt absolutely awful. One look at the woman and she could tell she'd been crying. "Oh, Trevor, please tell her that I didn't mean what I said and that my use of her language is rusty and—"

"It's not rusty, it's deplorable."

Ignoring his comment, Corinthians continued. "Please tell her I truly apologize for what I said and that I didn't mean it. I was trying to tell her I enjoyed my food."

In a soft, calming voice, Trevor began speaking in Portuguese. Corinthians noted the softening of the woman's features and the smile that stole onto her face. Whatever Trevor was saying was helping to smooth things over. When the woman looked at her and laughed before turning to leave, Corinthians raised a brow.

"What did you say to her?"

Trevor shrugged. "I told her everything you asked me to. I also shared with her a few thoughts of my own."

"A few thoughts of your own like what?"

He leaned back in his seat and looked at her. "I told her that unfortunately you had a habit of placing yourself in embarrassing situations. Today wasn't the first time I've been a witness to such an event, and I doubt it would be the last."

Corinthians's mouth dropped open. She couldn't believe he had said such a thing about her; and to a stranger at that. But the look he gave her said that he had. Totally peeved, she stood. "This was the last time you'll ever be a witness to any embarrassing situation I might endure."

"I doubt it."

Trevor couldn't help but grin when a very angry Corinthians Avery turned and walked off. He shrugged and resumed eating his food. So much for round one.

Chapter 3

Corinthians quickly left the restaurant and walked across the hotel's lobby, fuming. Her face was still stinging from the heat of embarrassment. Added to that was the humiliation of Trevor's words. She was so mad, her hands were shaking. As far as she was concerned, Trevor Grant was an arrogant and inconsiderate man. There was not a shred of decency in him. No respectable person would take joy in pointing out another person's misfortune.

Slowing her pace, Corinthians forced herself to slow her breathing and put a cap on her anger. He wasn't worth it. Exhausted and frustrated, she stopped in front of the elevator doors, then remembered she hadn't picked up her messages that day. Turning, she walked over to the hotel's front desk.

A few minutes later she was flipping through the numerous slips of paper that had been given to her. Trevor Grant and her brother, Joshua, were running neck and neck in the number of messages they had left. She crushed all the ones

from Trevor, feeling a sense of satisfaction in doing so. She
then turned her attention to those from Senator Joshua Avery.
She wondered which was worse, dealing with Trevor or
coming to blows with Josh. Although she loved her brother
dearly, he could be a monumental pain at times. He thought
since he was five years older, he had every right to boss her
around.

She sighed. He also thought he could manipulate her into
doing anything he wanted. As far as she was concerned,
becoming senator had gone to his head. Although some people
easily fell victim to his charm, she wasn't one of them. She had
to constantly remind him that at the age of thirty, she was a
grown woman who didn't need a big brother to boss her around.

Deciding not to wait until she returned to her room to
make the call, she picked up a courtesy phone off a nearby
desk and dialed the number Joshua had left on the messages.
It was to his office in Washington.

A few minutes later, his loud, authoritative voice came on
the line. "Senator Joshua Avery."

"Hi, Josh. I got your messages. What's up?"

"Your timing is perfect, Corinthians. Rasheed is here. Why
did you leave the country without letting him know when
you'd be returning? He thought you would be available to ac-
company him to the presidential dinner this weekend."

Corinthians raised her eyes to the ceiling. Joshua was
forever the politician looking for ways to make connections. He had talked her into attending a dinner party given
in Senator Nedwyn Lansing's honor a couple of weeks ago
with Rasheed Valdemon, the thirty-three-year-old son of a
sheikh from the Middle East. Rasheed's striking good looks,
a result of his Arab father and Egyptian mother, were enough
to make most women swoon. But not her. It had only taken
one evening spent in his company for her to realize the two
of them did not see eye-to-eye on a number of things. She
would never be able to tolerate his beliefs on certain

subjects, especially the rights of women. He was very proud of the fact that in his country, women were seen and not heard. And according to him, there was nothing wrong with a man having more than one wife if that's what he desired. He had phoned her a few times since then and had even flown from Washington, D.C., to Texas to see her, surprising the heck out of her when he'd appeared on her doorstep last weekend.

"I don't know how he could have thought that. I remember telling him I would not be going to that dinner with him."

"I guess he's not used to being turned down."

Corinthians frowned. She was getting fed up with arrogant men. "Then he needs to understand he's in America. In this country women have rights. I exercised mine when I turned him down. Now, if you'll excuse me, Josh, I need to go. Bye." She hung up the phone before her brother could say anything else. No doubt he would suggest that she talk to Rasheed, and she wasn't in the mood.

After hanging up the phone, Corinthians turned to find Trevor Grant standing across the lobby, leaning against the wall looking at her. He just stood there staring at her with an odd expression on his face. Even from the distance separating them, she could see something flicker deep in the depths of his eyes. It was something dark, compelling and seductive. He was looking at her as if he could see straight through the material of her gauzy white sundress; every revealing detail.

Angry at the way her thoughts were going, she gave him a cutting look before turning and walking over to the elevators. When the doors opened, she quickly stepped inside. When she turned back around, she saw his eyes were still on her. She met his stare with her glare. She was glad when the doors closed, shutting him off from her line of vision.

Trevor straightened his stance. He wondered whom Corinthians had been talking to on the telephone. Whoever it was had certainly teed her off. He had picked up on it even from across the room simply by reading her body language and facial expressions. A deep scowl covered his face. Him trying to get a rise out of her was one thing, someone else setting her off was another. He couldn't help wondering if the person she'd been on the phone with was a man. He suddenly loathed himself for even caring. The woman had already proven to him that she had no scruples. She'd all but hinted at dinner that she had not gotten over Dex. He wondered if she was an obsessive type of woman. He knew firsthand the destruction an obsessive woman could do. Hadn't Paris Sanders been the epitome of an obsessive woman when she had been responsible for his parents' breakup?

At the age of sixteen, he had taken his parents' separation hard, not understanding the reason for it. At home, his mother was always despondent, and whenever he and his sister, Regina, went to visit their father, his mood was just as downhearted. However, neither of his parents would reveal to their son and daughter the reason they had decided to live apart. And since neither of his parents had filed for a divorce, that had made the situation even more confusing to him. It was only years later, after he had finished school and joined the Marines, that he had found out the truth. Another woman had been involved.

At least that was what his mother had believed, although his father had staunchly denied having an affair with Paris Sanders. But the photo that had been delivered to his mother from Paris Sanders, a shot taken of his father holding a half-naked Ms. Sanders in his arms during a business trip, had sealed Maurice Grant's fate. Stella Grant had believed the worst.

Trevor placed his hands in the pockets of his pants as he continued to stare at the closed elevator doors. If Corinthians Avery thought she was going to make her move on a married man like Paris Sanders had done, she had another thought coming.

Washington, D.C.

"You Americans give your women too much freedom."

Joshua Avery leaned back in his chair and rubbed his temples upon hearing the statement from the man sitting across from his desk. "Look, Valdemon, I'm not my sister's keeper. According to Corinthians, she never agreed to be your dinner date this weekend. I mentioned to you two weeks ago that she was going to Brazil. Why didn't you find someone else to take?"

The tall, handsome man with dark, piercing eyes, skin the color of almond, and dark, straight black hair that reached his shoulders, gave Joshua a measured stare. "Because I assumed she would be back by this weekend."

Joshua almost told him he apparently assumed too much, then thought better of it. The last thing he needed was enemies from the Middle East. In his quest to become the first Black governor of Texas, the one thing he needed other than the support of fellow Texans were allies in the Middle East. With Texas being the oil basin in the United States and the Middle East being where the major oil-producing nations were located, there was a lot at stake. In order to get American oil companies that were based in Texas to support him, he needed to make sure their counterparts abroad were kept happy and content. The last thing anyone wanted was a repeat of the monopolized oil prices that had plagued the nation in the seventies. Although Valdemon's native country was not an oil-producing one, it was still located in the Middle East. And his father, the sheikh of Mowaiti, was well thought of in Washington, D.C., and Valdemon was his heir.

He smiled. "I don't think Corinthians will be back for another week, so I suggest you find someone else to take. I also suggest that if you're really interested in my sister, you take another approach. She doesn't like being told what to do. I don't care how you might handle women in your country, we do things differently here."

Rasheed looked aghast. "Are you suggesting that I let a woman rule me?"

Joshua raised his eyes to the ceiling. "No, I'm suggesting that you learn how to compromise."

Rasheed's gaze was hard as stone when he spoke. "I know how to compromise. However, I practice the art of compromising with world leaders, and not with defiant women." He stood and walked out of Joshua's office.

Prince Rasheed Valdemon left the Capitol building and stepped into a waiting limo. Once inside, he opened his briefcase and took out a manila folder. Flipping it open, he leaned back in his seat. Inside the folder was the profile on Corinthians Elizabeth Avery that he'd received six months ago. On top was a photograph of her. She was a strikingly beautiful woman. But unlike her brother assumed, her beauty wasn't what interested him. Her intelligence did. Specifically, her vast knowledge of the production and extraction of crude oil. Some claimed she had a sixth sense when it came to pinpointing the locations of unknown oil reserves.

A year and a half ago, she'd made history with her in-depth research and her uncanny ability to locate an unknown oil basin in the United States. It was the first to be found in more than fifty years. That had been quite an accomplishment and had gained her both national and international attention, especially in those countries whose main source of income was oil. Offers of employment had poured in from around the world, and she had turned them down, saying she was totally satisfied with her job as head geologist with an American-owned oil company, Remington Oil.

Rasheed shifted in his seat as he closed the folder. A deep, troubled look covered his face. His country had not been one of those who had offered her employment, but in truth it was *his* country that needed her the most.

The Middle East contained roughly seventy percent of all the world's oil reserves. Many of those basins rested within a few large fields, so most of the other countries in the region had relatively small quantities of oil or none at all. His homeland of Mowaiti was one of those countries that had none at all. The majority of his people were engaged in farming, and most lived harsh and impoverished lives. More than anything, he was determined to change that.

His father, Mowaiti's present leader, was ignoring the people's pleas of a better life. He regretted to say his father didn't have a vision. But Rasheed did. Unlike others, he believed there were oil reserves located somewhere in his country. What they needed was someone with the ability to find them.

Someone like Corinthians Avery.

Once the reserves were located, Mowaiti would emerge as a highly productive nation, and a powerful influence in OPEC. The discovery of oil over fifty something years ago had transformed Libya from a poor agricultural country, like Mowaiti was today, into one of the world's leading oil producers.

Rasheed placed the folder back in his briefcase. The decision had been made and a secret cartel had been formed. One way or another, Corinthians Avery would do for Mowaiti what she'd done for her own country. After spending time with her, he knew she would never leave the United States to live permanently in Mowaiti. He also knew the American government would never sanction her leaving the country for an extended stay in Mowaiti to help his country locate oil. To do so would be too political, and other impoverished Middle East countries would demand that the U.S. government provide the same services to them. And that would never happen for fear of the Middle East controlling all of the world's oil supply. Therefore, he'd been forced to take other measures.

Placing the briefcase on the floor by his feet, he finally turned his attention to the man who'd already been seated in the vehicle. "There better be a good reason why the Brazilian government did not follow my directive and apprehend Ms. Avery at the airport."

Chapter 4

Corinthians felt her breath catch as she glanced around Praca da Republica, the city of São Paulo's most lovely park. The forty-five-minute air shuttle from Rio de Janeiro had been well worth it. She checked the travel brochure she held in her hand for what would be her next stop, and decided she needed to get something to eat first. She had skipped breakfast to catch an early flight out of Rio.

She knew from the information she had read that São Paulo was the largest city in South America, and was considered the financial, commercial and industrial center of Brazil. It didn't have the suave beauty of Rio de Janeiro, but its wide variety of international restaurants, fabulous shopping districts and parks and museums made it a popular place for tourists.

Corinthians smiled when she saw, of all things, a McDonald's, and was in total awe of how elegant it looked. She then remembered reading in the brochure that the hamburger chain had restored one of the last remaining manors that had once been a millionaire's mansion.

Entering the McDonald's, she sat down at a table overlooking the São Paulo Museum of Art. She smiled at the waitress who came to take her order, feeling somewhat strange to get such personal service. In every U.S. city that she knew of, such service was not provided. Most McDonald's had drive-thrus and walk-up counters for service.

After her disastrous experience yesterday in trying to speak Portuguese, Corinthians thought it best to stick with English. After the woman had left with her order, she decided to pay a visit to the ladies' room before her food arrived. Standing, she made her way toward the area where the facilities were located.

Leaving the restroom a few minutes later, Corinthians noticed two men hanging around in the hallway. She made a move to walk past them and came to a stop when they blocked her path. She frowned and looked closely at them. She swallowed. Their expressions were anything but friendly.

"Excuse me," she said, and made another attempt to go around them and felt a sense of panic when they didn't move an inch.

Trevor entered the McDonald's and glanced around, not seeing Corinthians anywhere. He had been following her for the past hour or so, and she hadn't been aware of him doing so. Not that he had any complaints, since he had thoroughly enjoyed watching the sway of her hips as she'd moved through the streets of São Paulo. Her shapely thighs and small waist did a lot for the skirt and blouse she was wearing.

Deciding Corinthians must have gone to the ladies' room, he looked over in that direction. He stopped suddenly when he saw her surrounded by two men, and had a gut feeling they were up to no good. He cursed under his breath. Couldn't the woman go anywhere without getting herself into trouble?

Although there were a number of African-Brazilian

women in the city, an African-American woman stuck out like a sore thumb. Especially one as beautiful and one dressed as classy as Corinthians. She made herself an easy target for anyone committing crimes against tourists.

Knowing he had to intervene, but that he had to do so in such a way that would cause as little trouble as possible, Trevor boldly walked past the men and right up to Corinthians. He leaned over and kissed her lips, effectively silencing her startled gasp. "Sorry I got detained, sweetheart. Have you ordered yet?"

At first Corinthians was too surprised at seeing Trevor Grant to say anything. It was as if he'd materialized out of thin air. She couldn't help wondering where on earth he'd come from. But at the moment, she didn't care. Although she understood his game plan, she was too shaken up to answer his question. She merely nodded.

He gave her a reassuring smile. "Good, then come on before our food gets cold." Taking her hand in his, he turned and together they faced the two men.

Corinthians couldn't help wondering what the men would do now that Trevor was with her. She watched as he stared down at the two men with a look and stance that almost dared them to take him on. For a moment it seemed the standoff would go on forever, then finally the two men stepped aside and let them pass. Trevor continued to hold her hand as she led him to her table. Instead of them sitting down, he took some bills out of his pocket and tossed them on the table.

"Come on, let's get out of here. I know another place where we can eat."

Corinthians nodded and let him lead her out of the door. She took a quick glance over her shoulder. The men were gone.

"Are you all right?"

Corinthians drew in a deep breath before answering. "Yes."

After leaving McDonald's, Trevor led her over to a rental

car that was parked not far away. After he opened the door
she slid inside without asking any questions. She felt a sense
of relief when he walked around the car and got in beside her.

She gazed over at him. "I wonder what that was all about."

Trevor turned and stared at her before starting the engine.
He could not believe she'd asked such a question. Before answering he tried calming his overactive male hormones. Even
in the midst of danger, his body had immediately reacted
when he'd made the mistake of watching her when she'd slid
inside the car. The movement had inched her skirt up,
exposing plenty of leg and thigh. Just thinking about what
he'd seen made him ache in the worst way.

"What that was about was a simple case of thieves getting
ready to pounce on their next victim," he said slowly, starting
the car and pulling away. He tried putting a cap on the anger
he felt in knowing how close she'd come to that happening.
He wanted to give her the third degree for not being more alert
while alone in a strange city.

He glanced back over at her and could tell she was still
pretty badly shaken up over the incident. The last thing she
needed was for him to get on her case.

"But that doesn't make sense," Corinthians said, leaning
back in her seat. "I left my valuables at the hotel in Rio. I'm
not even wearing any jewelry."

"Yeah, but that Chanel purse of yours draws attention.
It's probably worth more than the shacks some of these
people live in."

"You're kidding."

"No, I'm not. Crime against tourists is high here."

A few minutes later Trevor brought the car to a stop in
front of a seaside restaurant. Even from the outside, the
smell of grilled fish made Corinthians's mouth water.
Whatever spices they were using had definitely tantalized
her taste buds. She'd heard that the largest single influence
on the preparation of Brazilian foods had come with the

arrival of African slaves many years ago. West African cooking was firmly established on the Brazilian palate. Then later, with new arrivals of other nationalities from Asia, Europe and the Middle East, each made massive contributions to make Brazil's multiethnic cuisine unique, delicious and the best in the world.

Corinthians stood by Trevor's side at the entrance to the restaurant while he spoke in Portuguese to a waiter. She did not understand a word they were saying, but her curiosity was piqued when the waiter kept looking at her and smiling. Moments later they were led up concrete stairs to a balcony. Surprisingly, the room was deserted, so they had their choice of tables. After giving them menus, the waiter left them alone.

"What did you say to him?" Corinthians asked. After what he'd said to the waitress yesterday, she wouldn't put anything past him.

Trevor shrugged as he glanced at his menu. "I told him we were newlyweds and wanted to be alone."

She leaned back in her chair and stared at him. "I can't believe you did that."

"It got results, didn't it? Would you have preferred staying below in that crowded room? I thought you'd enjoy the view from up here."

He was right. She did enjoy the view from up here. It was simply breathtaking. The photogenic beauty of the vast ocean that surrounded them moved her. Rising, she walked over to the edge of the deck and looked out, scanning the distance to where the blue sea ended and the coastal mountains began.

She turned to Trevor and smiled. "This is beautiful," she said. "Thanks for bringing me up here."

A hot stab of desire rushed through Trevor with Corinthians's smile. It was the first real smile she'd ever directed at him, and he suddenly felt off balance. She made a sultry image against the backdrop of ocean and mountains, while standing silhouetted in the sunlight. Of its own volition, his gaze took in everything about her, her outfit, her features, her hair…even the flat shoes she wore.

An exquisite pressure began building deep inside of him. He shifted in his seat, needing to regain control of his mind and most importantly his body. He didn't like the fact that she was putting him through changes.

"Don't mention it. And if you don't mind, we need to have our order ready by the time the waiter gets back," he snapped.

Corinthians's smile sagged. She then took two deep breaths. The first was to ignore the urge to pour the chilled pitcher of water that was sitting on their table over Trevor's head at the tone he'd suddenly taken with her. The second was to downplay the heroic image that kept flashing through her mind of him—one man against two. He'd been an imposing force to reckon with when he'd come to her aid. No matter how much she wanted to forget that, she couldn't.

"Fine with me," she snapped back. "I'm starving anyway."

She walked back over to the table, took her seat and began scanning the menu. After deciding on an entrée, she looked up to find Trevor watching her.

"Is there a problem?" she asked, glaring at him.

Yes, there is a problem, Trevor thought. But it was *his* problem and not hers. The one thing a Marine didn't do was lose control, but he was doing that very thing around her, constantly. Whatever trouble he was having in dealing with it, was no reason to be outright rude to her. "Look, Corinthians, I—"

She held up her hand to silence him, her anger had reached its limit, and she felt it was time to get him straight on a number of things. "No, *you* look. I've had just about enough of your—"

She stopped talking when the waiter returned to take their order. "I'll have your seafood platter," she said promptly, calmly. She decided to put her beef with Trevor on hold until after their meal. She could deal with him more effectively on a full stomach.

"And for an appetizer, I'll have some *pão de queijo*," she added, wanting to try their cheese rolls that were made with tapioca starch and grated cheese. "I'd also like a glass of white wine."

Trevor closed his menu. "I'll also have your seafood platter and some *pão de queijo*. However, bring me a glass of Brazilian brandy." Before the waiter walked off, he added. "And bring me some *malagueta* with my meal."

Corinthians shook her head. "Do you put hot sauce on practically everything you eat?"

"Just about," he answered, meeting her gaze. An uncomfortable silence grew between them. "I didn't mean to snap at you earlier, Corinthians," Trevor finally said. "But today has been one hell of a day."

"You can say that again," she said, taking a sip of water.

"Today has been one hell of a day."

Corinthians tried swallowing back the laughter that formed in her throat, but couldn't, and laughed despite not wanting to. She was glad they were the only ones out on the balcony.

"Thanks," she said afterward. "I needed that. And thanks for your help today. I don't know what I would have done had you not shown up."

She looked at him thoughtfully. "I'm really curious to know just why you were there."

Trevor's hand tightened on his glass, needing to feel something cool against his skin. Corinthians's laugh had been a breathy, sensuous sound that had made his body feel heated. "I was doing the same thing you were doing, taking a tour of the city. I told you at dinner yesterday that I was coming here today. I even suggested that we come together."

Corinthians nodded, remembering that conversation, then wishing she hadn't. "What time did you leave Rio?"

"Around ten. I got a late start because I requested a change in hotel rooms. Evidently the couple in the room next to mine are on their honeymoon. Their constant squeaking bed keeps me awake at night." He didn't add that it also reminded him of what he'd been missing.

Corinthians shook her head, smiling, not sure if he was joking or telling the truth about the amorous couple. At that moment the waiter returned with their drinks and appetizers.

"What made you decide to go into the Marines?" Corinthians asked after eating a *pão de queijo* and taking a sip of wine.

"I heard they were looking for a few good men, and I was cocky enough to believe that meant they were definitely looking for me."

Corinthians rolled her eyes. The man didn't lack any self-confidence. She looked at him speculatively. "I can see you as a Marine."

"Why?"

"Because you're hard."

Trevor smiled. She was right about that, but not in the way she had meant. He shifted around in his seat to ease the hard ache in the lower part of his body. "Marines aren't hard," he said smoothly. "They're tough. There's a difference."

Corinthians didn't think so, but decided not to tell him that. The man who had faced those two men in McDonald's that day had been both hard and tough. "I still don't understand how you did it," she said.

"How I did what?"

"How you got those guys to back off without saying one word to them."

Trevor took a sip of his brandy. "There're a number of ways to communicate. One is without words, but with the use of eye contact. People can read what you want them to know just by looking into your eyes. Another way is with body language. I used both eye contact and body language today. Those guys read me loud and clear. There was no mistake in what I was nonverbally telling them."

Corinthians nodded. "Weren't you afraid?"

"For you, yes. For myself, no. A Marine has no fear. It's not in our mind-set."

The waiter then returned with their entrées. Over lunch he told her more about the Marines and his decision to enlist. He told her how he had skipped college and entered the service. The recruiter that had come to his high school had offered him the chance to fulfill his lifelong dream of being a world traveler. He eventually got his college degree while in the Marines, serving his country for more than fifteen years.

What he didn't tell her was that he'd been so broken up over his parents' separation that he had needed to get away, and the Marines had provided him that escape. And what he had found was another family; a close-knit group of men and women who were ready, willing and able to fight for and defend their country.

After their meal the waiter brought over the check. Trevor paid for it.

"You didn't have to do that," Corinthians said. "You've done enough already."

Just wait until you get back to the hotel and find out what else I've done, Trevor thought as he stood from his seat. "Hasn't anyone ever told you that a woman shouldn't turn down a free meal from a man?"

Corinthians smiled. "No, probably because any smart woman knows that nothing is free, especially if it comes from a man. There are usually a few strings attached."

Trevor chuckled. "Trust me, there are no strings attached, so relax."

When they returned to the car, he said, "How about if we tour the rest of the city together?"

Corinthians grinned. "So there weren't any strings attached, huh?" She thought about it for a second then said, "How can I say no after you've fed me so well? You certainly can't be any more of a nuisance than those two men at McDonald's."

Trevor laughed. "Gee, I hope not."

They visited the São Paulo Museum of Art and spent some time in a number of the upscale shopping centers that were all over town. They even visited the Butanta Institute Snake Farm and went to a horse race at the Jockey Club.

It was late afternoon when they decided to call it a day and catch a flight back to Rio so they could be well rested for the research summit the next day.

"I'm walking you to your room," Trevor said when they both stepped inside the hotel's elevator.

"That's not necessary," she assured him, appreciating the offer. Although she didn't want to admit it, that episode in São Paulo had her still somewhat shaky. She knew she would be fine once she got a good night's sleep, and put the incident out of her mind. She still wasn't too keen on the idea of Trevor knowing where her room was located. She shrugged. She was probably being silly in trying to hide it from him anyway. It wasn't like he would force his way into her room or something.

"I know it's not necessary to walk you to your room, but I'll feel better if I do," he said when she punched the button for the fifth floor. "And we've both agreed that it's been one hell of a day."

Once they reached her room door, Corinthians turned to him. Their eyes met and held for a long moment before she broke contact by reaching down and taking her shopping bag out of his hands. "Thanks for carrying this. And thanks again for coming to my rescue today."

Trevor took a step forward, sandwiching Corinthians between him and the door. He reached out and let his fingers stroke the silken skin of her cheek. "It was my pleasure," he said huskily.

Corinthians's breath caught in response to the sensuality of Trevor's touch. She took a step back and found herself pressed firmly against the door. "I need to go inside," she heard herself saying to him.

"Invite me in."

Trevor's whispered plea was tempting. Too tempting, Corinthians thought. "I can't," she said, taking a deep breath and pushing away from the support of the door frame. Since Trevor didn't move back an inch, her movement brought her body right smack up against his. The sudden body contact was electrifying, arousing, stirring. It released fire, quickly followed by desire. The fire between them was hot and intense. The desire, strong and unyielding.

Trevor slowly leaned down and touched his mouth to hers, once, then twice. He slipped his hand under her mass of dark hair and cupped the nape of her neck. His eyes locked with hers.

"You *can* invite me in," he whispered, leaning closer to her lips. "And in a few seconds you'll wish you had."

Before she could draw her next breath, Trevor captured her mouth with his. His tongue, flavored with the taste of the hot sauce he'd had at lunch, inflamed her in sizzling heat as it penetrated the moist softness of her mouth, making a thorough sweep of the insides and capturing her tongue with his.

Corinthians felt his mouth move slow, steady and intense over hers as their tongues mated. The want and need she felt was potent, powerful. She couldn't think. She couldn't get a grip. Her body had never ached for a man before…and never like this. She wrapped her arms around his neck, giving just as good as she was getting, and admitting to herself that the real thing was a whole lot better than any dreams she'd had.

Trevor was drowning a slow, pleasurable death. A part of him had always known that kissing Corinthians would be like this, and that she would feel like heaven in his arms. And when he felt her move against him, it fueled his fire. He deepened the kiss, taking everything she was offering and still wanting more.

"Let's go inside," he whispered hotly, against her lips.

Somewhere in the distance Corinthians heard the sound of

a door opening and closing. It suddenly hit her that she and Trevor were standing in the middle of a hallway engaged in a kissing marathon. She quickly pushed him away just seconds before an elderly couple passed by them. But still they received strange looks from the lady and man. Corinthians couldn't help but blush in embarrassment.

When the couple had disappeared around the corner, Corinthians frowned up at Trevor. She'd experienced more embarrassing moments with him than at any other time in her life. "See what you made me do," she hissed, straightening her blouse.

"And see what you made me do," he countered with a teasing gleam in his eye. He straightened his own shirt and put it back inside his pants.

Corinthians sighed, feeling a sense of panic. Had she actually pulled his shirt from out of his pants? Oh, boy! She had to get away from Trevor and fast. She'd never carried on like this with a man.

"Look, I have to go. Good night, Trevor."

"Are you sure you want to end the night like this?" he asked, reaching out and lifting a finger beneath her jaw and tipping her face up to his.

At the moment, she wasn't sure of anything as the soft brushing of his fingers against her chin nearly pushed her over the edge. "Yes, I'm sure. We'll only have regrets in the morning."

Trevor's eyes darkened. "I won't."

"But I will," she responded truthfully.

He took a step closer to her. "No, you won't. You want me as much as I want you. Admit it."

Corinthians stiffened and glared up at him. "I won't admit anything."

Trevor smiled. "Yes, you will. I'm going to make sure of it." He took a step back. "If later tonight you have a change of heart, I'm in room 530."

It took a few seconds for Corinthians to remember that she

was in room 528. She stared at him, hoping she had misunderstood him. "Room 530?"

His smile widened. "Yes. Remember I told you that I changed rooms earlier today. My room is now next to yours. And there's a connecting door. I'll keep my side unlocked, so feel free to enter my room anytime you like. That should be easy enough for you, since you're an old pro at doing that sort of thing."

He took a step forward, again pinning her against the door. The look he gave her was serious. "But make no mistake about it, Corinthians, when you walk through that connecting door, it won't be for Dex. I refuse to be a substitute for any man. When I have you in my arms and make love to you, it will be my name you'll moan from your lips. No one else's."

Corinthians's anger reached full height and she saw red with a vengeance. Without saying a word she turned, opened her door and closed it behind her, slamming it shut in Trevor Grant's face.

Chapter 5

Corinthians couldn't stop pacing the floor in her hotel room. Trevor Grant had her boiling. It only took a few moments to realize her reaction was just what he'd probably hoped for. The man enjoyed rattling her, and again he had succeeded.

And to think she had actually let him kiss her. She had let him put his hands on her and touch her. "I didn't even like it when he—"

The lie she was about to tell died in her throat. Although it galled her to admit it, the truth of the matter was that she *had* enjoyed kissing him. She ground her teeth, annoyed with herself.

Trevor Grant had been a thorn in her side since the time they had met. She wasn't supposed to enjoy doing anything with him, least of all kissing him. And she definitely wasn't supposed to have enjoyed his company in São Paulo. She had unintentionally let her guard down and look where it had gotten her.

She began pacing again. The nerve of him saying the two

of them would be sleeping together like it was a foregone conclusion! The same cockiness that had convinced him he was one of the few good men the Marines had been looking for had evidently warped his brain. He would be the last man she slept with. The very idea made her…ache with desire and tremble with need. And to make matters worse, he thought she was still carrying a torch for Dex, which was hilarious.

With a hopeless groan, Corinthians dropped down on the love seat and covered her eyes with her arms. Little did he know, it wasn't thoughts of Dex that were confusing her emotions to the point of not making sense. It wasn't thoughts of Dex that filled her with sexual tension whenever Trevor was near. It wasn't thoughts of Dex that stirred a desire in her so strong that she felt the need to protect herself by keeping a constant feud going between them. And it certainly hadn't been thoughts of Dex that had made her behave the way she had less than an hour ago outside her hotel room door.

People who knew her would never have believed she'd acted that way. The Corinthians Avery they knew was temperate, rational, calm, polished and proper. But around Trevor, she was temperamental, explosive, irrational, volatile and passionate.

Passionate.

Corinthians felt her cheeks go warm at the thought. She took a deep, calming breath and tried to think through the situation in a logical way. But she couldn't. All she wanted to think about was Trevor in an illogical way. The taste of him, hot and spicy, was still on her tongue. The feel of his hands was still stamped on her body. And his scent, a male cologne that smelled husky and robust, still had parts of her body heated.

She momentarily closed her eyes remembering how easily her mouth had molded to his, how snugly her body had fit against his and…

Corinthians stiffened when she heard the sound of the shower going next door in Trevor's room. She nearly moaned at the thought that the walls were paper-thin, and there was a possibility he'd heard her pacing earlier. She felt flustered. How could one man make her come so unglued? How could one man make her so vividly aware of him?

She laid her head back against the seat, remembering the last time they'd had connecting rooms. It would be a night she would never forget because seeing him always made her remember. And to think she had actually passed out at his feet.

Her mind flashed back to that night…

"What happened?"

"You fainted."

Corinthians looked up at the man towering over her. He was still dressed in that darn towel. It took only a few seconds to realize she'd been placed on his bed. She made a move to get up.

"Lie still."

Ignoring his command, she sat up. This evening had become a nightmare, and it would be even more of one if what this man had told her about Dex was true. She suddenly noticed she wasn't wearing her robe and quickly jumped under the covers. "Where's my robe? Why did you take it off?"

"It's over there," he said, indicating the back of the chair. "I removed it after picking you up off the floor. I was concerned and thought that perhaps you had some sort of identification in your pockets. Instead, all I found were these."

Corinthians tinted when he held up the pack of condoms. She wished there was a way for her to crawl out of the bed and under it. This was getting more embarrassing by the minute. "Please hand me my robe. I want to leave."

"Lady, you're not going anywhere until I get some answers. Now who are you and what are you doing in my room?"

Corinthians closed her eyes and inhaled deeply. She reopened them. "I've told you. I thought this was Dex's room. I'd planned to spend an evening with him."

"Sounds kind of cozy for you and a married man."

Her eyes flashed fire. "I didn't know he was married. I talked to Dex a few days ago, and he didn't mention a thing about being married and having a child."

"And the two of you made plans to spend an evening together?" Trevor asked with disbelief in his voice.

"No. Dex didn't know anything about this evening. It was going to be a surprise."

"Aha! Clayton Madaris did put you up to this."

Corinthians became so mad she forgot just how skimpy her outfit was and angrily got out of bed. The next thing she knew, she was facing him, fuming. Her scantily clad body nearly touched his. All she could think about was the outrage she felt. This man was deliberately making things difficult for her. He had to be the most despicable man she'd ever met.

"I don't know what you're talking about. Clayton Madaris didn't put me up to anything. I don't even know Dex's brother that well. I only met him once."

"Then you have a lot of explaining to do. I want a name."

Corinthians's anger reached boiling point. "Why should I give you my name when you haven't given me yours?"

The expression on Trevor's face indicated he was stunned by her statement. "I don't have to tell you who I am. This is my room, not yours. You're the one who shouldn't be here."

Corinthians took a step forward, bringing her even closer to Trevor. The anger in her eyes grew. "Wrong, brother. My room is right through that door. We have connecting rooms and my company is paying for both. This room was strictly reserved for Dex Madaris and you aren't him. So you're the one out of place."

"I'm Dex's replacement."

"What?"

"I said I'm Dex's replacement. The name's Trevor Grant. I'm project foreman for Madaris Explorations. Dex couldn't make tomorrow's meeting, so I'm here in his place. All of this was cleared with your boss at Remington Oil."

Corinthians's anger drained abruptly. Complete humilia-tion took its place. She tried to take a step back, but Trevor Grant wouldn't let her. He placed his hand around her waist. "Take your hands off me, Mr. Grant."

Trevor gave her a crooked smile. "No can do. I won't run the risk of you fainting at my feet again. Now, where were we? Ah, yes, introductions." Trevor's gaze held hers intently. "I'm still waiting on a name."

"Then wait on."

A mirthless smile curved Trevor's lips. "All right, so you want to play hardball. I think I'll just call the head honcho at Remington Oil and find out what is going on. Maybe he'll be able to explain why some half-dressed woman entered my hotel room wearing a robe full of condoms, claiming to be an employee of Remington Oil."

Trevor's eyes darkened. "You can tell me who you are, or you can explain your actions to Mr. Remington himself. Got it?" he growled.

Corinthians glared up at him. "Yes, I've got it." She then swallowed deeply. "May I have my robe back first, please?"

Trevor's brows narrowed. He gazed at her thoughtfully before saying, "No. I happen to like what you're wearing." He continued to stare at her. "And don't pull some sort of stalling act. I'd like to have a name before midnight."

Corinthians knew that from this moment on, she would despise this man forever. "I'm Corinthians Avery."

Corinthians's thoughts returned to the present. Nothing had changed. She still despised him. And although she appreciated what he'd done for her earlier that day in McDonald's, she still despised him.

Who do you think you're fooling? her mind screamed. *You didn't act like you despised him this afternoon in São Paulo. In fact, you'd been thinking maybe he wasn't so bad after all.*

Corinthians let out a heavy sigh as her mind continued berating her. *And you certainly didn't have any problems*

*checking out his body in that shirt and those jeans. Surely you
remember that shirt, the one that had fit so snugly across his
broad chest and that had been tucked so neatly in his jeans.
It was that same shirt you almost tore off him while he was
kissing you in the hallway.*

Corinthians inhaled deeply and stood. She was fighting a
losing battle tonight with herself. What she needed was a
long, relaxing bath. Then afterward, she would go over the
reports for tomorrow's meeting.

She was determined to put Trevor Grant out of her mind
for the rest of the night.

After taking a shower and toweling off, Trevor slipped a
towel around his waist before leaving the bathroom.

Padding into the other room, he noticed the message light
on his phone was blinking. He picked up the phone and called
the front desk and found out the caller had been Dex. He
smiled. He and the three Madaris brothers, Justin, Dex and
Clayton, had been close friends since birth, growing up in the
same neighborhood in Houston.

Trevor sat on the edge of the bed. After his decision to get
out of the Marines, he had returned home at just about the
same time Dex had returned from Australia where he'd been
for two years working for Remington Oil. Dex wanted to go
into business for himself and Trevor had agreed to be his
foreman if he ever did. Within two years of that agreement,
Madaris Explorations was formed. Now, nearly three years
later, they were one of the most sought-after exploration companies in the country, especially after they had helped Remington Oil locate an oil basin near Eagle Pass.

And because Dex was a very generous employer, that
venture had given every employee of Madaris Explorations
a heftier bank account.

Trevor smiled. Because he'd had the good sense to invest
in Dex's company, he'd made a lot of money. And thanks to

the vast investment knowledge of Jake Madaris, Dex's wealthy uncle, over the past couple of years, he had watched his funds nearly triple. Some people would probably be surprised to discover just how much he was worth.

Money never fazed him. He lived comfortably, not flashy. And like Dex, he enjoyed the outdoors, and the physical labor of a job. Head foreman of Madaris Explorations was definitely his calling. And since the arrival of a new baby, Dex had passed more and more of the company's duties to him so that he could spend more time with Caitlin and their two daughters, Jordan and Ashley.

Trevor shook his head. Dex didn't have a clue how Corinthians felt about him. He considered her a good friend, nothing more. And Dex knew nothing about the hotel room incident. It was Trevor's and Corinthians's secret. Her fainting from shock that night had proven she honestly hadn't known Dex had gotten married. But now that she knew, Trevor couldn't help wondering if she would one day make an attempt to sabotage Dex's marriage. She hadn't made a move in that direction so far, but that didn't necessarily mean she wouldn't.

Before picking up the phone, he glanced at the connecting door. His side was unlocked just like he'd told Corinthians. It would be up to her to make the first move. But a part of him knew that she wouldn't.

He shook his head, grinning. The spitting sparks of fire that he'd seen in her eyes before she had slammed the door in his face had actually turned him on. He knew that whenever he did get her into his bed, the heat from her fire would torch him to flames. And like he had told her, he would not be a substitute for Dex. She would know with whom she shared the bed. Pleased with that thought, he picked up the phone to return Dex's call.

"Madaris here."

"Hey, man, it's Trevor. What's up?"

"Not much. I just wanted to touch base with you before tomorrow's meeting. How are things going?"

Trevor glanced again at the unlocked connecting door. "As well as expected. I've gotten in some sightseeing time. I've taken in a soccer game. This is a pretty nice place."

Dex laughed. "Don't get attached to it. You're needed here."

"Don't worry about any attachments. I'm getting homesick already."

"Have you seen Corinthians Avery yet? I understand she's Remington Oil's representative."

"Yes, she's here, and yes, I've seen her."

"And?"

"And nothing. The woman and I don't get along."

"Yeah, so I've noticed, and I don't understand it."

Trevor shook his head. Dex actually believed Corinthians was a prim, proper, well-bred woman and a real lady saint.

"There's nothing to understand," he finally answered. "She and I don't see eye-to-eye on a lot of things. In fact, we're like oil and water."

"That bad?"

"Worse. How're Caitlin and the girls?" he asked, deciding to change the subject.

"They're fine and send their love."

He smiled. "Tell them ditto from me. And how are the newlyweds?"

"Clayton and Syneda are fine. They moved into their new law office a few days ago. Can you imagine the two of them sharing office space?"

Trevor shook his head. Clayton and Syneda disagreed on just about everything. "No, I can't imagine it. I'm still in shock at the thought of them being married."

"You're not the only one. Take care, man."

"You do the same, Dex."

Chapter 6

Corinthians wondered how she managed to get through the entire day of the research summit without making a complete fool of herself, which she was sure she'd do after walking into the meeting room and seeing Trevor.

He'd been standing across the room talking to another man. Dressed in a dark blue suit, he looked suave, virile and sexy. He'd actually looked like he had walked directly off the cover of a magazine. And when he'd turned and looked at her, meeting her gaze with those deep, dark eyes and forcing her to remember the kiss they had shared the night before, she had almost come unglued right then and there.

She had tightened her fingers on the handle of her briefcase to hide her shaking hands, but it hadn't worked. In defiance, she lifted her chin and met his gaze for a long moment before finally conceding that for once, she could not maintain the disturbing contact and outstare him. Lowering her gaze, she had taken a seat at the table. Luckily for her, there had been an empty chair sandwiched between others that were already occupied, as well as those directly across from her. She'd sighed knowing that at least he wouldn't be sitting close by.

But that hadn't stopped him from getting to her. During the meeting, their glances would periodically meet, weakening her defenses, making her forget how much she didn't like him, and making it hard for her to concentrate on the proceedings.

After the meeting, the only thing she wanted was to leave as quickly as possible. She stood and began gathering up her things. Without looking up she knew the exact moment Trevor came to stand behind her. She could feel the heat of his body transfer to hers. Her pulse raced and her hands began shaking again. She took a deep breath and tried to calm herself as she haphazardly tossed her notepad and pen into her briefcase and closed it with a click.

Her heart was pounding intensely as she turned around and quickly noticed everyone else had left and she and Trevor were the only people remaining in the room.

"Mr. Grant. How are you today?" she asked professionally, yet coolly, detesting the attraction she felt for him. Her body was getting warm all over, and even warmer in certain places.

Trevor drew his brows together at the formality in her tone; he didn't like it one bit. He raised his gaze to the ceiling, then lowered it to the floor before it came back to hers. He leaned forward, bracing both hands on the table and neatly pinning her in.

"A warning, Corinthians. The next time you call me Mr. Grant and not Trevor, I'm going to do something about it. Something similar to what I did last night, but this time I'll go a little further."

Corinthians's cheeks became heated from just imagining just how far he would go. She then berated herself for even thinking about it. He couldn't go any further than she let him. "Don't count on it," she snapped.

She glared up at him. His face was so close to hers that she could inhale the masculine scent of his aftershave, and see the even lines of his shaven chin. She was tempted to reach out and touch his skin to see if it felt as warm as it looked. She knew he had to be at least in his midthirties, but there were no wrinkle lines anywhere. His features, although ruggedly handsome, still had a smooth, unmarked appearance.

He smiled. "Oh, but I am counting on it. In fact, I'm doing more than just counting on it. I'm looking forward to it, especially after spending a night like I did last night. I didn't get much sleep for thinking about you and remembering how you felt in my arms."

A shiver passed through Corinthians. He would be the last to know it, but she hadn't gotten a good night's sleep, either, remembering that very same thing. "Please don't," she said in a soft plea.

Trevor had no intentions of granting her that request. Last night his dreams had been worse than ever. Before last night he could only imagine how she tasted. Now he knew. The real thing was even better than he'd imagined. And knowing she was bedded in the room next to his hadn't helped matters. Before morning he had taken two cold showers.

"I can't help it," he said honestly, stubbornly and not too happily. He met her gaze directly. "I want you."

Corinthians felt her insides jolt. Her warm body suddenly got hot, aroused. She became angered because once again he had echoed her own sentiments. And they were feelings she was not ready to face. "That's tough because you *can't* and you *won't* have me. Ever. Now if you don't mind, I'd like to get by and you're blocking my way."

He gave her an easy smile, one that made her knees go weak. She got an uneasy feeling he had taken her statement as a challenge. He straightened his stance. "Sorry," he said moving aside. "I didn't mean to detain you."

Corinthians grew more and more tense as she headed

toward the door. In her haste to depart, she looked up just in time to avoid colliding with Armond Thetas as he entered the room. He looked to be in his midfifties and considered extremely handsome for his age. He was also known to be a very wealthy man. His oil company was one of the few located in South America.

"Ms. Avery, I'm glad I was able to see you before you left. The organization committee has planned a dinner party tonight in honor of all attendees. It will be held here in one of the banquet rooms. Then tomorrow, everyone is invited to my villa located in Buzios for an overnight stay. A chartered plane will transport you there and bring you back. I have made arrangements for a chartered bus to pick everyone up from the hotel tomorrow morning. You will be returned to the hotel in the afternoon of the following day."

Corinthians smiled. She knew that Buzios was a very nice and expensive resort area that jutted in the Atlantic on the Cabo Frio Peninsula. The community contained million-dollar villas that were nestled along one of the seventeen idyllic beaches set among sandy coves. She had seen photographs of the upscale resort area that had numerous fine shops and excellent restaurants. As far as she was concerned Mr. Thetas's invitation for an overnight stay was a special treat, one she planned to take advantage of.

"Thanks, I'd love to attend the dinner party, and I'll look forward to going to Buzios in the morning."

The older man's face beamed. "Wonderful. Just pack an overnight bag." He then glanced over at Trevor. "What about you, Mr. Grant? Will you be joining us?"

Corinthians turned and looked at Trevor. A part of her hoped to heaven that he had other plans and would not be joining them. Evidently he read her thoughts because he gave her a smooth smile before saying, "I wouldn't miss it. Please count me in."

Armond Thetas nodded. "I'll look forward to seeing you both tonight. Good day."

After the man left, Corinthians turned back to Trevor and glared at him. Her anger flared when she saw the smile that lit his eyes. Clutching her briefcase more firmly in her hand, she headed for the door. She didn't miss the sound of his deep chuckle as the door swung shut behind her.

Rasheed Valdemon stepped from behind his desk and faced the man who had delivered the bad news to him. He raised an arched, angry brow. "What do you mean you still don't have Ms. Avery? I was counting on you, Santini. Now twice you and your people have disappointed me."

Raul Santini came to his feet in defense of both himself and his men. "It's not as easy as you think to snatch an American woman off the streets of Brazil. These things take time. Do you have any idea of the repercussions we'll face if the North American government finds out about your plan and connects us to it?"

Rasheed looked long and hard at his old friend. During their teen years, the two of them had attended a private academy in France. Santini's father was an ambassador from Argentina. "You agreed to help me, Santini."

"And I will. At least I will try, Monty," Santini replied, calling Valdemon by the name his friends had given him at the academy. "But just like you have to be careful to protect your country, I must do the same for mine, my friend. I can't take any unnecessary chances."

Rasheed sighed deeply and ran a hand over his face. "You have nothing to worry about. I told you that in the very beginning. American tourists disappear in foreign countries all the time, and the only people who make any noise about it are their families. They soon quiet down once they see their government won't do anything. Some tourists have been missing for years. Americans traveling abroad are on their own."

"But this isn't just any American, Monty. Ms. Avery is the sister of a United States senator."

"So what? As far as I am concerned, we'll be doing Joshua Avery a favor. He can't seem to handle her anyway. I'm sure that initially there may be some sort of an investigation, but in time, that, too, shall pass."

He came and sat on the edge of his desk and faced his friend. "Remember that if I succeed in this, your country will be rewarded greatly. You know me well enough to know that I never forget my friends."

Santini sighed, knowing that was true. Valdemon had secretly helped his country on a number of occasions. While at the academy several of them, all sons of important political figures from various nations, had formed a pact, a secret cartel. If there was anything one of them could do that would benefit the other's homeland, then they would do it. He had called on his friends in the cartel several times. However, this was the first time one of them had called on South America for help.

"We would have grabbed her yesterday had that man not shown up," Santini finally said, breaking the silence.

Rasheed blinked at the unexpected news. He stood. "What man?"

"The American who arrived before my men could do anything. And according to them, the man seemed to be a close friend of Ms. Avery. Possibly even her lover. He handled her with too much familiarity to be anything less."

Rasheed frowned. According to Joshua Avery, his sister was not romantically involved with anyone. "And your men couldn't handle one man?"

"Not this particular man. He's had extensive military training."

Rasheed's frown deepened. "And how do your men know that?"

"Because he wears *the* ring."

"What ring?"

"The Force Reconnaissance ring."

Any military man, no matter what country he was from,

had heard about the Force Recon group. They were an elite, highly skilled, specially trained group of men in the United States Marine Corps. A special breed of warriors, they were a close-knit group, almost like a brotherhood, who proudly wore their signet rings to prove it. To anyone else's observant eye it would look like just another signet ring. But to another military man, no matter what branch of service and no matter from what country, that ring had significant meaning.

"Are you sure?" Rasheed asked quietly, thoughtfully.

"I'm positive. The two men who reported back to me are former military men with the Argentine government. They would know."

Rasheed's mood darkened. "This changes nothing. I won't be satisfied until I receive the news that Corinthians Avery is on her way to Mowaiti."

"And the American protecting her?"

"He's your problem. You deal with him."

Santini shook his head. "You're taking a big chance, Monty."

"Am I?" he challenged. "Can you say you wouldn't do the same to save your country if given the chance, big or small?"

Santini thought about his love for his own country and knew there was nothing he wouldn't do for his people. "No."

Rasheed smiled. He knew his friend understood. He walked over to him and touched him on the shoulder. "Once I have Ms. Avery and she finds oil, Mowaiti's troubles will be over. Out of friendship and honor, please continue to help me on this."

Santini nodded. "I will."

Trevor glanced around the crowded banquet room. Most of the people present had attended today's meeting and represented more than fifty major oil companies from around the world. They were people who were well-trained in scientific and technical skills in ways to extract oil reserves. The purpose of the all-day meeting had been to share as much of that knowledge as possible without leaking any company secrets.

He couldn't help but be proud of the way Corinthians had handled herself. He hadn't missed the look of admiration and respect in a number of the men's eyes. She had done something a lot of them had yet to do, and that was to use her vast knowledge and skill to locate an oil basin. As far as he was concerned, that said a lot for someone who was the only female head geologist in the group. When she had given her presentation, a lot of eyes had been on her. Some, he'd noticed, for reasons other than the information she was providing. Her physical beauty had entranced them. And he had to grudgingly admit, he hadn't liked it one bit. At first he had convinced himself that he hadn't cared that other men were looking at her with male interest. But later he'd been man enough to admit he'd lied to himself.

He had cared. More than he had wanted to.

He was reaching for another glass of wine off the tray of a passing waiter when the room suddenly became quiet. He turned to see what had caused the silence and felt his stomach tighten. Corinthians stood in the doorway and she looked absolutely gorgeous. Trevor took a quick glance around the room. Some of the men were openly drooling. His anger heightened. You would think they had never seen a beautiful American woman before. Even Armond Thetas appeared spellbound.

Trevor's gaze hardened as he looked at Corinthians again. A sudden knot formed in his throat. He himself had seen numerous beautiful American women, but never like this. She had really outdone herself tonight. He blinked once, then twice, to make sure he was seeing straight. She was dressed in—of all things—a virginal white, flowing evening gown. The gown's color was a stark contrast against the dark hue of her skin. But the combination of coloring made her look absolutely stunning, breathtaking.

Trevor glanced back around the room. A number of the men, although married, had not bothered to bring their wives with them on this trip. They were the main ones slobbering at the sight of Corinthians. The sight was totally disgusting.

His gaze moved back to the doorway. He could gather from Corinthians's expression she had also noted the fact that she was on display. She stood transfixed in place, scanning the group as if to make up her mind whether or not she really wanted to enter a den filled with salivating wolves.

Trevor noticed she kept glancing around the room as if looking for someone. He suddenly realized she was searching for him. He was surprised, given the on-going feud between them. He quickly reached the conclusion that to her way of thinking, he was just one more brazen, salivating wolf among many, *but* he was the one Corinthians assumed she could handle.

What the heck, he would let her assume whatever she liked, he thought, moving toward her. And he would let the people here tonight assume whatever they wanted to think, he thought further, picking up his pace. A few seconds later he was standing directly in front of Corinthians. He immediately saw the look of both relief and gratitude in her eyes.

For the space of several timeless moments, he didn't move. Then he leaned slightly and brushed his lips against hers in way of an affectionate greeting, effectively telling everyone present that Corinthians Avery was already taken.

Corinthians had seen the kiss coming, but hadn't had time to prepare herself for it. Although Trevor had barely brushed his lips against hers, her body had begun tingling all over. When he straightened his tall form, her gaze covered him from head to toe. If she thought Trevor had looked handsome in his dark suit at today's meeting, he looked doubly so in his white dinner jacket and dark slacks.

"For some reason, Trevor, I think you enjoy rescuing me," she whispered.

He smiled as he reached out and took her hand in his. "I do." He looked down at her. "You look great."

"Thanks."

The room was no longer silent. People were once again engaged in conversations. However, Trevor knew those same slavering wolves were discreetly watching them. "I may have disappointed a lot of men here tonight," he whispered to Corinthians.

Corinthians looked up at him. "How so?"

"When you entered the room dressed in all white, because of the customs, traditions and beliefs in their countries regarding women wearing white, they saw you as a maiden virgin. I may have destroyed that image with my kiss, especially since it was in front of everyone at a professional gathering. Rumors will probably begin circulating that we're lovers." He angled his head, studying her intently. "What do you have to say about that?"

She smiled up at him. "Nothing, since you and I know better. Tonight, we're merely playacting."

"Are you sure about that?"

Before she could answer, he led her over to the table where dinner would be served.

Rasheed stood in front of the window in his Washington, D.C., apartment watching the rain. In Mowaiti, the rain was always welcomed. His people needed it for the growth of their crops. For the past few years, occasional drought had ravished the lands, making it harder for the people to earn a living, and making it harder still for them to feed their families. These things seemed to worry him more than they did his father, whose only concern was with gaining allies to keep the country safe. He had closed his eyes to the bleak circumstances surrounding his people. If it continued, Mowaiti would no longer exist as a country.

The soft knock at the door interrupted his thoughts. A few minutes later, Swalar, his valet, announced the arrival of Yasir Bedouins, a man who had been his father's adviser and close confidant for a number of years. Rasheed had once loved this man like a father because when his own parents hadn't had the time to listen to his youthful woes, Yasir had. But because of Yasir's close relationship with Sheikh Amin Valdemon, and his strong sense of dedication and loyalty to him, their once-close relationship was no more, especially now since he was no longer a child, but a man with his own views and a mind to express them. Rasheed regretted that, like his father, Yasir's ambition in life was not in making Mowaiti a stronger and powerful nation, but in keeping it safe and preserving its present state of existence.

"Yasir, to what do I owe this visit? Is something wrong with Father?" he asked with genuine concern in his voice when the older man entered his office. Even with their differences, he loved his father deeply.

"No, your father is fine. A little tired tonight more than usual, but he's fine."

At that moment, efficient as ever, Swalar brought in coffee. And as Swalar went about pouring the brew in each of their cups, Rasheed studied Yasir, trying to decipher his mood and most importantly the reason for his visit. However, no words were spoken until after Swalar had finished his task and left the room, closing the door behind him.

"How long has he been serving you?" Yasir asked before taking a sip of the coffee.

Rasheed frowned. "Who? Swalar?"

At Yasir's nod, he answered, "Since I was thirteen years old. Why?"

"I think he's getting too old for the task. You need a younger, more able-bodied man to—"

"I don't want anyone else," Rasheed interrupted. "I like Swalar just fine, and he still serves my needs extremely well." He took a sip of his own coffee before adding, "He and I understand each other."

Yasir lifted a brow. "In other words, he's still very efficient in keeping your secrets."

Rasheed knew better than to play cat-and-mouse games with Yasir. The man was too sharp-witted for that. But tonight, just to humor him, he would make an exception. "I suppose he's as efficient at keeping my secrets as you are in keeping my father's. Should I try and guess why he's so tired tonight?"

Yasir met his gaze directly and unswervingly. "Your father has special needs."

Rasheed smiled faintly. "Evidently. But isn't it enough that he has a harem full of women back home in our country. Does he have to create another one here in this country, as well?"

Yasir shrugged. "The American women are willing enough, and he's not hurting anyone."

Rasheed snorted. "No one but himself. He turns sixty-one this year. How many women a night is he up to now? Last count it was five."

Yasir shifted in his seat, not out of mortification or disgrace, Rasheed concluded, but merely to find a more comfortable position. "I don't keep tabs on such matters," he replied gruffly.

"Maybe you should. He's not immune to AIDS you know. And I love my mother very much. I wouldn't want my father's private, sordid affairs to ever cause harm to her health."

"I take care of such matters."

Rasheed shook his head, not doubting that he did. A part of him couldn't help wondering just to what extent Yasir did so. "Are you going to tell me why you're here, Yasir?"

The older man sat back in his chair. "I've heard things…" Yasir said slowly. "Senator Joshua Avery has boasted to others of your interest in his sister. Your father and I saw the two of you together last month at that dinner party for Senator Nedwyn Lansing."

Rasheed took another sip of coffee. "So, what of it? She's very beautiful. And I happen to like American women…like my father."

Yasir's smile was slow. "If anything, you would not like them because of that very reason. So I've been curious as to why Ms. Avery has interested you. To appease my curiosity, I did some checking into her background. What I discovered is very interesting."

"And just what have you discovered, Yasir?"

"Knowing your modern views on how you believe you can save Mowaiti, I think your interest in Corinthians Avery speaks for itself." Yasir leaned forward. "But don't be a fool, Rasheed. Take this advice from someone who cares for you like a father. Whatever you're into, get out of it. The United States is one of our biggest allies. We don't need you to bring bad blood between our countries because of your foolish, boyish dreams. Are you determined to destroy the good, solid relationship we have with this country that your father has worked years to cultivate?"

Rasheed leaped out of his chair. "Is it foolish and boyish to want better for our people?"

"No, but you have no proof there is oil anywhere in Mowaiti. If there were, don't you think it would have been discovered by now?"

"Not necessarily. Look at Libya, and how—"

"I don't want to hear about Libya. When are you going to realize we are a totally different country?"

Rasheed narrowed his eyes. "And when are you and Father going to get your heads out of the sand and out from underneath the American women's skirts, and take note of what's really happening in Mowaiti? You're so busy keeping Father's secrets and he's so busy creating more secrets for you to keep that neither of you can see what's happening. Neither you nor him have been to Mowaiti in months."

Yasir stood. "I refuse to continue this conversation with you, Rasheed. I expect you to take heed of my advice. If I have to, I will alert your father of what you're about. I take my job as his confidant and adviser seriously."

Without saying another word, Yasir Bedouins turned and walked out of the room.

Corinthians finished packing the overnight bag she was taking to Buzios, and placed it next to her bed. According to Armond Thetas, the chartered bus that would take them to the airport would arrive at dawn. She had decided to pack tonight instead of rushing about doing the chore in the morning.

She had left the dinner party more than an hour ago. Trevor had remained close by her side the entire evening, and she had appreciated that. At the end of dinner, he had escorted her back to her room. She'd been mildly surprised when all he'd done was brush a kiss on her cheek before saying good-night. She refused to admit she was disappointed he hadn't taken her into his arms and kissed her senseless like he'd done the night before.

Corinthians was so absorbed in her thoughts that the shrill ringing of the telephone startled her. She reached out and grabbed it before it could ring a second time. "Hello."

"Corinth? What's going on, girl?"

Corinthians smiled. Her best friend, Brenna, was just the person she needed to talk to. The two of them had been friends since childhood and had no secrets.

"Brenna, when did you get back?" For years Brenna had been a Fashion Fair model, but had given it up a couple of years ago after complaining of being burned out and getting up in age. Photographers were looking for younger women these days, Brenna claimed, and not women who were hitting thirty. However, she had jumped at the opportunity when *Ebony* contacted her six months ago to coordinate the fashion shows for them. Although it meant constant travel, it had been an opportunity for her to remain a part of an industry she loved.

"I got back yesterday, but let's cut the small talk. Tell me, how's Trevor Grant?"

Corinthians laughed as she stretched out on the bed. "Trevor Grant is doing fine, I guess."

"Did you see him today?"

"Yes, we attended the same dinner party tonight."

"Umm. And you're alone now?"

Corinthians raised a brow. "Yes, why?"

"Then I bet the brother isn't doing fine. I bet he's taking a cold shower about now."

Corinthians smiled at Brenna's assumption. She could actually hear the shower running in Trevor's room. But that didn't necessarily mean the shower he was taking was a cold one. "All right, Brenna, let up, girl. Pull back."

"If you insist. But if I were you I wouldn't let him get away, Corinth. Good men are hard to find."

Corinthians chuckled when she remembered something Trevor had said yesterday. "I bet I know where a few of them are."

"Really? Where?" Brenna asked, more than mildly curious.

Corinthians scooted over in the bed to the side closest to the wall. Trevor's shower, she noted, was going full blast. "In the Marines."

Nothing like a cold shower to cool a man off, Trevor thought as he dried off his wet body before placing a towel around his waist. There was only so much temptation that a sane man could take. And tonight he had nearly reached his limit. His lips twisted into a smile as he made his way out of the bathroom. Tonight Corinthians had been all grace, finesse and elegance. It hadn't been the flowing gown that covered, yet tantalized every curve of her body. Nor had it been the way she'd had her hair fixed atop her head in a bevy of curls that crowned her features with innocence. To his way of thinking, it had been the way she had carried herself, so vibrantly alive yet the carefully controlled, dignified and proper lady.

The envious looks he'd receive from numerous men had stunned him with the knowledge of just what he hadn't realized until tonight. There were two sides to Corinthians Avery. One was the wanton seductress, who had appeared half-naked in his hotel room that night, and the other was the prim-and-proper Ms. Avery. He couldn't help but wonder which Corinthians Avery he liked best. He then decided he liked them both. And deep down he knew he wanted them both.

Trevor bit back a groan when thoughts of having her sent blood rushing through his veins. When he had walked her to her room, it had taken all the control he could conjure from years of military training not to take her into his arms for a repeat of last night. He couldn't run the risk of tasting then devouring the sweetness of her mouth again, without being tempted to taste the rest of her.

He leaned back against the wall to get his bearings. This kind of sensual attraction was a first for him. Never had he been so captivated with a woman. And if that didn't beat all, this magnetic pull had lasted nearly two years. Even knowing that she was in love with another man—a man who happened to be his best friend—hadn't stopped him from desiring her, hungering after her. And that realization cut him to the core.

Reaching down, he picked up his overnight bag and began filling it with the things he needed for his overnight stay in Buzios. The only reason he had accepted Thetas's invitation was because the look Corinthians had given him had dared him to. He shrugged. He was a sucker for a dare, especially one from Corinthians.

Chapter 7

Someone was in her room.

That thought suddenly registered in Corinthians's groggy mind and she came awake instantly. She sat up in bed and frantically glanced around the room. It was dark and she couldn't see a thing. Fear knotted inside of her. She pushed aside the covers and was about to ease out of bed when someone pulled her up from behind. A large, rough hand covered her mouth, effectively silencing the scream she was about to make.

"Don't make a sound. We have to get out of here. Now."

Trevor's deep voice cut through Corinthians's near hysteria. Her body became calm when she realized who the intruder was, and she automatically relaxed against his hard frame. She then became angry, almost livid. Had he lost his mind? The nerve of him entering her room in the middle of the night and frightening her. And how on earth did he get in? She squirmed against him, and when he twisted her around to face him, she glared up at him, barely making out his features in the darkness, but ready to give him a piece of her mind. She would have done so if his hand hadn't still been firmly clamped over her mouth. But in her furious state, she was not about to let that stop her. She tried talking against the palm of his hand and couldn't. She groaned her frustration, getting even madder.

Trevor pulled her over to an area where a small pool of light flowed in through the window blinds. "Shh. Listen to me, Corinthians. Listen like your very life depends on what I'm about to tell you because it just might. A group of terrorists have taken over this hotel."

He saw her dark eyes widen and blink as she comprehended what he had said. He felt the chill that swept through her body and momentarily froze her in place. "I couldn't sleep and decided to go downstairs. I took the stairs instead of the elevators." Trevor decided not to mention the reason he had taken the stairs was because he'd felt the need to work off some frustrated sexual energy. Being around her at the dinner party had made his desire for her stronger than ever.

"When I got to the bottom floor I saw them. They're holding some of the hotel personnel at gunpoint, as well as some of the people in our group who decided to stay late at the dinner party. I ducked back in the stairway before they saw me. It's my guess that eventually they'll make a clean sweep of this hotel and take anyone they can as hostages, especially Americans. I don't plan on being among that number, and I don't think you want that, either. So we're getting out of here. Understand?"

Corinthians nodded her head. She could tell from the look on Trevor's face and from the troubled sound of his voice that he was dead serious about the hotel being under terrorist attack. She took in a deep gulp of air when he removed his hand from her mouth.

"Come on, we have to move quickly before they reach our

floor," he whispered close to her ear. "I've jammed the elevator and blocked the stairway door but that will only buy us—"

"Why don't we just call the police?" Corinthians cut in. Following his lead, she kept her voice low.

"I tried, but the phones are dead. And because this hotel is located on an isolated stretch of beach the cell phones haven't worked since day one, and there's no place we can go to for help that's close by."

He sighed deeply. "We're wasting time. You need to change out of what you have on and put on something else. Wear something dark, and put on a pair of comfortable shoes. And you're going to have to get the items out of your closet without turning on the lights."

It suddenly hit Corinthians that she was dressed in her sleepwear. But at the moment, being modest was the last thing on her mind as she quickly moved to her closet. She couldn't worry about Trevor seeing her dressed in her short, silk nightshirt. There wasn't much light in the room for him to see too much and besides, he'd once seen her in a whole lot less.

No woman's body should be that perfectly shaped, Trevor thought as he watched Corinthians rush to the closet and begin pulling items off hangers. And no woman's body should feel that soft. He couldn't help but remember how she'd felt against him a few moments ago when he had pulled her out of bed. His hand hadn't been what he'd wanted to use to cover her mouth. The deep desire he always felt around her had tempted him to cover her mouth with his own, and again taste her passion and her fire. What he had wanted to do with his hand was to run it over her body, to feel her softness while he continued to kiss her, and elicit from her that sweet, deep, throaty moan he'd gotten out of her last night while kissing her.

He mentally chastised himself for letting his mind concentrate on seducing her and not on the important matter at hand, which was getting them to safety. "While you're getting dressed I'm going to throw a few things we might need in a bag," he whispered, glancing around the room. He needed to look at anything in the room but at her right now, especially her legs and thighs that were exposed from underneath her short nightshirt.

"I packed that bag earlier tonight to take with me to Buzios," Corinthians said, pointing to her overnight bag next to the bed. "Everything I might need is in it. We'll be able to return to the hotel in a couple of hours, won't we?"

Trevor wished he could answer yes to that question, but he wasn't sure. "I hope so," he said leaning down and picking up her bag. He frowned. It was heavy, way too heavy.

"Where are we going?" Corinthians asked, tossing the items that she had taken out of the closet on the bed.

"In the jungle. We'll hang out there until the authorities get things back under control here."

She nodded. "How did you get into my room?" she asked, after reaching down for her shoes and socks.

"I picked the lock," he answered absently. He couldn't keep his gaze off her legs.

When Corinthians dashed off into the bathroom to change, Trevor sucked in a deep breath to regain control of his senses before quickly walking through the connecting door and into his room to get his own overnight bag. They would have to combine their stuff into one bag, preferably his since it appeared to be the sturdier of the two.

Going back into Corinthians's room, he opened her night bag and began going through it, only taking out the things he thought were necessary and packing them in his. His hand trembled when it came in contact with silky and lacy material. He took a deep breath when he pulled out a pair of lacy underwear and a matching bra. He put them back inside her bag.

Corinthians came out of the bathroom dressed in a pair of dark-colored jeans and a black top. She had on a pair of sneakers.

"We can only take one bag, so I'm putting our stuff together and using mine," Trevor said, turning to her.

She nodded. "Did you get everything I need?" she asked as she watched him zip up the bag.

Trevor thought about her underthings he hadn't placed in his bag. "I took out everything I'm letting you take. Too much stuff will slow us down and we don't need that."

He tossed her wallet to her. "Keep this on you at all times. You may need your passport."

Corinthians nodded, stuffing her wallet into her back pocket. "How are we going to get out of here?"

"Just follow me and do what I tell you to."

Corinthians took offense with the bossiness of his tone of voice. She glared up at him. "I'll do what you tell me to do as long as it makes sense."

"I won't do it, Trevor. It doesn't make sense. There has to be another way," Corinthians said moments later as they stood on the balcony of her hotel room.

Trevor turned and met her gaze. "What do you suggest that we do? Use the elevators or the stairs to get down?" His voice was low and agitated. He was beginning to lose his patience. "This is the only way we can make it down without being seen. It's not as bad as it looks."

Corinthians wasn't convinced of that, as she looked down over the balcony's railing to the ground that was five stories below. She then looked at the fire escape ladder that over the years had grown covered with trails of burgeoned vines. Evidently periodic safety inspections weren't required here. "I disagree. I think it's as bad as it looks."

Trevor frowned. "Then suit yourself. You can stay here if that's what you're inclined to do. But I'm going down using that ladder. I suggest you do the same and follow. Believe me, the last thing you'd want is to stay behind. Female hostages, especially the ones who're attractive as you are, don't fare well with terrorists. I'm sure you know what I mean."

Corinthians shuddered. She knew exactly what he meant. Last year the newspapers had reported how an American businessman and his wife, who had been vacationing in Central America, had been abducted by a group of revolutionaries. The man had been killed and his wife had been gang raped before she'd been left for dead.

She took a deep breath. Revolutionaries or terrorists, they were all the same in her book. Both groups had causes and beliefs they were willing to die for; causes and beliefs they would do just about anything to draw worldwide attention to.

Corinthians glanced again at the ladder. It didn't look like it could hold one person's weight, let alone two. "I might fall," she finally said softly in a shaky voice.

Trevor saw the fear in her eyes, and he heard it in her voice. A part of him wanted to reach out and pull her into his arms and soothe her, reassure her. "You won't fall. I won't let you. Trust me."

Their eyes met for a moment, then Corinthians nodded. She would trust him. For some reason she believed he would get them to safety.

"Come on, Corinthians. We need to get a move on, and the fire escape is our only way. I'll go first and you follow. With me ahead of you, I'll be between you and the ground."

Corinthians nodded and watched Trevor. With the overnight bag in one hand, he hefted his body over the side railing. After getting the proper footing, he reached out and grasped the vine-covered ladder with his free hand.

He glanced back at her. "Just follow me down."

Trevor had gone down the rungs a few feet before looking up at Corinthians. She hadn't moved from her spot on the balcony. "Come on, baby, you can do it."

Corinthians took a deep breath. The fear attacking her was

immediately wiped away with Trevor's term of endearment. The word *baby* had flowed like soft honey from his lips. Looking deep into his dark eyes, Corinthians leaned over and clutched the metal ladder with her hands. She then lifted her body over the side. After getting firm footing and saying a silent prayer, she began following Trevor down slowly, rung after rung, one step at a time. At one point, she almost slipped, but Trevor's hand reached up and cushioned her backside to keep her from toppling over. She breathed a prayer of thanks to God when her feet finally hit solid ground.

She turned to Trevor to thank him for his help when suddenly there was a burst of gunfire that seemed to be all around them. He snatched her down to the ground and covered her with his body, shielding her. When it was apparent the shots had been fired from inside the hotel, he lifted his body off hers.

"Sounds like all hell has broken loose. Let's get out of here," he whispered urgently. "See that area over there?" he asked her, pointing to what appeared to be a wooded cove.

Corinthians shook her head. "Yes."

"We're going to make a run for it. I want you to run as fast as you can and no matter what, don't look back, and don't stop. I'll be right behind you."

Corinthians nodded. Although Trevor hadn't said so, she knew that by being behind her, he would be protecting her back. His instincts to protect and defend completely amazed her. Although she feared the unknown, she felt her life was safe in his hands.

"Run, Corinthians."

Taking a deep breath, she did as he'd instructed and took off running with him right behind her. When they reached the wooded area, he grabbed her hand and stopped her from going any farther.

"Wait," he breathed in her ear and gently tugged her behind him. "Let me go first now. Just stay close."

Corinthians nodded as they walked deeper and deeper into

the overgrown thicket of trees and foliage of numerous plants. A gentle breeze wafted through the trees and the surrounding dense undergrowth. Moonlight glistening across the land provided them with an adequate degree of light as they kept walking, moving farther away from the hotel.

A few minutes later when Trevor stopped suddenly, she almost bumped into him. He quickly dropped to the ground and pulled her down beside him. Placing a finger to his lips, he whispered, "Shh."

Moments later she understood why he'd requested her silence when she heard voices. Trevor sandwiched their crouched bodies tightly between the trunks of two huge blossoming trees, placing her behind him. The low-hanging branches shielded their presence from view.

Corinthians tried ignoring the flutter in the pit of her stomach from the feel of them being so close and their bodies touching. Trevor's back felt warm and sturdy against her chest. Neither the material of her shirt nor the material of his was thick enough to diffuse the heat passing from his body to hers. From her body's reaction, they may as well have been skin-to-skin. Her breasts were tingling from the contact, and her body was trembling.

Trevor felt her shiver and misinterpreted it as her being frightened. He reached behind him and took hold of her hand, entwining their fingers. He didn't want to question why it was important to him that she felt safe. He tightened his fingers around hers, willing her to believe things would be all right, and that he would take care of her.

Corinthians held her breath when, in the sparse lighting cast to earth from a quarter moon, the figures of two men came into view. Whatever they were saying was being spoken in Spanish.

She wished she could follow their conversation, but she didn't know Spanish any more than she knew Portuguese. But from the way Trevor's body stiffened, she could tell he somewhat understood them. At one point during the men's conversation, he snapped his head around and looked at her with questioning eyes.

It seemed that a full twenty minutes had passed before the men finally moved on. Corinthians was grateful. Her body was hurting from remaining in one position for such a long period of time, and the smoke from one of the men's cigarettes had begun stinging her eyes.

When Trevor was sure the men had moved a safe distance away from them, he stood and pulled Corinthians up with him. "That was a close call," he said. He began stretching to work the kinks and tightness out of his cramped body.

Corinthians followed his lead and began doing the same thing. "Did you understand what they were saying? Who are they? I could swear they're the same ones from McDonald's. But with those bandannas tied around their heads, I can't be too sure."

Trevor stopped stretching and turned to fix his gaze on Corinthians. He'd wondered if she would notice that they were the same two. But until he found out what was going on and how she was involved, he wouldn't tell her that. "I understood a little of what they were saying, but not enough to make any sense out of it," he replied truthfully. "Come on, I'm going to find a safe place where I can leave you before I go."

Corinthians's eyes widened. "Go where?"

"Back to the hotel."

"Why? Shouldn't we stay put until the police come?" she asked, not caring that her voice was quivering.

The look Trevor gave her was deep, intense and protective. "I'll be back, Corinthians, but I need to go back to the hotel to see if I can help the others."

He picked up the overnight bag. "Come on, let's keep moving."

Trevor left Corinthians in what he considered a pretty safe place. Using extreme caution and all the survival skills he possessed as a former member of the Marine's Force Recon group, he made his way through the jungle of dense vines, overhanging trees and thick underbrush.

He tried to ignore the surge of adrenaline pumping through his bloodstream, and the rush of energy consuming him. As much as he didn't want to admit it, out here in the wilds underneath the predawn sky, and the possibility of danger nipping close at his heels, he was within his element.

One of his special skills as a member of the Marine Corps Force Reconnaissance unit was his survival expertise. Within the special, elite group of highly trained men who engaged in special Marine operations, his fellow peers had considered him one of the best in that field. Because of the nature of the Force Recon, they had to be well trained on how to survive if they were ever caught behind enemy lines. All of them had been taught ways on how to escape their captors, how to hide out in the thicket of a jungle, and how to travel with special emphasis placed on what roads and paths to avoid.

Trevor crouched down when he saw the hotel in the distance through the trees. There had been approximately twenty-five people who had stayed at the hotel for the research summit. And no telling how many others had been there just for a little rest and relaxation. It would take quite a number of terrorists to handle a group that large of panic-stricken and hysterical people.

He had only seen five armed men when he had gone downstairs. At the time, after weighing all the factors and considering all his options, he had decided not to be foolish and to try doing anything heroic. His main thought had been on Corinthians and getting her out of the hotel. For some reason it had been of monumental importance to keep her safe.

Trevor sighed deeply, not fully understanding why he had felt such a strong need to protect her at any cost; even at the cost of his own life. Even now he was worried about her. He had discovered a steep slope that had been well-hidden by a cloak of trees whose overhanging branches had formed a canopy, making it the perfect hideout. And although he felt she was pretty safe for now, he didn't want to leave her alone for too long. He had given her strict orders to stay put.

When he got closer to the hotel, Trevor tensed, ready for action. He slowly and silently made his way toward the regal six-floor structure. All was quiet. Too quiet, he thought, as he slipped into the dark alley of a vine-covered walkway that was adjacent to the hotel. All his senses were astute and on alert. His facial features became void of any expression. In the pit of his stomach he felt there was something about the situation that wasn't right. Being careful not to be seen, he eased his body close to a window and peeped in. The lobby area of the hotel was empty. There wasn't a single person in sight. He slowly eased his way around the other side of the building to check out the hotel from another angle. He then saw everything.

The large banquet room, the same one the dinner party had been held in that night, was in shambles. Tables had been overturned and the stage where the live band had performed had been destroyed. But what caught his eye was the fact that there were people in the room. Most of them were dressed in their sleepwear. Evidently they had been accosted from their rooms in the middle of the night. They were sitting on the floor as if in a trance and afraid to move.

Trevor frowned as he analyzed the situation before him in full detail. There was a look of total fear on all of their faces, from the youngest person in the room to the oldest. Why? As far as he could see from within the window's perimeter, there wasn't an armed terrorist around. So what was keeping these people immobile? He felt around the window for a latch to open so he could get inside.

"No, *senhor!* You mustn't!"

Trevor swung his body around quickly, automatically going into attack position, ready to defend. With his body poised, his feet spread apart and his hands in midair with palms arched, his stance was symbolic of lethal readiness. The Force Recons's special fighting skill consisted of four different types of martial arts that were blended together for maximum use. And his mind and his body were high-toned, keen and as sharp as a fine cutting edge.

"Please, *senhor*, don't hurt me. I just wanted to warn you."

Trevor's body somewhat relaxed when he looked into the young boy's tired and frightened face. He couldn't have been more than twelve or thirteen years old. He'd remembered seeing him serving as a waiter during dinner, and had thought at the time that the labor force in this country started rather young.

Trevor wondered how the kid had managed to escape the terrorists. He even considered the possibility that the boy was one of them. It wasn't uncommon for revolutionaries or terrorists to pull into their folds young innocents, who possessed a zeal for making changes, even drastic, radical ones. He tilted his head back and studied the boy. And the more he did so, the more his features depicted someone who was truly frightened and genuinely concerned. "Warn me about what?" he finally asked.

"The bomb."

Trevor frowned as a wave of apprehension flowed through him. "What bomb?"

"The one those bad men left behind in the hotel. I was in the back when they came into the hotel. I was able to get out without being seen."

The muscles of Trevor's forearms hardened beneath the sleeves of his shirt. A cold knot formed in his stomach as he thought about the people inside the hotel. "What makes you think there's a bomb?"

"Those men said so. They told everyone that a bomb has been planted in the hotel, somewhere in that room. And that any sound or any slight movement would set it off."

The unwelcome knot that had formed in Trevor's stomach

moved higher to his chest, making it feel as if it would burst
as he comprehended what the boy was saying. No wonder the
people were all sitting around like zombies, afraid to move.
"How many terrorists were there?"

"In the beginning there were about five, then another four
men showed up later."

"Where are they now?"

"They left around half an hour ago and took some of the
people with them, all Americans."

Trevor wasn't surprised they had taken American hostages.
"Which way did they go?"

"Half of them headed toward the mountains with the
hostages. The others went through the jungle looking for the
African-American woman. The one you were with at the
dinner party tonight."

Trevor's body tensed and a pensive shimmer appeared in
the shadows of his dark eyes. "How do you know that?"

"I overheard them talking when I was hiding out in the
kitchen. I can't remember everything they said, I only
remember them saying that their leader was angry that she
could not be found. I can only assume she was the one they
were talking about because she's the only African-American
woman who's been staying at the hotel. The leader told his
men who went into the jungle not to return without her."

Trevor's face hardened. "How many men went into the
jungle?"

"Three of them." He glanced at the hotel. "*Senhor,* what
can we do to help those people inside? Do you really believe
a bomb is planted in there?"

Trevor knew enough about terrorists to know they were
good in backing up their threats. In fact, to cause destruction
for what they believed in was an honor. "Yes, I believe it."

At that moment the sound of sirens could be heard in the
distance. Help was coming. Trevor's eyes darkened with intensity as he thought about everything that the kid had told

him. He had to get back to Corinthians. She wasn't safe alone in the jungle with three men looking for her. And until he was able to piece together what was going on and what part she played, it would be best if they hid out in the jungle for a while longer. He didn't feel safe trusting the Brazilian police right now. He looked back at the young boy who was watching him with something akin to fear in his eyes.

"What's your name?" Trevor asked the boy.

"Giovano."

Trevor nodded. "Giovano, when the police get here, I want you to tell them exactly what you've told me about the bomb so they won't go barging into the hotel. But under no circumstances are you to mention to them that you saw me here tonight or anything you've told me about the terrorists' interest in the African-American woman. Understood?"

Giovano nodded his head yes.

Trevor reached into his pocket and pulled out a wad of American bills. "This is for you," he said, handing him the money. "I want you to do me a favor."

Giovano's eyes widened as his hand closed around the money. "What, *senhor?*"

"I have something I want delivered to Colonel Ashton Sinclair at the American Embassy. I don't want it given to anyone but Colonel Sinclair. Understood?"

The boy nodded again. *"Sim, senhor."*

Trevor took off his Marine Force Recon signet ring and handed it to him. "Get this to him as soon as you can after you've finished up here. Tell him I'm somewhere in the Rio jungle. And you can tell him about the American woman."

Trevor then turned and slipped away in the darkness.

Chapter 8

When Trevor returned to the hideout, to his surprise, he found Corinthians sleeping like a baby. She had taken the lightweight jacket he left with her and had used it as a pallet, and had used his overnight bag as a pillow. Her face was pressed against the palm of her hand to protect her skin from the rough material.

There was both delicacy and strength in her features, and her hair fell in a graceful slant around her face and over her shoulders. Even lying down, her breasts were uplifted and pressed firmly against her shirt, and her hips were well-defined and exquisitely curved against the fabric of her jeans.

He couldn't help but remember the feel of her backside cushioned in his hand when he'd stopped her from falling off the ladder back at the hotel. The sweat that had formed on his brow at the time had had nothing to do with the danger surrounding them, but had had everything to do with the tempestuous feelings that had ripped through him when he had touched her so intimately.

Trevor moved closer and knelt beside her, unable to resist the temptation to reach out and gently move a few loose tendrils of hair out of her face. Asleep she looked peaceful, serene and, if possible, even more beautiful.

He watched her slow breathing and knew she must have been extremely tired to fall asleep in this wild, impenetrable place. The distance they had covered since leaving the hotel had taken its toll on her. He was used to occasionally operating under severe hardships, but she wasn't. Yet she hadn't complained or whined to him about anything. Even when he had left her here alone in the dark, she hadn't voiced her disapproval. In the past couple of hours, he had discovered a strength about her that was at odds with some of his earlier assumptions. Corinthians Avery never ceased to both amaze and surprise him.

Trevor sighed deeply as he glanced down at his watch. From the looks of things, their exodus from the hotel was only the beginning. Until Ashton found them, they would have to move deeper and deeper into the jungle. There was no doubt in his mind that once his ring was delivered to his good friend at the embassy, he would organize a search party to find them. And he *would* find them. Half Cherokee Indian and half African-American, Ashton Sinclair had been one of the best trackers the Force Recon unit ever had.

Trevor glanced again at his watch. He hated waking Corinthians, but knew he had no choice. It was now daybreak, and they would be at a disadvantage traveling through the jungle during daytime hours. But it wasn't safe to remain here in this place any longer. It was bad enough to be pitted against one hunter, but they had to somehow elude three. If the situation had been different and he'd only had himself to think about, he wouldn't elude them at all. He would set a trap and let the hunters become the hunted and take care of them in his own way. But he couldn't think of doing that now. Corinthians's safety was at stake.

He looked thoughtfully at her for a moment, wondering why the terrorists specifically wanted her. He shook his head. Maybe he was reading more into it than there really was. It wasn't that the terrorists only wanted her, they'd apparently been interested in taking all the Americans who were key players of the research summit team as hostages. And she had definitely been a key player.

Corinthians stirred in her sleep. Trevor reached out and stroked the side of her face. Her skin felt soft and smooth to his touch. He then advanced his hand lower, toward her chest. He caught himself and stopped within a few inches of her firm, high-perched breasts.

For crying out loud! What in the blazes was wrong with him? He'd been about to fondle her while she slept. Touching her should have been the last thing on his mind. What he should have been focusing on was getting them out of this area and moving them deeper into the jungle.

Angry with himself, he stood and backed away. "Corinthians, wake up," he said more roughly than he'd intended.

His deep voice awakened Corinthians. She had a tendency to fall into a state of deep sleep whenever she was extremely tired, sometimes sleeping as long as twelve hours straight. She looked up at Trevor through sleep-filled eyes. With daylight breaking through the trees, the shadow of his unshaven face gave him an even manlier aura. His massive shoulders filled his shirt, and his stance emphasized the force of his presence. The way he stood over her was both appealing and compelling. An air of firm strength and virile command exuded from him.

She saw a muscle clench along his jaw, eliminating any traces of softness around his mouth and eyes. And when he continued to stare at her with those dark eyes of his, she felt a quickening in the pit of her stomach. She wanted to reach out and stroke his hard jaw and let her fingers slide across his smooth skin and…

Corinthians took a quick, sharp breath, surprised at where her thoughts were going. She momentarily turned her face away from him, afraid he might be able to read her mind. Evidently she was more tired than she had originally thought to even think such things. Sitting up, she turned and faced him again. His dark eyes were still on her. She refused to let him unnerve her and leaned her head back and met his stare, noting the tightness around his jaw was even more profound. She couldn't help wondering what had him in such a bad mood.

It suddenly occurred to her that his mood might have something to do with what he had found upon returning to the hotel. A part of her was almost afraid to ask if that was the case. Before she could do so, his voice boomed out at her.

"We need to move on. Now."

She blinked as the words he had spoken cleared her fatigued mind. "Why? Are the terrorists still at the hotel?"

"No, they left before I got there. Unfortunately, several persons were taken as hostages."

Corinthians pushed herself into a standing position. The thought that any of the people she had met this week were among the ones taken was very disturbing. "What about the others left behind?"

"I didn't see any casualties."

She sighed deeply, relieved. "Thank God for that."

"But the terrorists did leave their mark."

"How so?" Her stomach clenched tight. She was afraid she was not going to like what he was about to say.

Trevor told her about the bomb. "But the authorities were arriving when I left. Hopefully, the bomb experts will be able to get everything under control."

"I hope and pray they will. So now can we start heading back?"

"No."

Corinthians's brows raised inquiringly. "No? I don't understand."

Trevor wondered just how much he should tell her. The last

thing he wanted or needed was a hysterical, worked-up and overwrought woman on his hands. His dark eyes met hers as she waited for an answer. "You and I are going deeper into the jungle to hide out for a while."

Corinthians's eyebrows slanted in a confused frown. "Why?"

"I think it will be for the best."

She glared up at him, not understanding why he would feel that way. Evidently he liked being out here in the jungle playing soldier. If that were the case, he could look for another playmate because she wasn't interested. "Well, I don't think it will be for the best. I see no reason why we can't go back to the hotel."

The narrowing of Trevor's eyes revealed his irritation and anger. "Well, I do."

"Why? You just said the police had arrived," she managed to say through stiff lips. Getting information out of him was like shedding cellulose from one's thighs. It was nearly impossible.

"It's not safe to go back there just yet."

Corinthians sighed out loud in frustration. "That doesn't make sense. Why wouldn't it be?"

"Because not all the terrorists went back to where they came from. There are three of them wandering around out here in this jungle somewhere," he said in a deceptively calm voice.

"Then that's all the more reason we should get out of here and go back to the hotel." She reached down to pick up the overnight bag and found it was too heavy for her to lift. She wondered how on earth Trevor had carried it.

"You, of all people, can't go back."

Corinthians glanced back at him, narrowing her eyes. "And why not?"

"Because it appears the terrorists are interested in the American key players of the research summit. Those men lurking around out here have strict orders to capture you and take you to their leader."

"That's insane."

"Then you tell that to Terry Mills, Sidney Wells, Keith

Johnson and a few other Americans that were taken as hostages. That is, if you ever see them again. Their lives are now at the mercy of those terrorists. It's a good thing Armond Thetas got called away unexpectedly from dinner last night. With all his money, he would have been a good catch for those terrorists although he isn't from the United States."

Corinthians nearly collapsed down onto the overnight bag. Her body began shaking. It was impossible to calm the alarming quakes that had suddenly torn at her insides when Trevor had mentioned the names of several persons who had been taken as hostages. They were men she knew professionally. They were men who just last night had laughed with her, had held conversations with her and had eaten dinner with her.

"But shouldn't that be all the more reason we should seek police protection?" she asked quietly, still feeling stunned and disoriented by the news.

"Right now I don't trust anyone. And neither should you. I have a lot of questions about all of this. And until I get some answers, I think we should stay lost for a while. I'm asking you to trust me on this."

Corinthians's brain was in tumult. She took a long, deep, steady breath to control her swirling emotions. She stood silent for a few moments, trying to absorb everything Trevor had told her. She knew what she would do. The bottom line was she did trust him. He had proven ever since that incident with those two men at McDonald's that he was concerned with her welfare. And last night he had shown her just how far he would go to protect her when he had placed his body over hers when they had heard the gunfire at the hotel. He had used his body as a human shield to protect her. Although he could be an infuriating, exasperating and irritating man at times, deep down she knew he would protect her with his life. He had already proven it.

"But what if we get lost out here?"

"We won't. And I've already sent word to a good friend of mine at the American embassy. He'll find us in no time."

"And you trust him?"

"Yes. He's a fellow Marine who's now a colonel. We started out in boot camp together in South Carolina and have worked together on a number of missions. I trust him with my life."

Trevor took a few steps that brought him closer to her. He stood before her. The gaze that bored into her burned with heated intensity. "But most importantly, Corinthians, I trust him with yours."

Corinthians shivered with the forcefulness of Trevor's words. She was caught off guard by the tenderness in his voice. It wasn't what he had said, but rather how he had said it. He had spoken the words as if her life meant everything to him. She took a deep breath, trying to control her thoughts, which were now running wild.

Get a grip, girl. Trevor Grant doesn't even like you, remember. He's just a man who possesses an instinct to protect, take charge of and defend. His attitude has nothing to do with you personally. Don't be stupid and read any more into it than that. You mean nothing to him.

"And you think he'll come?" she finally asked.

"He'll come."

She nodded. "But will he be able to find us out here?"

"He'll find us. That's the least of my worries. Now come on, we need to leave this place. It isn't safe for us to hang around here any longer." After she stepped out of his way, he reached down and effortlessly picked up his overnight bag.

Corinthians sighed, feeling dispirited. "I wish there was some way we could let our families and friends know that we're okay. Once news of the terrorist attack hits the airwaves and we're listed as missing, they'll think the worst."

Trevor nodded. He thought about his parents; his sister, Regina; and his close friends the Madaris brothers. "Hopefully, they won't have to worry for long."

But even as he said the words, he had a gut feeling it would be longer than he hoped.

Houston, Texas

Maurice Grant entered the barbershop where he had been getting his hair cut for well over forty years. Most of the men who came here had started coming as teenagers. And later as grown men they had eventually brought their sons here. Those sons were now bringing their own sons. It wasn't uncommon to find three generations of men patronizing Mister P's Barbershop.

"Good morning, Zack."

"Same to you, Maurice. Go ahead and take a seat. You're next in the chair."

Maurice nodded. It seemed to him that Zack Peterson had worked here forever. He had originally opened the shop back in the early fifties. During that time a mom-and-pop drugstore had operated out of the building next door and had had a reputation of selling the best soda fountain drinks around. Unfortunately, the drugstore hadn't been able to compete with the super–chain store pharmacy that had opened around the corner, and had been forced to close its doors a few years back. Now the building had been turned into a hair and beauty supply store.

Survivorship hadn't been a problem for Mister P's Barbershop. Even during the late sixties and early seventies when the Afro was popular and haircuts had been on the decline, business at Mister P's hadn't suffered. No one around town could wear a "'fro" and not let Zack give it a neat tapering or a smooth trim. He had a way of giving your Afro that special Mister P's look. Now, although Zack was getting on up in age, he was still a very popular barber around town. Everyone knew that during his lifetime he had cut the hair of such notables who'd passed through Houston as Dr. Martin Luther King, Jr., Thurgood Marshall, Sidney Poitier, Smokey Robinson and most recently, actor Sterling Hamilton and movie producer, Spike Lee. One wall in the shop was plastered with photos of Zack with all those famous people and quite a few others.

Before taking a seat, Maurice went over to a counter and

picked up the current issue of *Jet*. The television set in the shop was turned on to the *Jerry Springer Show*. The talk-show host was interviewing a couple claiming to have been kidnapped by space aliens last year. Having no desire to listen to what the couple was saying, Maurice flipped through the magazine to find an interesting article to read.

"How's the family, Maurice?" Zack called out to him.

A pain cut through Maurice like it always did whenever he thought about his family. Although he maintained a very close relationship with his son, Trevor, and his daughter, Regina, he and his wife, Stella, had been living apart for more than twenty years.

"Everybody's fine," he said, taking his seat. Maurice began reading an article about movie star Sterling Hamilton's recent marriage. He looked up when Zack turned up the volume on the television set.

"There's some kind of news flash, and I want to hear what it's about," Zack said by way of an explanation. "These days I can't hear as well as I used to."

Maurice nodded an understanding and was about to return to reading the article when the news anchorman appeared on the television screen. "We have just gotten word that terrorists stormed the La Grande Hotel in Rio de Janeiro before daybreak, taking several hostages, all of them Americans, and leaving others in a room with a bomb set to go off at the slightest movement. We understand the bomb has been found and discharged without any injuries. We are, however, awaiting word on the identities of those six Americans that were taken as hostages. We will keep you updated on…"

The magazine Maurice had been reading fell to the floor when he suddenly jumped from his seat.

"Maurice? What's wrong?"

Maurice stared numbly at the television. In the back of his mind he heard Zack talking to him, calling his name.

"Maurice? Maurice, are you all right?"

He turned and looked at Zack. "It's Trevor."

Zack frowned. He knew Maurice's son, Trevor, very well. He had given Trevor his very first haircut and had continued to take care of his head all the way through high school. Even now he considered himself Trevor's barber. "What about Trevor?"

"He's there," Maurice said, pointing to the television.

Zack's frown deepened as he tried to make sense of what Maurice was saying. "Trevor's where?"

Maurice's gaze bored into Zack, imploring him to understand. "Trevor's over there in Rio de Janeiro on a business trip. And he was staying at that hotel."

"The one that got hit by terrorists?" Zack asked in alarm.

"Yes." Maurice frantically searched his pants pockets for his car keys. "I've got to go and tell Stella. I hope I can get to her before she sees any of this on television."

Without saying another word, Maurice Grant rushed out of the barbershop.

"Since you're the one who invited me to lunch, I assume you're picking up the tab."

Clayton Madaris shook his head, grinning. "You can afford to pay for your own meal, Dex."

Dex Madaris eyed his brother thoughtfully. "So, what's up? What's so important that you had to meet with me today?"

Clayton sat back in his chair. "I have a great idea. To be honest with you, it's really Syneda's idea, but I happen to think it's great, too."

Dex lifted a brow. "That's scary."

Clayton frowned. "What is?"

"The thought that you and Syneda actually agreed on something."

Clayton's frown turned into a wide grin. "Yeah, it is kind of scary when you think about it, isn't it? Trust me, it doesn't happen often."

Dex nodded. He could believe that. Clayton and his wife Syneda rarely agreed on anything. "So what's this great idea?"

"How does the Madaris Building sound?"

Now it was Dex's turn to frown. "The Madaris Building? What are you talking about, Clayton?"

"I'm talking about me, you and Justin, along with Uncle Jake, of course, getting together and pooling our resources to build an office building somewhere in downtown Houston."

Dex sat back in his chair. "An office building? Why?"

"Because during my and Syneda's search for a place to accommodate our law firm, we discovered what a good investment rental property can be. We can build a nice building with at least three or four floors and use the area that we need, then lease out any unused space. You can even move your office there. Just think of the money you'll save."

Dex rubbed his chin, thinking about the possibility of being in the same building day after day with Clayton and Syneda. Their constant bickering would probably drive him batty. He would rather fork out the money and stay in his present building just to maintain his sanity. There were certain things in life that you couldn't put a price tag on and his peace of mind was one of them. "I'll pass on the idea of sharing office space with you and Syneda, but the idea concerning the building itself has merit."

"Excuse me. Mr. Madaris, you have a phone call."

Both Dex and Clayton glanced up at the waiter.

"Which one of us?" Clayton asked, smiling.

"You, sir, Clayton Madaris," was the waiter's reply. "The telephone is located this way."

"Where's your mobile phone?" Dex asked Clayton when he stood to follow the waiter.

"Syneda has it. She, ah, kind of borrowed it for a while."

Dex shook his head. Knowing Clayton and Syneda, there was probably more to the mobile phone story than Clayton was telling, but Dex decided the less he knew, the better. He resumed eating his food after Clayton left.

A few minutes later he looked up to see Clayton heading back to their table. There was an odd expression on his face. "Hey, man, what's wrong with you?"

Clayton sighed deeply, wondering what would be the best way to break the news to Dex. He decided to just come right out and tell him. "That was Justin."

Dex lifted a surprised brow. Their brother Justin was a physician who lived in a small town outside of Dallas. "Why would Justin be calling you here?"

"He called the office and Syneda told him where we were. There was a news flash on television."

Dex frowned. "What sort of news flash?"

"Terrorists stormed a hotel in Brazil last night taking several Americans as hostages."

An uneasy feeling settled over Dex. "Where exactly in Brazil did this attack take place?"

Clayton hesitated briefly before answering. He met his brother's gaze directly. "Rio de Janeiro."

As soon as the words left his mouth, Clayton saw the immediate reaction they had on Dex. "But that doesn't necessarily mean anything, Dex," he rushed on to say.

"Like hell it doesn't."

Dex stood and reached into his pocket and pulled out several bills. He threw them on the table. When he met Clayton's gaze, pure rage covered his face. "Come on, let's go."

Clayton lifted a brow. "Go where?"

"To Rio de Janeiro if we have to."

The two Madaris brothers quickly left the restaurant.

Chapter 9

Corinthians put the canteen to her mouth and took another sip of the cool, refreshing liquid. It had a fruity taste that included some ingredients she did not recognize. A few hours ago Trevor had left her alone again to go on a jungle excursion in search of something for them to eat. He had returned a short while later with the frothy drink that she had desperately needed.

She asked him how he had put together such a cool, refreshing and delicious drink out here in the jungle. He'd told her about all the different kinds of fruit he'd come upon, as well as an ice-cold spring nearby. And he had further explained that in addition to being tasty and filling, the fruity beverage would provide her with vital nutrients that were needed to sustain her body for a while, since she hadn't eaten anything solid since dinner last night.

Peering up at the sky, she figured it was close to early afternoon. They had plenty of daylight hours left, and the scorching heat and high humidity were getting the best of her. Her clothes were beginning to stick to her skin and her tired, sore feet were aching. They had walked most of the day at a pretty steady pace, moving farther and deeper into the jungle. Now, according to Trevor, they were in a part of the jungle he referred to as a tropical forest.

Corinthians glanced over to where Trevor was hard at work rubbing the tip of a bamboo rod against a huge rock, trying to give it a sharp, pointed edge. He had explained that he needed to make some sort of a weapon for their protection, and that he had felt inadequate and defenseless without one.

She couldn't think of using words such as *inadequate* or *defenseless* to ever describe Trevor Grant. As far as she was concerned, his motto in life definitely had to be, "Where there's a will, there's a way." The drink she was holding in her hand was a testimony to that, as well as the very fact that she was here with him and not a hostage like the others. He had literally, single-handedly, kept her safe. Even now he was busy seeing to her welfare.

It suddenly occurred to her just how little she knew about him personally other than what he had shared with her about his time in the Marines. She knew he and Dex were childhood friends, and that he had a rather close relationship with the other two Madaris brothers, Justin and Clayton, as well. The one other thing she knew about Trevor was that more times than not, he unnerved her.

Corinthians sighed. There was so much about Trevor that she didn't know. And she wasn't sure why, but there was so much about him that she wanted to know. Except for when he occasionally educated her on their surroundings, there had been little conversation between the two of them as they had moved through the jungle. And now, as she sat with her back resting against the trunk of a huge tree and sipped her drink, she couldn't help but watch him. She was incredibly aware of him physically. He had a magnificent body, lean, strong and dark-toned.

Her gaze followed his every movement with interest. He had removed his shirt and the taut, hard muscles of his shoulders and chest outright fascinated her. They seemed to flex with each and every movement he made, whether it was bending down, leaning over or reaching upward. He moved with the kind of sure agility that came from a man who evidently enjoyed the outdoors and the physical side of life. The man definitely possessed an attractive male physique. And without his shirt, his jeans showed the force of his thighs and the firm slimness of his hips.

Corinthians took another sip of her drink, suddenly feeling hot. She blotted moisture from her face with the palm of her hand and tried ignoring the tingling sensation she felt in the pit of her stomach. You would think she had never seen a man with a good-looking body before. She had to get a grip. Trevor's body had been the cause of many sleepless nights over the past two years. And it seemed she was getting herself in even more trouble by being out here alone with him in the wilderness. She was beginning to have plenty of wild and primitive thoughts about him. They were thoughts she did not need and could not afford to have. It bothered her that he could inspire such thoughts from her. She couldn't help but remember the feelings she got whenever he touched her. When he had placed his body over hers to protect her, she had marveled at the hard strength of him. She couldn't help but wonder how that strength would feel lying in his arms.

Annoyed at the way her thoughts were going, she looked away from him. She drew up her legs, hugged her knees and rested her head on them. She wanted to think of something else besides Trevor. She wondered if the police had been able to dismantle the bomb and if everyone was all right. She thought about the men who'd been taken as hostages and sent up a silent prayer for their safe return. She then wondered if her parents, Josh and Brenna had heard about the terrorist attack yet.

Corinthians began thinking of even more things to occupy her mind, and the next thing she knew she'd begun feeling overly tired and sleepy.

"Don't go to sleep on me now. You have to take a dip first."

Corinthians's drooping eyelids shot up. She lifted her head and looked up into Trevor's face. At times he could move as silently as a cat. She had not heard him approach.

"A dip?"

"Yeah. I think we've done enough walking for one day. This might be a good spot for us to settle down for the night. But first we need to take a dip in that stream over there to refresh our sweaty bodies and to wash away our scent. That way we won't make it easy for those guys looking for you to find us. Out here in the jungle your body's scent can give away your location."

Corinthians nodded. "How much longer do you think it will be before your friend at the embassy comes looking for us?"

"He'll come as soon as he gets my message," he replied, holding up the bamboo rod that had now taken the shape of a spear. "Come on, let's go. I think you need to cool off a bit. It's been a long day," Trevor said, extending his hand to her.

Corinthians accepted it and he pulled her to her feet. She accidently brushed her chest against his. The body contact almost took her breath away, and she took an immediate step back. The sudden movement nearly made her lose her balance. Instinctively and instantly, Trevor reached out an arm to place around her shoulders to steady her.

"Be careful," he said huskily.

His touch sent an unwelcome surge of pleasure through her, and she grudgingly admitted it also provided her with the comfort of his nearness. She felt remarkably safe with his strong arms on her shoulders. She gazed up into his eyes to find he was staring back at her. She watched as his gaze shifted from her eyes and dropped to her mouth.

"You said I needed to take a dip," she said shakily, dropping her gaze from his and saying the only thing she could think of at the moment. It was all she could do to force herself not to reach up and run her fingers along the strong, firm angle of his stubbly chin.

For a tense moment he just stood there, saying nothing. Then he spoke; his words were murmured low in his throat. "Yes, I did, didn't I." He lowered his hand from her shoulders. "We both need to take a dip. You go first and I'll watch."

Corinthians's brows drew together. "What do you mean you'll watch?"

Trevor's face broke into an irresistibly devastating grin. "I'm not going to watch you take a bath, if that's what you think. I'm going to be the lookout to make sure we don't get any unwanted company."

Corinthians nodded, feeling like a fool for having jumped to conclusions.

"Besides," Trevor continued. "You need to take the dip with your clothes on then change out of them after you're through."

"Why?"

"That way you'll wash your scent out of your clothes. You can lay them across the tree branches overnight to dry."

"All right." Corinthians felt a lot better knowing she wouldn't have to get undressed around him. When she did have to change out of her wet things, he would be occupied by taking his own turn in the stream.

"Is the water safe?" she asked. Sudden images of old Tarzan movies she had seen with crocodiles and snakes nipping at Jane's heels suddenly popped into her mind. The thought of washing off in a cool stream of water was heavenly, but she didn't want to become some animal's dinner doing so.

Trevor suppressed a smile. "Yeah, it's safe. I've checked out both sides of the stream. But if you'd like, I can always forget about standing guard and join you in that dip if you're afraid."

Corinthians tilted her chin up and glared at him. "I'm not afraid." She turned and walked off toward the stream.

Stella Grant looked up when the tinkling of the bell over the door of her store signaled she had a customer. She shook her head to clear it in utter disbelief. Maurice had just entered. In the five years since Stella's Books and Gifts had opened, he had never patronized her store.

As always, she thought Maurice Grant was a good-looking man. Over the years, age had only added distinctive grace and maturity to his overall appearance. His bone structure had strong, defined lines, and his dark figure was tall and powerful. His looks were classically handsome. Those prominent attributes had been passed on to their son.

She straightened her shoulders when he came nearer. His expression, she noted, appeared tense and serious. "Maurice, this is a pleasant surprise," she said truthfully, when he reached the counter. She tried keeping her features deceptively calm and composed.

"Hello, Stella. Is there someplace where we can talk privately?"

She lifted a brow before replying. "Sure. We can go into my office. Just give me a moment to let Amos know where I am."

"Amos?"

"Yes. You probably don't remember him, but he's Sarah Fields's grandson."

Maurice nodded. Sarah Fields had been their neighbor when he and Stella were married. He drew in a deep breath upon remembering that legally, they were still married. During the twenty years of their separation, neither of them had bothered to file for a divorce.

He followed Stella as she led him toward the back of the store. At any other time, he would have stopped and taken the opportunity to admire the place that had been a fulfillment of her lifelong dream. But now, he couldn't. Today he had news to share with her. It was news that would possibly shatter her.

He paused as he watched her stop and speak briefly to a young man who appeared to be around the age of sixteen. The youth smiled and nodded him a greeting before heading toward the front of the store.

"My office is this way," Stella said as they continued walking toward the back of the store. "I need to warn you that it's kind of junky right now. I haven't had a chance to put out the new stock yet." They entered the cluttered room and Maurice closed the door behind them.

Stella turned to face him. "What is it, Maurice? What is it that you want to talk to me about?" A part of her couldn't help wondering if he was finally getting around to asking her for a divorce. She inhaled deeply, preparing herself for the pain that would come if that was the reason for his unexpected visit. Her lack of trust and faith in him had destroyed their marriage, and she had spent every day of her life since regretting it.

She braced herself as Maurice walked toward her and stopped when he stood directly in front of her. He slowly bowed his head for a few seconds before finally lifting his head to meet her questioning gaze.

"It's Trevor, Stella."

A bemused frown covered her face. "Trevor? What about Trevor?"

"It's been all over the news. The hotel he was staying in while in South America was hit by terrorists last night. From all accounts, around six to eight Americans were taken as hostages. There's a strong possibility he was one of those taken."

Stella stood shocked and emotionless in the room as the weight of Maurice's words hit her. "*Our* Trevor?" she finally asked quietly, not wanting to believe what she'd just been told.

Maurice's body ached at the sight of the tears that began forming in her eyes. "Yes, our Trevor. But we have to believe he's okay."

Stella nodded slowly just moments before her body broke down with racking, heart-wrenching sobs. Immediately, Maurice pulled her into his arms. He held her tight, closer to him, absorbing her trembles with his body and sharing her pain. He took a deep, unsteady breath as he continued to hold her.

He suddenly realized that this was the first time he had held his wife in his arms in more than twenty years.

"Excuse me, *senhor.*"

Major Lawton Snow looked up from the pile of paperwork on his desk. The boy who was standing on the other side of it looked rather nervous about something. "Yes, what can I do for you?"

"I'd like to see Colonel Sinclair. I have a message for him."

Major Snow's brows raised questioningly. He couldn't help but wonder what kind of message this kid could possibly have for the colonel. "Colonel Sinclair isn't here."

"He isn't here?" the young boy asked in surprise.

"No, he left the country to return to North America."

"Will he be returning, *senhor?*"

"Yes, we expect him back late tomorrow."

Major Snow saw the worried expression that appeared on the boy's face and couldn't help but wonder the reason for it. "You can leave the message with me and I'll pass it on to him."

Giovano remembered the explicit instructions the American had given to him. He was supposed to deliver the message and the ring to Colonel Sinclair, and no one else. He had been detained in coming here because the Brazilian police had questioned him intensely about the terrorist attack at the hotel. "No, thank you. I need to see Colonel Sinclair."

"I work for him. You can leave the message with me. I'll make sure he gets it," Major Snow said, trying again to assure the young boy.

"No," Giovano said. "But thank you anyway. I'll be back when I think Colonel Sinclair is here."

Major Snow watched as the boy turned and quickly left the embassy.

Chapter 10

Trevor told himself not to look…but he couldn't help himself and looked anyway.

Feeling defeated, he emitted a tiny, hopeless sigh when he turned toward the area where the stream was located. He glanced across the thicket of trees and watched while a fully clothed Corinthians stood in the stream and bent to cup water in her hands to wash her face.

He shoved his hands in his pockets and leaned back against the tree. He was well aware of the blood rushing through his veins when she splashed water over the top part of her body. Evidently that didn't satisfy her need for cleanliness, and she dropped to her knees, making the water completely cover her body up to her shoulders.

When she stood again Trevor's mouth went completely dry. It didn't matter to him that she was fully clothed. The sight of the wet clothes clinging to her body aroused him to a degree that he hadn't known was possible. He never knew a man could be driven to want a woman so badly. But over the past two years, he had come to discover just how much that was possible. There seemed to be some kind of a powerful, invisible force that drew him to her whenever they were in close proximity to each other.

As he continued to watch her, in his mind he imagined joining her in the stream and undressing her. He imagined how it would feel to remove every stitch of her clothing, piece by piece, by slow degree; and how it would feel when his mouth touched every inch of her wet skin.

He inhaled deeply as thoughts floated through his mind of how it would feel to caress her breasts and other parts of her body, and how it would feel to lay down with her and sink his flesh into hers, merging their bodies as one.

Trevor jerked his gaze away at the same time that an angry sound rumbled deep in his throat. Every instinct he possessed once again warned him that he was headed down a dangerous path with such mental activities, and the best thing to do was to get rid of them once and for all. Getting involved with Corinthians Avery would only complicate his life. She was completely wrong for him. There was nothing right about her.

And to make matters worse, he knew she had not gotten over Dex. But even knowing that, he still wanted her. And although he fervently wished he didn't, he had to face the truth and admit that he was deeply attracted to her.

With his back resting against the tree, Trevor considered the possibility that the only thing he felt for Corinthians was a deep case of lust, pure and simple. But he knew that was not true. He wanted her for a number of reasons, and he wished he could say sex was foremost in his mind…but it wasn't. What he felt went deeper than just sex. Even if she weren't capable of stimulating his male hormones like she could so effortlessly do, he would still want her.

He wished he could even say that he wanted her because she was a challenge to him. And he enjoyed challenges. He had never encountered a woman who could get next to him as Corinthians could. It was hard just being in the same room with her. Although she had the ability to ruffle his feathers like no other woman could, that wasn't it, either. That was not the reason he wanted her.

Trevor rubbed the palm of his hand across his face. Although he wished he could, he found no excuses for what he was feeling. Nor could he find the reason he was drawn to her like a moth to a flame. But he knew what he had to do. He had to stay strong and to continue to do what he'd been doing for the past two years, and that was to fight whatever feelings he was developing for her every step of the way. There was no way he would allow himself to be a substitute for another man. He refused to let any woman invade his heart, knowing she would end up breaking it and destroying him.

In all his thirty-seven years, no woman had ever held any power over him, and no woman ever would.

Rasheed Valdemon angrily paced the floor of his study. News of the terrorist attack in Rio had dominated all of the major television networks throughout the morning. He was furious. How had such a thing happened? He had given Santini explicit instructions not to draw attention to Corinthians Avery's abduction. Not only had attention been drawn, but now the entire United States government was in a complete uproar with the news that a number of Americans were missing and presumed taken as hostages.

"Mr. Valdemon, Mr. Santini is here."

Swalar's voice interrupted Rasheed's thoughts. "Send him in immediately."

Rasheed stood rigid with his feet braced apart. His expression was hard and derisive when Santini entered the room. Before he could speak, Raul Santini's words stopped him.

"We had nothing to do with what went down in Rio last night, Monty. Those were not my men who attacked that hotel."

At first Rasheed was too startled by Santini's statement to speak. He soon recovered his voice. "If they weren't your men, whose were they?"

"I don't know, but I have some of my people finding out. It was our plan to snatch Ms. Avery from her hotel room last night. But my men reached the hotel just moments after the terrorists had forced their way inside by gunpoint. When they saw what was happening, my men escaped through the jungle without being seen."

"And they have no idea what happened to Corinthians Avery?"

"No. They didn't stick around to find out. I can only assume she's been taken as a hostage."

Rasheed took a deep breath. His nostrils flared with fury and Arabic curses fell from his mouth. "As soon as you find out who's behind that attack in Rio, I want to know."

After making sure Trevor was taking a dip in the stream, Corinthians quickly began removing the wet clothes from her body. Although the hour was moving into the late afternoon, it was hot and the humidity remained relatively high. At least for the moment she no longer felt sticky and dirty.

Once she had removed all of her clothing, except for her underthings, she leaned down and opened Trevor's overnight bag in search of her lingerie. She frowned. Other than her comb, hairbrush, toothbrush and deodorant, everything else in the bag were items belonging to Trevor. Surely her things were somewhere. By the looks of all the items in the bag, Trevor had looked out for his own needs, but not hers. He hadn't even bothered to pack her makeup. And for crying out loud, she didn't see any of her underthings!

She willed herself to stay calm and not to panic. The rest of her belongings had to be here somewhere. Thinking that Trevor had possibly packed them in another compartment, she calmed herself and continued her search. She released a sigh of relief when she saw that there was another compartment, nearly hidden.

With eager fingers Corinthians unzipped the compartment and opened it. Reaching inside, she pulled out a pack of condoms.

She went speechless as she stared at them. She couldn't help but notice the pack's distinct designer label. These could only be purchased from an exclusive lingerie boutique. It was the same boutique where she had purchased the negligee she had worn the night she had planned to seduce Dex.

Something elemental picked at her brain as she continued to stare at the pack. Then it hit her. They were the same ones she had purchased nearly two years ago that were guaranteed to last a lifetime with no expiration date; the same ones Trevor had taken out of her robe when she'd fainted.

Suddenly, his threatening words of that night came back to her…

"Aren't you forgetting something?"

Corinthians turned around. "What?" she snapped.

"These." He held up the pack of condoms.

She tinted furiously, but not to let him get the best of her, she lifted her chin and gave him her haughtiest glare. "You can have them."

Trevor smiled and Corinthians thought she would melt then and there. He had the sexiest smile.

"Thanks," he said. "I'll be saving them to use one day. Maybe when I see you again."

Corinthians's thoughts returned to the present. She shivered upon realizing that although her and Trevor's paths crossed a number of times since that night, their encounters had always been business related. Out here in the jungle with him was actually the first time they had ever been alone together for any length of time in a totally secluded environment.

Angry lines formed on Corinthians's face. Did he think he would take advantage of their situation and make good on his threat about the condoms? Did he think for one minute that he *would* be using them on her?

Whirling around, she stomped off toward the stream then stopped upon realizing she only had on her bra and panties. Walking quickly back to the overnight bag, she pulled out one of Trevor's T-shirts and slipped it on. The shirt covered her to midthigh. Satisfied for now that she was sufficiently covered, she once again stomped off toward the stream and didn't stop walking until she had reached the water's edge.

"Trevor Grant, how could you?"

Trevor looked up. Corinthians was standing on the bank wearing his T-shirt. Although it fit large on her, his shirt clearly defined her body's nubile curves, agilely firmed hips and rounded breasts. And it didn't help matters that the wet underclothes under the T-shirt were nearly transparent. Seeing the angered look on her face, he thought better of devoting his full concentration to her body, and shifted his attention to whatever had gotten her all riled up.

"How could I do what?"

"You didn't pack any of my things. Just what am I supposed to wear?"

He looked at her from head to toe, pinning her with a long, silent scrutiny. "What you're wearing now looks good to me."

Corinthians's anger flared. "You had no right!"

Trevor released an exasperated sigh. "I had every right. Like most women, you don't know the meaning of traveling light. I only brought along those things I deemed necessary."

Corinthians sputtered, bristling with indignation. "Only those things *you* deemed necessary? Then how do you explain these?" she asked furiously, holding up the pack of condoms for him to see.

Trevor stared first at her, then the condoms, then back at her before calmly saying. "There's nothing to explain."

Corinthians's expression became thunderous. "In that case, these definitely aren't necessary, either," she stormed. With a pitch that would have impressed even baseball great Hank Aaron, she sent the pack of condoms flying out of her hand and over Trevor's head. The pack hit the water and disappeared underneath. Satisfied with what she had done and pleased with the look of surprise and anger on Trevor's face, she turned and walked off.

Trevor's anger had not cooled by the time he'd gotten out of the water and found Corinthians. He leaned against a huge rock and watched her as she sat under a tree, pouting. She glanced up when she saw him. The look she gave him was cold and deadly. Instead of turning around and leaving her alone like any man with an ounce of common sense would have done, he walked toward her.

Mindless of the fact that he was soaking wet, he dropped down on the ground beside her. He laid a restraining hand on her arm when she made a move to get up.

"What you did back there was pretty childish, Corinthians."

His words made something inside Corinthians snap. "Childish! You think what I did was childish? You have a lot of nerve. Just who do you think you are to assume that we—"

Trevor held up a hand to silence her. "Will you listen to what I have to say? There's no way I could have carried both bags."

"I didn't ask you to. I could have carried my own bag."

"No, you couldn't have. I'm capable of handling a lot more weight than you, and I could barely pick up your bag back at the hotel when I was in your room. I had to do what was needed to lighten our load. I did what I thought was best for the both of us."

"And you thought you would be accomplishing that by leaving all my stuff behind?"

"I didn't leave all of your stuff. I brought what I considered were your necessities."

"My necessities? And just what am I suppose to do for clothing?"

"There wasn't enough room for both of our things so we'll have to compromise and share." One corner of Trevor's mouth pulled into a slight smile. "I can envision you sleeping in my T-shirts and boxer shorts more so than I can see myself sleeping in one of your nightgowns."

Corinthians stared at him, not the least bit impressed by his attempt at humor. "What about those condoms, Trevor? Apparently you found room for them in your bag. Those are the same ones you took out of my robe that night two years ago. Why did you keep them?"

Trevor looked at her levelly. "Yeah, they're the same ones and I didn't have to find room for them, Corinthians. Those condoms have been in that bag ever since that night. The reason I kept them is because I forgot they were in there. But in all honesty, even if I had remembered they were there, I would not have thrown them away. If I remember correctly, it was your idea that I keep them. I merely took you up on it. So what's the big deal?"

"The big deal is the threat you made *after* I suggested that you keep them. You insinuated that you would be keeping them to use one day when…" Corinthians tinted. She was too embarrassed to finish what she was saying.

Trevor pulled his body up in a crouching position and turned to face her. He stared at her with dark eyes. "When what, Corinthians? Contrary to what you may want to believe, I did not intentionally bring them along to take advantage of our situation out here in the jungle. When I left that hotel, my only thought was getting out of there and keeping us both alive. Like I said before, I had completely forgotten they were in that bag."

He leaned closer to her. "But I would be telling you a lie if I said that I've never envisioned using them when we did make love one day."

"We'll never make love," she said, her breath coming out in a barely audible whisper.

Trevor's eyes turned warm, almost challenging. "Oh, yes, we will. Count on it. It may be days from now, even weeks or months, but one day we will," he assured her quietly. "And do you know why I'm so certain of that, Corinthians?"

A deep, penetrating heat seeped through Corinthians's body as she continued to gaze into Trevor's eyes. "No."

Slowly, Trevor leaned closer to her. He reached out and took her chin between his fingers, forcing her to look even deeper into his eyes. "Because we're attracted to each other. You might be in love with someone else, but you're attracted to me. Just like I'm attracted to you. That kind of attraction can only lead to one thing. And I think you'll agree that we have a score to settle."

An unexpected tormenting pain swept through Corinthians at the thought that Trevor felt what was happening between them amounted to nothing more than a score to settle. "You think a woman can be that fickle and love one man yet be deeply attracted to another?" she asked quietly. Her lashes flickered downward, shielding her gaze from his.

"I wouldn't call it being fickle. I think of it as having shaky and unsteady emotions. Few things are solid as a rock, especially love."

Corinthians wondered what had happened during his lifetime to make him feel that way. But with Trevor's mouth leaning closer to hers, she didn't want to dwell on the things they were talking about any longer.

"I want you, Corinthians, so I guess my attraction to you is pretty solid since it has lasted nearly two years," he said in a deep voice, leaning even closer to her.

Corinthians didn't want to admit it, but her want of him seemed pretty solid, too.

"Somehow and someway you've gotten into my system, and I refuse to let you stay there. I know of only one way to get you out, and that's by making love to you," Trevor added hoarsely.

"To settle a score?"

"Yes."

For a moment, he just gazed at her. The only sounds were those of the birds flying overhead and other distant sounds of the forest. It seemed that suddenly everything else got quiet. Desire clouded Corinthians's eyes.

Her grip on reality wavered when Trevor leaned even closer to her, and the first thing she thought was that even after just washing off in the stream, he smelled tantalizingly male. She held his gaze and wished her mind wasn't so quick to remember the way his mouth tasted the last time they'd kissed, all hot and spicy. And she wished, with all the strength she possessed, that she didn't reciprocate the hot, fiery look of fire and desire in his eyes.

A shudder of unleashed passion tore through her the moment Trevor touched his mouth to hers. He tilted her head up to have full access to her mouth as his warm and tender lips took total control of hers. It moved gently back and forth slowly. The gentleness in his kiss was so different from the last one they had shared that night after returning from São Paulo. Then, his kiss had been hot, urgent and intense.

Corinthians let herself go, holding nothing back as she willingly returned it, accepting his tongue when he flicked it inside her mouth. She held on to it as sensation after sensation began at the top of her head and rapidly spread down to her toes.

She didn't know Trevor had pulled her to her feet until she felt the roughness of the tree against her back. But the slight discomfort didn't matter. At the moment, nothing mattered. She was in too deep a state of sensual bliss. Her mind and her body were consumed with the taste of Trevor in her mouth and the feel of his hard body pressing against her.

Deep inside her, nerve ending pleasure threatened to explode to the point that she felt her knees buckle. But

Trevor's firm hands held her as he continued to kiss her. Then, suddenly, the tempo of the kiss changed and his mouth became firmer and demanding.

It became solid.

Instinctively, she pressed her body closer to his, mindless of the fact that his wet clothing was soaking through to the T-shirt she wore. She returned his kiss, stroke for stroke, caress for caress, the action making heated and unsaturated desire flow through her entire body.

And when she felt the light touch of his finger on her thigh, the part of her not covered by his T-shirt, she nearly lost it and released a deep, throaty moan. She wound her arms around his neck, as the fire he had started within her became an all-consuming flame.

A sudden sound of rustling leaves brought Trevor to full awareness. He broke off their kiss. His senses were instantly put on alert and he quickly turned around. "Shh," he whispered. "I think we have company."

No sooner had Trevor whispered those words than a huge man appeared from behind a thicket of trees.

And he was holding a gun on them.

Chapter 11

The man began speaking in rapid Portuguese. From the tone of his voice and the look on his face, Corinthians knew that whatever orders he was giving them, he wanted them followed. She also knew from the defiant stiffening of Trevor's body that he did not intend to be obedient.

A lump of fear formed in her throat and terror ripped through her heart. She tightened her grip on Trevor when the man barked another order at them. "Who is he and what does he want?" she whispered in Trevor's ear, looking past him to the man. Deep down she knew the answer to both questions, but asked anyway on the slight chance she was wrong.

"He's one of the terrorists, and he wants you," Trevor said quietly. "But don't worry, to get you he'll have to kill me first." He chuckled lightly. "Although from the looks of things, he may be planning to do that anyway."

Corinthians's heart thumped against her rib cage. She wondered how Trevor could make light of their situation when every fiber of her body was quaking with fear. She tensed even more when the man barked yet another order at them.

"He wants you to move away from me," Trevor said steadily. "And I advise you to do what he says. I doubt he'll harm you since he's gone to a lot of trouble to find you."

Corinthians wasn't so sure of that. A vicious glint shone in the man's eyes, and his cheek muscles stood out when he clenched his jaw. Realization struck her. The man may not intend to hurt her, but from the cold, hard look he was giving Trevor, there was no doubt in her mind he intended to hurt Trevor once she got out of the way. And she wasn't going to let that happen.

"I won't move, and you can tell him that for me." She tried to make her voice sound forceful and commanding, but knew she had failed. Even to her own ears, it sounded weak and shaky. She moved closer to Trevor, pressing her chest against his solid back. Then in an act of defiance, she wrapped her arms around his waist.

Trevor swore and his muscles tightened. "Do what he says, Corinthians."

"No!"

"Do it!"

"I won't! If I move out of the way, he'll hurt you."

Trevor knew there was a strong possibility what she'd just said was true. But he didn't have time to dwell on that fact now. What he had to do was concentrate on the man. He wanted to be ready to take advantage of any mistake the man made that could be used against him.

It appeared he was a South American. His face was like a hard mask. He had a mustache that looked like it had been marked by a felt tip pen and a nose so sharp it could probably slice cheese. The hand that held the gun was steady…too steady, Trevor thought. The man apparently wasn't nervous, which meant he evidently felt he had everything under his complete control. It was then that Trevor noticed the gun was not an automatic.

Trevor's eyes narrowed when the overconfident man took a few steps forward. The look on his face indicated he wasn't happy that Corinthians had not followed his order. "Do what he says, Corinthians," Trevor said curtly, prying her arms from around him. "Now."

"But—"

"Just do it and move away slowly. We don't want to agitate him any more than we already have. I'll get us out of this mess, trust me."

Cold chills touched Corinthians's body. Fear knotted even more inside of her. Slowly, reluctantly, she eased from behind Trevor and moved away from him. And as she did so, the man kept his gun carefully aimed on Trevor. But the terrorist made the mistake, just for a split second, of shifting his eyes from Trevor to Corinthians, clearly interested in how the wet T-shirt clung to her curvaceous body.

Unknown to Corinthians, that distraction was the man's mistake, and the one Trevor had been waiting for and immediately took advantage of.

She watched in utter amazement as Trevor's body twirled in quick, rapid, fluent motion. His movement was so sudden and so swift, she didn't have time to blink. He was using some type of martial arts she'd never seen before. He swung his right foot up in the air to knock the gun from the terrorist's hands, making the blow connect with the lower part of the man's body. Then Trevor's left foot immediately followed with a sharp kick to the man's face. In pain, the man doubled over and dropped to his knees, then fell flat on his face.

Moving quickly, Trevor picked up the gun and stuffed it in the waist of his pants. "Bring me the thick cord from my bag," he called over his shoulder to Corinthians. "We need to tie him up before he comes to. Then we need to pack up our things and leave here as soon as possible. There are two others out there somewhere, and I don't plan to get caught off guard again. We have to put a lot of distance between us and them."

When Corinthians handed him the cord he'd asked for, he looked up at her. He could tell she was trying desperately to hold herself together. It should never have come down to this. If he hadn't been so intent on finding pleasure in her arms, he would have been on his guard. But he hadn't been, and because of it, he had placed them both in inexcusable danger. Her safety hinged on him being alert and on guard at all times. He didn't need any distractions. It wasn't her fault that she was the most desirable woman he'd ever met. Nor was it her fault that he wanted her in a way he'd never wanted a woman before. And it certainly wasn't her fault that he was falling for her…and hard. He remembered how she had refused to move from behind him when she thought that his life was in danger. She had put her arms around him to protect him. The thought of her doing that touched him.

"Thanks," he said, taking the cord from her and using it to tie up the man. "Do you think you're up to doing some more walking?"

"Yes, but we won't have much daylight left."

"I know, but it's something we have to do, even if we have to travel during the night."

Trevor looked down at the unconscious man. When he had feasted his beady eyes on Corinthians, and Trevor had seen the sudden lustful look in them, something inside him had snapped. As far as he was concerned, the man was lucky he was still alive. If he had touched his woman…

His woman? Now where did that thought come from? Corinthians Avery was not his woman. It had been years since he had thought of any woman as being his. He had always preferred being noncommittal in any relationship, since he never liked being tied down to any one woman. He couldn't boast of having the player-player reputation Clayton Madaris used to have, but he had never gone lacking for female companionship, with no strings attached, whenever he'd wanted it.

"Corinthians?"

When she didn't answer him right away, he turned his attention to her. He noticed her eyes were glued to the unconscious man tied up tight on the ground.

He sighed. The last thing he needed was for her to start freaking out on him, getting nervous, scared and jumpy. "Corinthians, how about gathering up our things so we can leave as soon as I finish up here."

She managed a nod.

His hand shot out and stopped her when she turned to walk away. Startled, she looked up at him. "Everything's going to be all right. We're in this together, and we'll make it back home. Trust me."

A faint, nervous smile wobbled on her mouth. "I do trust you, Trevor." Then she turned and walked away.

Rasheed Valdemon checked his watch. He had hoped to receive a call from Santini more than an hour ago. He walked over to the window and looked out. It was a beautiful night. The stars were as bright as he had seen them one night in his homeland. He was touched with a sense of loneliness and compassion for Mowaiti and his people. They needed so much and he wanted to give them so much.

Out of the corner of his eye he saw a movement. Without turning around, he said, "What is it, Swalar?"

"I'm not Swalar. I told him that I would announce myself."

Rasheed swung around. "Why are you here, Yasir?"

The older man closed the door before walking farther into the room. The expression he wore was furious. "How dare you do the very thing that I warned you not to do?"

Rasheed shrugged. "I have no idea what you are talking about, Yasir."

Yasir's eyes narrowed. "Are you saying that you know nothing about the terrorist attack in Rio? And the fact that a number of Americans were taken as hostages? There is a possibility that Senator Joshua Avery's sister was among them?"

Rasheed's expression showed no emotion. "That is unfortunate."

Yasir's gaze darkened. "Yes, it is, and I think you are taking it extremely well for a man who was hot on her heels just a few weeks ago."

Rasheed frowned. "You evidently misread my interest."

"No, Rasheed, I do not think so. And I hope you had nothing to do with what happened in Rio. Because if you did—"

"I had nothing to do with what happened in Rio, Yasir."

Yasir gazed at him with deadly concentration. A muscle flicked angrily at his jaw. "I hope you are being honest with me. If I find out you are lying, and that you have risked the peace and tranquility we have shared with this country for a number of years, I'll have your father place you in exile."

Rasheed's anger flared. He knew it was not a threat to be taken lightly. Yasir had great influence over his father. "You have no right to threaten me, Yasir."

"I have every right. Just remember you are the prince and not the king. Your father will do as I advise him. He will not let you cause him embarrassment in this country. So for your sake, Rasheed, I hope you have told me the truth and you were not involved."

Yasir turned and, after opening the door, walked out of the room.

The two men exchanged salutes.

"Good evening, sir. Welcome back."

"Good evening, Snow. I understand there was quite a bit of action around here while I was away. Who's handling the investigation on that terrorist attack in Rio?"

"Captain Richards of the Army Green Beret is heading

that, sir. And I understand he's narrowed down the list of people who were registered at the hotel but not yet accounted for."

Colonel Ashton Sinclair nodded gravely. Things were always touchy in any type of terrorist attack. He was glad Richards was working on identifying those taken as hostages. It was of the utmost importance that the State Department officially notified their families. "Let Richards know I've returned and that the Marines will assist with the investigation in any way we can. The Pentagon is antsy about this one, especially with the number of Americans involved."

"Yes, sir."

"And Snow, I have quite a lot of paperwork to go through this evening. Make sure I'm not disturbed unless it's of grave importance."

"Yes, sir."

Colonel Ashton Sinclair walked into his office and closed the door behind him.

Chapter 12

"Hold up, Corinthians. We'll stop here for the night."

Feeling a sense of relief, Corinthians stopped walking. It seemed they had been moving through the jungle for hours. Other than the two times they'd stopped when she had requested potty breaks, they had kept moving at a pretty steady pace. Now more so than ever, she was aware of her sore, aching feet, as well as the aches and pains of her tired body.

The night air was warm enough to make her glad that because her jeans and shirt were still wet, she'd been forced to keep on Trevor's T-shirt. The cotton material was lighter and cooler, and it provided more freedom of movement than her jeans and shirt would have. However, she felt uncomfortably exposed romping through the jungle wearing an oversize T-shirt with just the bare necessities underneath. But her major complaint was occasionally fighting off the few pestering mosquitoes from attacking her arms, legs and thighs.

It was full dark and had been for quite some time. Their

only light was from the pale glow of the moon. She wondered how Trevor had been able to lead them through the cluster of large trees, overgrown brushes and overhanging vines. At times, the foliage was so thick and dark, they had barely had enough light to see their way.

Corinthians turned around and almost stumbled. Not surprisingly, Trevor's strong arms reached out and tightened around her as they had done a couple of other times that night.

"Come on," he said, drawing her closer to his side. "Let's get you settled in before you take a nasty fall."

Too exhausted to argue, she let him guide her to an area surrounded by huge sheltering trees. She stood and watched while he knelt and spread a blanket on the ground over a bed of leaves. He held another blanket under his arm.

"Where did you get those blankets?"

He turned to her and smiled. "I borrowed them."

Corinthians then remembered him mentioning that he had come across the terrorist's backpack not far from where the man had found them. Trevor had apparently helped himself to whatever supplies he felt they would need.

"The only thing that's left is for me to give you a rubdown."

When he saw that she was about to protest, he said, "Without one, you'll be too sore to move in the morning. And we have to cover as much ground as we can tomorrow before it gets too hot out here."

He stood. "Just stand right there for a second. I'll be right back." He then disappeared into the darkness.

Trevor returned in no time. Corinthians hadn't been given a chance to think twice about the mistake she would be making by letting him put his hands on her.

He knelt down before her with a variety of plants she'd noticed him gathering earlier that day. She watched as he snapped the stem off each plant and let the milky substance from them flow into the palm of his hand.

He stood. "Hold out your arms. This contains a healing balm and will ease the soreness in your muscles, as well as soothe your skin that's been irritated by the shrubs and vines that came into contact with it. It will also work as a repellent to help fight off the mosquitoes."

Corinthians did as he instructed. After pushing the short sleeves of the T-shirt up out of his way, he began rubbing the milky substance over her arms.

Her breath caught in her throat. Despite her tiredness, her body automatically responded to him. His touch was warm, gentle and soothing. As if in a trance, she watched his hands move slowly and methodically down her arms. With every stroke, her pulse intensified and her breathing became labored.

She closed her eyes when he knelt before her and began working on her legs. His fingers were tender as he massaged the soothing substance on her knees and downward to her ankles. She became so absorbed in the tranquilized pleasure he was making her feel that when she noticed him lifting the hem of the T-shirt to rub some of the substance onto her thighs and stomach, she couldn't move. She couldn't even think. All she could do was stand there while his fingers worked their magic over her body. She could feel the slow warmth spreading through her with unabashed intensity. The muscles of her thighs and belly flexed with his touch.

"I'm finished, Corinthians. Go ahead and get some sleep," Trevor said in a deep, husky voice.

Corinthians slowly opened her eyes and noticed he was standing directly in front of her. His dark gaze held hers. The look in his eyes was starkly sexual. It stirred her body, making her feel hot, and making firebolts of desire take off within her.

He didn't say a word. Neither did she. All she could do was stand there and gaze up into those incredible dark eyes of his while silently acknowledging the sexual electricity that sparkled between them. He took a step forward. And when she saw his lips part and felt her own doing likewise, she was tempted to lean up and join his mouth to hers. But then she remembered what happened the last time they'd kissed, and how the terrorist had caught them off guard. Reluctantly, she took a step back, forcing the pulsing intensity in her body to subside.

"What about you?" she asked, taking a deep breath and lowering her body onto the bed he'd made for her. "Aren't you going to sleep, too?" She began removing her shoes and socks to busy her trembling fingers. They were aching to reach out and touch him.

"Later. There are a few things I have to do first."

Corinthians nodded and tried to ignore the deep huskiness in his voice, but her body wouldn't let her. A quiver surged through her veins. "Good night, Trevor."

"Good night."

Trevor watched as she curled her body up in the blanket and fought to control his swirling emotions. He felt his sanity under attack. He'd been about to do the very thing he'd said he would not do again, and that was to lose control. And he was very uncomfortable with that thought.

When he turned and walked away, he struggled with the realization that their closeness out here alone in the jungle was proving to be incredibly tempting, too incredibly tempting. And because of it, he was finding himself ill-equipped to deal with Corinthians Avery. The woman was proving to be too much for him to handle, and she was getting deeper and deeper under his skin.

He would have to rethink his strategy.

Corinthians released a deep sigh, feeling an odd sense of wariness when Trevor finally walked away. Her gaze followed him as he moved across the clumps of shaggy grass, his form barely visible in the darkness.

It seemed that everything was beginning to happen to her all at once, and she didn't know how she was going to deal with it. First, there was this feeling of fear that had taken its hold on her. Never in her wildest dreams had she imagined anything like this happening to her. Here she was in the deep jungles of South America on the run from terrorists. Something like this is what you saw in movies with Harrison Ford or Sterling Hamilton in the starring role. If nothing else, coming face-to-face with that man at gunpoint had made her realize just how serious her situation was. It also made her aware of just what a competent man Trevor was.

Trevor.

He was the cause of her other fear…the physical emotions he was making her feel. Never in her life had she acted so wanton, so loosely and so out of control with a man. Even when she thought herself in love with Dex, she'd never felt this way. Her planned seduction of him had been conceived as a way to make Dex finally notice her. The idea had not been the result of any out-of-control emotions that had overpowered her.

Corinthians looked up at the stars, feeling oddly displaced. No matter how hard she tried to convince herself otherwise, she knew that Trevor Grant was getting next to her. He was getting next to her in a way that no man had ever gotten next to her before.

The sound of him returning shattered Corinthians's reverie, and she closed her eyes to pretend sleep. She watched through lowered lashes as he knelt to make his bed a few feet from hers. She should have felt relief, but instead she felt disappointment that he was putting any distance between them. That was her very last thought before sleep finally overtook her.

Ashton Sinclair looked up from the report he was reading when he heard the commotion outside his office door. Tossing the papers aside, he walked over to the door and snatched it open. He frowned when he saw Major Snow and Sergeant Porter trying to subdue a young South American boy.

"Major Snow, Sergeant Porter, what's going on out here?"

"Sorry to disturb you, sir, but this kid wanted to see you. When I told him you were busy, he tried forcing his way into your office," Major Snow said in way of an explanation.

Ashton frowned as he looked at the boy. "Are you sure he wants to see me?"

"Yes, sir. He came here yesterday asking for you. He claims he has a message that he can only give to you."

Ashton walked over to them. "Let him go." And with that order the two men released their hold on the boy. He saw the scared look on the kid's face. Evidently Snow and Porter had frightened him out of his wits.

"I'm Colonel Sinclair, and I understand you want to see me."

At first, he thought the boy was not going to say anything. Then he spoke. "The American told me to give this to you." He reached into his pocket, pulled something out, and handed it to Ashton.

Ashton took the ring from the boy, recognizing it immediately. He held it up to the light and read the initials engraved inside. He frowned. "Where did you get this?"

Giovano took a step back at the sharp tone of Ashton's voice. When Ashton saw that he had scared the boy, he asked the question again in a less demanding voice.

"The American man gave it to me. He said to give it only to you and to tell you he went into the Rio jungle."

Ashton's frown deepened. "Where was he when he gave this to you?"

"At the hotel."

"The one that was attacked by terrorists?"

"Sim, senhor."

Ashton turned his attention to Major Snow. "Find Captain Richards. Tell him that I need to take a look at that list containing the names of the people who were registered at the hotel at the time the terrorists attacked."

"Yes, sir."

Then he looked over at Sergeant Porter. "This youngster has come a long way to bring this message to me. How about bringing him something cold to drink and something filling to eat."

"Yes, sir."

Ashton looked back down at the boy. "When you saw this American was he alone?"

"*Sim, senhor,* he was alone, but he has the American woman with him."

Ashton lifted a dark brow. "What American woman?"

"The one the terrorists want."

"Go ahead, Stella, and drink this. It will help you to relax."

Stella Grant shook her head. "I don't want to relax, Maurice. I want news about Trevor."

Maurice Grant sighed deeply. "I know, Stel. I'm sure we'll hear something soon."

"But we should have heard something long ago. The wait is killing me."

Maurice studied his wife's features. He, too, was worried and concerned with the length of time the government was taking in letting them know something. The only thing they'd confirmed was that Trevor had been registered at the hotel at the time of the terrorist attack. However, the Brazilian government could not verify or deny if he'd been one of the Americans taken as a hostage. After he had broken the news to Stella at her shop, he had driven her home and together the two of them had been waiting patiently by the telephone ever since.

Their daughter, Regina, was out of town on a business trip. Luckily, he'd been able to catch her at the hotel. Like everyone else, she had heard about the terrorist attack in Brazil, but had not connected it to Trevor. After being told about her brother, she had cancelled the rest of her trip and was now on her way home.

"Go ahead, Stella, and drink the tea."

Stella frowned and looked up at him. "You don't have to get so bossy, Maurice. If it's going to make you happy, I'll drink the stuff." She took a sip then settled back on the couch, tucking her feet under her.

Maurice shook his head. He wasn't the least fooled by Stella's gruffness. He knew her well enough to know, bossy or not, she did just what she wanted to do. He also knew that when it came to her children, she was one protective woman. That was only one of the many things he'd always admired about her. She had been, and still was, a wonderful mother to his son and daughter.

"I wonder what's taking Gina so long. She should have been here by now," Stella said, sipping more of her tea.

Maurice rammed his hands in his pockets, and took a deep, silent breath while doing so. "That's something I need to tell you."

Stella lifted a brow. "What?" she asked as she leaned forward and placed her half-full cup of tea on the table beside the couch. "What do you need to tell me?"

"Gina called from the airport. Her flight out has been delayed. It will be morning before she gets here."

Stella looked confused. "Gina called? But I didn't hear the phone ring."

"She didn't want to disturb you, so she called me on my mobile phone. It was on vibrate. I called her back while you were in the kitchen making the tea."

Stella nodded and tried to take a deep, calming breath. With Trevor missing, the mother in her needed to see her daughter to make sure she was safe.

She met Maurice's gaze and knew he comprehended what she was feeling and somehow he understood that need within her.

"Gina told me to tell you not to worry. She's fine and will be here in the morning. We also have to believe that wherever he is, Trevor is fine, too."

Stella blinked back her tears. "Oh, Maurice, I want to believe that."

He reached out his hand to her. "We both have to believe that, Stella."

She squeezed the hand he'd given her, taking some of his physical strength. But a part of her could not forget the danger their son could be in.

Maurice looked down at their joined hands and remembered other times they'd done this—held hands to feed off each other's strength. There was the time at the funeral of the grandmother he had loved so much, the one who had raised him when his own mother had refused to do so; then there was the time at Stella's parents' funerals. They had died within a year of each other. Then more painstakingly, he remembered the time at the funeral of their baby son, the one who'd been born with a large hole in his heart. He'd been their first child, the one they never brought home from the hospital.

The ringing of the telephone made them both jump. Maurice picked it up before Stella could even think about reaching for it.

"Yes, Maurice Grant here."

Maurice's face was emotionless as he listened to whatever the caller was saying to him. Occasionally, he would answer with an, "I understand," or a "yes." When he finally hung up the phone, Stella nervously got to her feet.

"Who was that? Was that news about Trevor?" she asked in a trembling voice.

Maurice reached out and again took her hands in his. "That was the State Department. They have valid reason to believe Trevor is not one of the hostages." He felt the tension flow from Stella's hand with his statement.

"Does that mean he's on his way home?" she asked cautiously.

His hand tightened on hers. "Not exactly."

She frowned. "Not exactly? I don't understand. Then what is it exactly?"

"Trevor and another American, a woman, are believed to have escaped into the jungles."

He felt the tension in Stella's hand return. "The jungles? Out there with snakes, wild animals, poisonous plants and—"

"Think about it, Stella. Think about it for a second. Trevor was in the Marines for more than fifteen years. During much of that time, he was part of that special unit. Remember he once told us that living out in the jungle was something they had taught him to do. I feel better with him out there in the jungle than with him being a hostage."

For the first time since hearing about the terrorist attack, Maurice Grant felt he had a reason to smile. "Yeah, Stella. I got a feeling our boy is going to be all right. I just know it."

He took a quick glance at his watch. "I better call Dex. I told him I would let him know if we heard anything."

When he released Stella's hands to pick up the phone to call Dex, a sudden feeling of loss came over him. For some reason, he still needed her touch. Over the years, he had gone to a lot of trouble to keep her at arm's length. But tonight, it was important to keep that physical link to her, even if only for a little while.

Chapter 13

Corinthians woke the next morning to the smell of fresh coffee and grilled fish. At first she thought her nose was playing tricks on her, but after sniffing the air, it seemed that wasn't the case.

Sitting up, she rubbed the sleep from her eyes and glanced around. Trevor was sitting about six feet away around a campfire. Coffee was brewing in a worn-out pot, and he had concocted a man-made grill to cook two large pieces of fish.

Food! And she was starving!

She scrambled to her feet, still clutching the blanket around her, and moved quickly toward him.

"I wondered how long it would take for you to wake up and notice food," he said, casually sipping his coffee. He leaned over and handed her a cup of the hot, steaming brew when she took a seat across from him.

Corinthians eagerly accepted his offer, inhaling the aroma

before taking a sip. She released a satisfied sigh. There was nothing like caffeine in the morning to get one's senses stirred. The coffee was a wee bit stronger than she would have liked and it was minus any cream or sugar, but when you were out in the jungle, you couldn't be too picky about such things. As far as she was concerned, it tasted heavenly and served a real purpose.

She lifted one eyebrow ever so slightly. "Thanks. How did you manage this?"

Trevor's mouth twitched. "In case you've forgotten, this is South America, the coffee capital of the world. It's not hard to find a wild coffee plant growing someplace, even out here in the jungle."

"What about the fish?"

"I got up early and went fishing. There's a stream not far away that's loaded. I didn't have the convenience of a pole so I used that bamboo rod to spear them."

"And the cooking supplies?"

He grinned. "I borrowed them."

Corinthians couldn't help but return his grin as she stared across the open fire at him. He had that unshaven look and it made him appear dark, dangerous and desirable. She thought it should be against the law for any man to look that good so early in the morning. The man was also very resourceful, to say the least, which prompted her next question. "How do you know so much about surviving out here in the jungle?"

Trevor took another sip of coffee before answering. She was full of questions this morning, he thought. "I've already told you I was in the Marines."

She nodded. "Are all Marines taught jungle survival as part of their basic training?"

He shrugged. "Pretty much, but my training was more intensive that usual."

She lifted a dark brow. "Really? Why?"

"I was part of the Marines Special Forces."

The dark lashes shadowing Corinthians's cheeks flew up. She knew that the Army had the Green Berets, the Navy had their SEALs; and the Marines had…

Her mouth dropped open. "You were a member of the Force Recon unit?"

When he didn't answer immediately, she repeated her question. "Well?" she demanded. "Were you?"

"Yes," he finally answered, enjoying the shock on her face.

A smile softened Corinthians's eyes. "No wonder you know so much. That really explains a lot."

He frowned. "A lot like what?"

"It explains why you're so competent out here, and how you've managed to keep us safe."

"I almost blew it yesterday," he said as he looked at her steadily. "At the time, I was involved in something I shouldn't have been and let my guard down. It won't happen again."

Corinthians knew there was an underlying message in his statement that had been meant for her.

"Here," he said, handing her a tin plate with a large piece of grilled fish. "Eat enough. It has to last a while. Until we make camp again later today, we'll be munching on berries."

"Did you enjoy being a part of the Force Recon unit?"

"It had its moments." The memory of his last assignment that claimed the lives of two of his close friends suddenly appeared to him. As always, whenever the old pain tried to raise its ugly head, he shoved the memory to the back of his mind.

"But did you enjoy it?" Corinthians asked.

"Yeah, overall, I guess you can say I enjoyed it."

The path they were now taking was rough and mountainous. It required that they watch their footing carefully. Corinthians wished Trevor had chosen another way for them to go, but he'd said it would be advantageous for them to go this way. The men looking for them would not expect them to take such a risky route. After nearly an hour or so of such strenuous exertion, she hoped he was right.

"How long were you a part of it?" she asked him. She wished he would turn around. She hated talking to his back.

"A part of what?"

Corinthians raised her eyes heavenward. "The Force Recon."

"I was a part of it long enough," he said as he continued his climb up a steep ledge with her following behind.

"How long?"

Trevor stopped walking and turned around. "You sure are full of questions this morning," he said, studying her intently with a glare in his eyes.

Corinthians shrugged, wondering about his mood. He'd acted decent enough over the campfire at breakfast, but then later after she'd returned from getting all cleaned up and changing clothes, his mood had darkened. "I was just trying to keep conversation going to pass the time."

"Oh, is that what you're doing?" he asked sarcastically before turning back around to resume their climb.

Corinthians narrowed her gaze at him. Trying to keep the conversation going was only part of it, but she would never admit it to him. What she was really trying to do was to get to know him better. She'd already spent two days alone with him and there was a lot about him she didn't know. Her only problem was that he was being difficult and not cooperating. But she was determined not to give up.

"Have you ever been married and do you have any children?" she came right out and asked him. She decided it would be a waste of time beating around the bush with Trevor.

He was surprised at her question and found himself answering before he reconsidered. "No."

"So tell me about your family."

"Who said I had one?"

"Oh." She stopped walking and swallowed past the lump

in her throat. She hadn't thought of the possibility that he didn't have any family. "I'm sorry, I just assumed that—"

"No need to apologize. I do have a family. Both of my parents are alive and well."

Corinthians heaved an exasperated groan. "Why did you just let me think you didn't have a family?"

"You're the one who jumped to conclusions."

She glared at him and wished he would take the time to turn around and see the look she was giving him. "So tell me about your family," she asked through clenched teeth.

He took his time answering. "What do you want to know?"

"Where do they live?"

Trevor walked over to a huge boulder, turned around and leaned against it. "They're living in Houston where they've lived all their lives. My dad lives on Chelsea Court and my mom lives on Washington Street."

Corinthians nodded in understanding. "They're divorced?"

"No, they're separated."

"Oh. How long have they been separated?"

Trevor shook his head, wondering if at any point during their conversation did she consider her questions too personal. Evidently not, he thought when she repeated herself.

"How long have they been separated?"

"They have been separated for more than twenty years," he finally answered her.

"That long? Why don't they get a divorce?"

He stared at her. She had asked the same question he and his sister had asked each other a number of times over the years. "Your guess is as good as mine."

The squinting of Corinthians's forehead showed she was in a state of deep concentration. "My guess may be better than yours. I may have an idea as to why they haven't gotten a divorce."

Trevor looked at this watch. They were wasting precious

time just standing around chit-chatting. "Really? Then how about sharing it with me."

She shrugged. "They probably don't believe in divorce. The Bible teaches against it."

Trevor crossed his arms over his chest. "You don't say? I guess you of all people would know, being a preacher's daughter and all."

Corinthians became irritated by the critical tone she heard in his voice. "How did you know my father is a minister?"

"There is a lot I know about you, Corinthians Avery."

Her eyebrows slanted in a frown. There was a lot he thought he knew about her, but as far as she was concerned, he did not know her at all, and probably never would. He would continue to base his opinions on her actions that one night two years ago.

"And there's a lot about you that I *don't* know, Trevor Grant," she said.

Trevor met her gaze directly. "You know as much as you need to. The main thing you need to know is that I plan to keep us both alive to make it back to Texas."

He said the words with anger in his voice. He resented the fact that she looked so desirable bathed in the early-morning sunlight while standing beside a medley of overwrought and overgrown bushes and vines. She was providing immense beauty to an otherwise dreary piece of scenery.

He fixed his eyes on her seductive frame as she stood glaring at him with her hands on her hips. She had changed back into her jeans and top. He much preferred seeing her romping through the jungle with just his T-shirt covering her. He had appreciated looking at every bit of uncovered flesh his T-shirt hadn't hidden. He shifted his position as desire, hot and rampant, began settling in his gut. He tried forcing those feelings away. He had to stay in control.

"Come on," he growled. "We better keep moving. And lay off the questions. You're giving me a headache." *As well as another sort of ache,* he thought to himself.

Corinthians's glare sharpened. If he could be in a bad mood, then so could she. The very least he could do was to try to be a little bit more civil. However, if that's the way he wanted it, then that's the way he would get it.

"Dex?"

"Umm?"

"You're still worried about Trevor, aren't you?"

Dex Madaris glanced down at the woman he held in his arms. He thought she had gone to sleep hours ago after they had made love. His eyes lit up with love when he gazed down at her. There wasn't anything he didn't love about her. He leaned down and brushed his mouth across hers.

"Yeah," he said, bringing her closer to him. "I'm still worried, although I agree with Trevor's father. It's good that he's out there in the jungle instead of being held as a hostage."

Caitlin Madaris shifted in her husband's arms and glanced over at the clock that sat on a small table near the bed. It was just past three in the morning. She reached up and wrapped both arms around his neck and snuggled even closer to him. "If you really believe that, then why are you still worried?"

"Because although it has not been officially confirmed, I think Corinthians Avery is the woman that's out there in the jungle with Trevor. That's good news for the Avery family if that's true because I think Trevor is capable of keeping them safe until they're rescued. But…"

"But what?"

"You may not have noticed, honey, but Trevor and Corinthians don't get along."

He paused and sighed. "To be more frank, I really don't think they like each other."

A knowing smile softened Caitlin's lips. Oh, she had been noticing things all right. She could not help but notice on a number of occasions whenever Trevor and Corinthians were within ten feet of each other, how they could not keep their eyes off each other. Especially when they thought the other one wasn't looking. Trevor and Corinthians may not like each other, but there was no doubt in her mind that the two of them were attracted to each other.

"Oh, I think in the end they'll get along just fine. They only have each other to depend on until they're rescued. In fact, I happen to find their situation out there in the jungle rather interesting," she said as the smile on her face widened.

Dex raised a dark brow as he looked down at Caitlin. "Interesting in what way?"

"You know what happened to Clayton and Syneda when they went on vacation together to Florida. They couldn't get along, either, but they discovered something special while alone during that time. They discovered they had deep feelings for each other."

Dex shook his head. "If you're getting any romantic notions about Trevor and Corinthians, forget it. Although Clayton and Syneda never agreed on anything, they did get along and considered themselves friends. The same isn't true with Trevor and Corinthians. I truly and honestly don't think they like each other. Period."

Caitlin's lips twitched. She wasn't as convinced of that as Dex seemed to be. "Well, I think it's time for Trevor to settle down. He'll make some woman a good husband and some child a wonderful father. You see how great he is with Jordan and Ashley."

Dex nodded when he thought about how good Trevor was with his two daughters. They simply adored him. But he doubted the woman Trevor would settle down with was Corinthians. He had to admit the possibility of Trevor and Corinthians being a twosome had crossed his mind on occasion. But the last time he had spoken to Trevor, he'd said that he and Corinthians were like oil and water—they didn't mix.

"I think Corinthians would make some man a nice wife, too," Dex said of the woman he used to work with and considered a friend. "She's such a classy, well-bred lady. All polished and refined. I often wondered why she's never gotten serious about anyone."

Caitlin wondered what her husband would say if he knew that for years he had unknowingly been the object of Corinthians's secret affections. She moved closer to Dex. "I think things will eventually work out fine. At least let's hope and pray they do. Everyone deserves to be as happy as we are."

Deep love burned in the depths of Dex's charcoal-gray eyes when his strong arms pulled Caitlin closer to him. "Now, *that* I agree with," he said before leaning down and kissing her with all the love he had in his heart.

The heavyset man took a quick glance out of the window. "Are you sure you weren't followed?"

"I'm positive," was the terse response from the man in the dark suit. "Why did you call this meeting? Now isn't a good time for me—"

"I've heard from Araque. The woman got away."

The man in the dark suit slammed his fist on the table. His anger was apparent. "How did that happen?"

The heavyset man surveyed the man who was apparently upset that things had not gone as planned. "She escaped into the jungle with the other American. Araque has sent some of his men after her."

The man in the dark suit nodded. He desired her with a passion. She had looked so beautiful that night at the dinner party. She would be another beautiful woman to add to his collection of others. But she would be different. She would be more intellectual and intelligent than the others. He would make her his favorite pet. He planned to take her away to his secluded hideaway where no one would ever be able to find her. "I want her found," he said. The look on his face was intense.

"We will do our best."

"I hope your best will be good enough," was the man in the dark suit's terse reply.

"Araque wants to know what you want him to do with the other Americans?"

The man in the dark suit rubbed his forehead in frustration. "I want him to do what's expected and ransom them off so no one will be suspicious of anything. I don't want anyone to know the woman was our sole target. She's the only one I'm interested in, so make sure she's found."

Chapter 14

There wasn't any doubt in Trevor's mind that Corinthians was teed off with him. Her less-than-subtle hints did more than suggest the possibility. The woman had not opened her mouth for more than an hour. And every time he glanced over his shoulder to make sure she was keeping up with him, the glare she gave him spoke volumes. If given the chance, she would probably smack him right into next week. She was just that mad with him.

It was better this way, he thought. Her anger meant there would be distance between them, and that was the way he wanted it. She would be much easier for him to deal with that way. He had enough to worry about without being concerned with losing control around her.

Trevor stopped walking when they came to a huge waterfall that tumbled over a massive group of boulders and rocks. He looked up at the sky when the sound of thunder rumbled across the land. Blast! A jungle downpour was the last thing they needed.

Turning to Corinthians, he said, "Stay put while I go find some sort of shelter for us. It's going to start raining at any minute."

The only acknowledgment she gave indicating she'd heard what he had said was narrowing her gaze at him. He shrugged. The woman definitely knew how to take being mad to a whole new level.

He returned to her in no time with what he thought was good news. However, whether she agreed it was good news was questionable since he didn't get any type of reaction from her one way or the other. Just for the sake of doing so, he repeated himself.

"I said we're in luck. There's some sort of cave behind that waterfall. It'll provide the shelter we need from the storm, and it's roomy enough for us to hide out in until Ashton finds us."

Trevor released an exasperated sigh. If a response was what he had expected from her, then a response wasn't what he was going to get. Her expression was one of absolute indifference. She actually had the nerve to look uninterested in what he was telling her.

He looked around while he silently counted to ten and tried focusing his thoughts on something else. Because of the route they had taken, he felt comfortable in deciding that this would be the ideal spot for them to stay put and wait for Ashton to come. The peak was high enough for him to see anyone who approached without them seeing him. He had been careful to wipe out every trace of their camp that morning before they had started out. He'd also taken every precaution to cover their tracks. He didn't intend on taking any chances of someone else surprising them again.

He turned and watched Corinthians intently when he said, "I'm going to clean out the cave. The last thing we want is to share it with lizards, scorpions or snakes."

He inwardly smiled. Although she remained tight-lipped, he saw her body tense at the mention of the jungle critters. "And don't go wandering off. I saw jaguar tracks not far away," he added for good measure.

"What?" she asked him in a jerky voice. "Did you say that you saw jaguar tracks?"

Trevor crossed his arms over his chest. "Oh, so you've gotten your voice back, hmm?"

He watched her lift her chin and harden her glare. "There's nothing wrong with my voice, only with the company I'm forced to keep." She turned to walk off from him.

His hand closed over her shoulder and pulled her back. "Get used to the company, Miss Avery. Like it or not you're stuck with me for a while."

Against his will, Trevor's body responded to touching her. Swearing under his breath, he released her and walked away.

Corinthians was satisfied that she had found something to keep her busy without having to be near Trevor. He hadn't asked for her help in cleaning out the cave, and she hadn't volunteered. The thought that she might encounter a lizard, scorpion or snake was enough to send frightening chills up her spine.

"What do you think you're doing?" Trevor asked from behind her, startling her.

Corinthians dipped her hand in the water as she rinsed out the blanket. She didn't bother to look around or to stop what she was doing. Trevor had the tendency to catch her unaware. She had not heard him approach.

"What does it look like I'm doing? I'm washing this blanket. Then I'm going to put it in the sun to dry so I can use it again tonight."

"It won't be dry by then."

"Sure it will. As hot as it is out here, it will be good and dry by tonight."

"No, it won't. It's going to rain later."

"It looked that way earlier, but the sky is bright now. It cleared up while you were inside that cave. It won't rain."

"Yes, it will. The reason it looks so clear is because you're up on a high peak. It's probably raining cats and dogs down below on the lowland. I'd say a thunderstorm will probably hit us hard later today."

"I doubt it."

"Suit yourself. Don't say I didn't warn you when later tonight you have to sleep without a blanket."

Corinthians glared at him over her shoulder. "Then I'll just sleep without one. It was almost too hot for a blanket last night anyway."

"Up here in the mountains will be different. Be prepared for cooler nights. And after the rain, it just might be down-right cold."

Corinthians gritted her teeth as she stood and turned around to face him. The man thought he knew everything. "Thanks for the warning. Now if you don't mind, I'd like to finish what I'm doing."

With a sigh of relief, she watched as he walked away and went back into the cave.

It wasn't just raining cats and dogs—someone had evidently thrown a few cows and horses in the mix, Corinthians thought as she sat huddled in front of the fire. She listened as the hard force of the rain beat down on the top of the cave. That sound, along with the one from the waterfall gushing down at the cave's opening, was capable of drowning out any other sounds.

She had just placed her blanket neatly across a huge rock to dry in the sun when suddenly the clouds overhead had begun gathering. Before she had a chance to seek shelter, the torrential rain had come pouring down, nearly knocking her to the ground.

Corinthians had been surprised when she entered the cave

for the first time. The area was the size of a small room, and with the fire Trevor had started in the center of it, the place looked downright cozy and intimate—too cozy and intimate.

She didn't have a clue how the cave looked before Trevor had cleaned it out, but now, all she saw was a large, neat space whose rocky floors had been brushed clean.

Because the rain blotted out whatever light would have filtered through a number of cracks in the rock wall, the area was dark. It was so dark that even with the fire, she could barely see Trevor as he stood leaning against a wall, glaring at her.

She glared right back at him. Even sitting in front of the fire she was cold. And she didn't think it was from the dampness of her clothing that was getting dry from the fire's heat. Trevor had been right. It would be a cold night. Already she felt the temperature dropping. And she didn't have a blanket!

Drawing her legs up, she wrapped her arms around them for warmth. Trevor, she noticed, was still standing in the same spot, watching her, but saying nothing. He had not said anything to her since she had entered the cave. She was grateful for that because she could not bear to hear his, "I told you so." Silence lengthened between them, but she refused to be the one to break it. Evidently, he felt the same way, so they ignored each other.

At least, Corinthians thought, she tried ignoring him, but she had discovered long ago that ignoring Trevor Grant wasn't easy. With a will of their own, her eyes followed him whenever he moved around the cave.

Chills once again touched her body, making her shiver. She would do anything to have her blanket to wrap around her right now. Glancing across the room, she saw the one Trevor had used last night neatly folded and placed on top of his over-night bag. Tempted as she was, she refused to ask him if she could use it for only a little while.

A little later she knew it had gotten dark outside. Out of the corner of her eye she saw Trevor go to the blanket and spread it on the hard, rocky floor and stretch out on it. She tried to once again ignore him and placed her attention on listening to the sound of the hard rain as it continued to beat against the top of the cave.

Corinthians jumped when she looked up and saw Trevor standing next to her as he leaned down and placed some more wood on the fire.

"Do you plan on sitting here all night?" he asked shortly, glaring down at her.

"What choice do I have? I have to stay warm. It's cold in here," she snapped back.

"I'd be willing to share my heat with you."

Corinthians lifted a dark brow. She wondered what heat he was referring to. She didn't think he meant the fire since she was hoarding that already. She could only assume he meant he would share his blanket with her.

"You're willing to give me your blanket?" she asked.

"No, but I'll let you share my bed. Together our bodies will generate enough heat to keep us warm through the night."

Corinthians gave Trevor a sidelong glance in utter disbelief. *He would let her share his bed?* He made it sound as if he'd be doing her a favor. Did he for one minute actually think she was that gullible? He had already said he was more than certain that one day they would make love. Did he think he would get her over to his bed with the pretense of keeping her warm?

Fat chance! She knew exactly what kind of heat their bodies might end up sharing. She glared up at him. "Trevor Grant, you are the last man I'd willingly sleep with. The only way you'll get me in bed with you is to hog-tie me and force me."

Corinthians heard him mutter a few not so nice words before she suddenly felt herself being lifted in his strong arms.

"Suit yourself, woman, it was your call," he grumbled in her ear.

"Put me down this minute! I mean it!" She struggled to get out of his arms, but he was holding on to her tight.

"Be still before I drop you on the floor. It would be a pity if you broke any bones on this rocky surface," he said as he carried her over to his blanket. "I refuse to watch you sit your butt over there and freeze to death."

He leaned down and placed her on the blanket. Without giving her a chance to scoot away, his strong arms clamped around her as he wrapped their bodies in the blanket.

The floor was hard, but that wasn't the only hardness Corinthians felt. Her backside was spooned against Trevor's front. Even through their clothing, she could feel his body. It was hard and solid all over. Her breath caught when she felt his hand on her arm, urging her closer.

"Stay still and go to sleep," he ordered.

Corinthians didn't think that she would be able to sleep, given her position in his arms. She doubted if her eyes would be willing to close. Her heart rate had accelerated and blood was gushing fast and furious through her veins. She lay there waiting, dreading the moment when he would try to make a move on her. She had already plotted out in her mind what she would do when he did. She would turn around and knee him real good in the area of his body that men cherished the most. After tonight, he would think twice about ever trying to take advantage of her again.

She waited for him to come on to her, but he never did. Seconds turned into minutes, and those minutes became a full hour and still he just held her in his arms without trying anything. His strong arms were wrapped tight around her and his hard body was pressed close to her, keeping her warm. His heat seemed to penetrate through his clothing and come straight through to hers. She felt warm, cozy and secure.

Corinthians tried to fight the sleep she felt descending upon her, but couldn't. When she felt herself drifting off repeatedly, she knew she had to say something before sleep claimed her.

"Go ahead and say it," she said quietly, sleepily. "I know you're just dying to say it."

"Say what?" Trevor's voice was like a husky whisper against her ear. His breath fanned her skin, making it tingle.

"Go ahead and say that I was wrong and that you tried to warn me but I was too stubborn to listen. Go ahead and say I brought this all on myself, and that if I had listened to you, I wouldn't be in this predicament."

His body shifted and Corinthians didn't have to turn around to know he was leaning over, dangerously close to her face. Almost too close. Even his body had shifted and he was nearly on top of her. She couldn't stop looking up at him, gazing up into the darkness of his eyes.

"You just said everything for me. I couldn't have said it better myself. Now please be quiet and go to sleep."

Corinthians frowned. The last thing she thought when sleep finally claimed her was that Trevor Grant was an infuriating man.

So much for putting distance between us. I want her now more so than ever before.

That was the only thing Trevor could think of with Corinthians sleeping with her body so close to his. Even with their clothing still intact, he felt their bodies generating heat. Heaven help it if they had their clothes off. They would probably burn into cinders. He was pretty close to scorching right now. Each and every time she shifted her body, her backside fitted more snug against his lower part, and he would have to inhale a deep breath. His body reacted each time she moved. He wondered what he had done to deserve this torture.

The sound of rain continued to beat down upon the cave, and thunder rumbled across the mountains. But the woman in his arms was sleeping like a baby. And for a brief moment, knowing she had drifted off to sleep with his protective arms around her, a strange feeling of deep contentment flowed through him.

He inwardly groaned when Corinthians again shifted in her sleep, wiggling her backside against him. His heart pounded and blood rushed through his veins. He had an impulse to flip her on her back and take off her clothes and have his way with her.

"Cool it, Grant," he muttered to himself. "That's not your style. Besides, you'll only be asking for trouble."

But then, he thought as he lifted his hand from around her waist and let it close warmly over her breasts through the material of her shirt, torture was fair play. And if he was going to be tortured, he may as well gain some benefit from it. He rubbed his hand over the firmness of her breasts.

Suddenly feeling guilty at taking advantage of a sleeping woman, he removed his hand and tried concentrating on something else. Glancing across the room, he watched as the flickering dance of the fire cast shadows on the rocky wall. When in his mind those shadows turned into images of something sexy and sensual, he felt desire for Corinthians grip his body again. Nothing like this had ever happened to him before. Why did she have the ability to make him lose control? How could this woman claim a part of him that he had never offered to any woman before?

In answering those questions, he knew he could no longer deny one monumental fact: He had fallen in love with her. And although he had tried not to, and although he had tried to fight it every step of the way, he had to finally admit that he was deeply in love with the woman he held in his arms. There was no other reason for him acting the way he'd been acting for the past two years. Corinthians had done more than just get under his skin. The woman was deeply embedded into his heart and the very soul of him. He could no more not love her than he could order it to stop raining.

He thought back to a conversation he'd had with Clayton Madaris last year while the two of them had been dining at Sisters restaurant. That night Clayton had revealed to him that he had fallen in love. That bit of news had come as a shocker because everyone knew Clayton had always been Houston's number-one player. The man had a history of having more women than the NBA and NFL had players combined. But that night Clayton had poured his heart out to him, and had told him of the love he felt for this particular woman, who surprisingly had turned out to be Syneda Walters. But on that night at Sisters, Clayton had asked him if he had ever been in love. And without thinking about it, Trevor had immediately thought of Corinthians. Chances were he had loved her even then. He just hadn't acknowledged it yet in his mind and his heart. All he knew at the time was that he could not get a good night's sleep without her invading his dreams, without thinking of her at some of the oddest times, and without wanting to make love to her each and every time he saw her. He knew that just like Clayton had had problems with Syneda at first, before she had come around and accepted her love for him, he would have problems with Corinthians.

He slowly caressed his initials into her arm, branding her his. He acknowledged in his heart and soul that this woman was his. His woman. And he would not share her with anyone, nor would he allow her to share her heart with someone other than him. He wanted all of her, not just the part she could spare him. The thought that she still loved Dex was a weight he would have to bear for now. But he was determined that someday and somehow, he would make her love him just as much as he loved her. That was a startling promise he made to himself, and he would make sure it was one he kept.

Clayton Madaris took the BlackBerry from his pocket. The device had gotten him in trouble when he'd found himself sending sensuous, explicit messages to his wife throughout the day, resulting in them never getting any work done. To teach him a lesson, Syneda had hidden the mobile phone for several days and had just returned it to him last night. He knew he was probably headed for trouble again, but he punched in a message to his wife. *I want you.*

He chuckled when seconds later he received her reply. *You always want me, Madaris.*

He punched in his reply to her message. *That's true. By the way, I got news about Trevor.*

Clayton cut off the BlackBerry, replaced it in his pocket and checked his watch. He would give her less than a minute. Bingo! he thought when she breezed into his office and closed the door behind her.

"What have you heard about Trevor?" she asked, coming over to him. She moved his calendar out of the way to find space to place her rear end on the edge of his desk. Her skirt was short, and when she sat on his desk, a good portion of her thigh was showing. Clayton's gaze immediately became glued to the sight of it.

"Clayton, for heaven's sakes, pay attention. What have you heard about Trevor?"

Clayton forced himself to stop looking at her thigh. He leaned back in his chair. First, he would tell her what she wanted to know, and then…

"Dex got a call from Trevor's father. The State Department contacted him and Mrs. Grant. It appears that Trevor was not taken as a hostage, but escaped into the jungles of South America. Word has it he's hiding out in the jungle with some woman."

"A woman?" Syneda asked, lifting a brow. "Who?"

"Dex thinks it's Corinthians Avery."

"Corinthians!" Syneda's eyes lit up. She had recently become friends with the woman who worked as head geologist for her father, S. T. Remington, president and CEO of Remington Oil.

"How charming," Syneda said as a smile touched her lips.

Clayton let out a short, dry laugh. "There's nothing charming about it. Trevor can't stand the woman."

Syneda frowned. "And how do you know? Did he tell you that?"

"No, but it doesn't take a rocket scientist to see the two of them don't jell. Have you even seen them in a room together?"

Syneda frowned in deep concentration. "Yes, at that Businessman of the Year Awards Banquet for Dex, and then at our wedding. Why?"

"You wouldn't believe the daggered looks they give each other. I can't imagine them being alone anywhere, especially a jungle." He chuckled. "I guess one advantage is that Trevor can feed her to wild animals if she gets on his nerves. No one would ever know."

Syneda didn't share Clayton's amusement. In fact, she found his comment downright tacky. "If you recall at our wedding, Trevor caught the garter you tossed out and Corinthians caught my bouquet. Which means, by tradition, they are both next in line to marry. Now isn't that a coincidence?"

"I'd call it a bad catch on Trevor's part," Clayton said, resting his eyes on his wife's thigh again.

Syneda saw where his gaze had wandered. She adjusted her position to pull down her skirt to cover herself from his ravenous eyes. "Well, if you ask me, it means something."

Clayton shrugged. "Trust me, for Trevor it doesn't mean a thing."

"You don't know that."

"I know Trevor."

Syneda narrowed her eyes. "Yeah, and everyone thought they knew you, too, but look at you now, Clayton Madaris. You're a happily married man. If you can conform, anyone can."

Clayton smiled. "That's true." He reached out and pulled Syneda to him. "I want you."

Syneda glared at her husband before standing. "I have work to do, Madaris. My client's due in the office within an hour."

"They can wait."

Syneda laughed. "Is this the professional Clayton Madaris talking?"

"This is the Clayton Madaris who wants to make love to his wife. Now."

He stood and gave a quick inspection of Syneda's attire. The two-piece suit was classy, and no doubt was as costly as it was short. The skirt hit her way above the knee. He hoped she wouldn't have a reason to bend over today. He forced himself not to say anything. He had learned a long time ago not to tell her how to dress. Although he had to admit that whatever she put on her body, she looked absolutely good in it.

"Stay here and don't move," he ordered her before walking over to the door and locking it.

When he turned around, he noticed Syneda was no longer standing next to his desk, but had gone to a corner of the room and was removing her skirt. He frowned. He had wanted to undress her himself. "I told you not to move, Syneda."

She grinned. "I don't take orders very well, Madaris." Then she removed her panty hose.

Clayton rubbed his hand across his beard as he watched her. Her not taking orders very well was an understatement. He walked over to stand in front of her after she had removed her jacket, leaving her clad in a mint-green bra and matching panties. Both were lacy and silky, and looked as soft as the shapely body the lingerie barely covered. "Is there anything that you do take very well, Syneda?"

A sensuous smile tugged at the corners of her mouth. She tilted her head and looked up at him. "Yes, Madaris. I take you very well. All of you."

Clayton's breath caught in his throat. During his bachelor days he'd feared committing himself to a woman would eventually lead to boredom. He'd been married one month and two weeks, and hadn't experienced a second of boredom with Syneda.

"Come here, baby." He reached out for her and she willingly came into his arms.

Frustration was clearly etched on Rasheed Valdemon's face when he looked up to see Raul Santini enter his office. "Do you have any information for me?"

Santini nodded as he took a chair across from the desk. Frustration lined his features as well. "Yeah, and it's not good news."

Rasheed tilted his head back, wondering how much more disappointment he could handle. "What is it?"

"It appears that a man by the name of Araque was behind the terrorist attack. He's a lowlife from my country with a band of cutthroats for followers. I can't imagine him masterminding anything of this magnitude. I think he's working with someone. He—"

"I don't care about him, I want to know what you've heard about Corinthians Avery. Is Araque holding her as a hostage along with the other Americans?"

"No. It seems she and that Force Recon guy are somewhere in the jungles. Somehow they were able to escape. My source has informed me that because Araque knows Ms. Avery's worth to Remington Oil, he has sent some of his men into the jungle to find her. I also heard the United States government has gotten wind of it and has sent a team of military men into the jungle to rescue them."

For the longest moment Rasheed didn't say a word, making Santini wonder what was going on in his head. "What are you thinking, Monty?"

Rasheed met Santini's gaze. "Are you sure that other than a plot to kidnap the Americans for ransom, there is nothing I need to concern myself with? Are you sure there's not anyone in your country who wants Ms. Avery as much as I do?"

Santini shook his head. "Our country already has oil,

Two Kimani™ Romance Novels
Two exciting surprise gifts

PLACE
FREE GIFTS
SEAL
HERE

168 XDL EVGW   368 XDL EVJ9

FIRST NAME	LAST NAME

ADDRESS

APT.#	CITY

STATE/PROV.	ZIP/POSTAL CODE

Thank You!

BUSINESS REPLY MAIL

FIRST-CLASS MAIL   PERMIT NO. 717   BUFFALO, NY

POSTAGE WILL BE PAID BY ADDRESSEE

THE READER SERVICE
3010 WALDEN AVE
PO BOX 1867
BUFFALO NY 14240-9952

Monty. It may not have as much as the Middle East, but we have enough. I don't think the terrorists' attack had anything to do with Corinthians Avery personally. She just happened to be in the wrong place at the wrong time."

Rasheed nodded. He was undecided what he would do. Yasir's threat hung heavily over his head. But exile or not, he did not intend to walk away from the situation in Mowaiti.

"Something else you need to know, Monty," Santini continued. "Because all the hostages are Americans, their government is blaming my country for what they see as a plot against the American oil companies. The president of this country is demanding Araque's capture immediately. Since my father is ambassador, his hands are full trying to appease the United States government. At the same time, he's working with the South American government on capturing Araque and returning the hostages unharmed before any ransom is paid. I have no doubt in my mind Araque will be captured. He has gone too far. My question to you is what do you want me to do now?"

"Let's do nothing for now. If we tried to make another move on Corinthians Avery anytime soon, it will be too coincidental and will raise suspicious brows. But I won't give up my plans. Mowaiti still needs her."

Chapter 15

Corinthians woke up the next morning and knew she was alone. She had no idea when Trevor had left or where he had gone. The fire was still blazing in the center of the cave. A pot of coffee sat steaming nearby along with a pan of grilled fish. She snuggled under the covers, thinking he had apparently found another loaded stream and had gone spearfishing again.

She closed her eyes as she remembered how the heat from his body had kept her warm during the night. There was no part of her that had gotten cold. He had wrapped them in his blanket and she had gone to sleep tucked securely in his arms with her body snuggled close to his.

Corinthians clutched the blanket more tightly around her when a deep emotion took hold of her. She shifted her body to face the fire, and let her mind go back to when her and Trevor's paths had first crossed. She had originally set out to seduce one man and had ended up falling for another.

There was no way she could convince herself that that night two years ago had meant nothing to her but one embarrassing moment. Deep down she knew it had meant everything. Her life had not been the same since. And she now knew why.

She had fallen in love with Trevor Grant.

But the sad thing was that he didn't love her in return. Not only did he not love her, he didn't even like her. He actually thought she could love one man and be deeply attracted to another. He had accused her of having shaky and unsteady emotions. She may have been confused about her emotions two years ago, but today she knew her heart. There was no doubt in her mind that she was in love with him.

But knowing what he thought of her, the obvious question was what was she going to do to set him straight? With a groan, she turned over onto her side, shifted her gaze away from the fire, and looked at the rocky wall. She could tell him her true feelings, but what would she gain by doing that? Especially since he disliked her anyway. However, by his own admission, he was attracted to her. She could use that attraction to her advantage. She immediately tossed out that idea. She wanted more between them than physical attraction. She wanted love.

But she knew for Trevor to fall in love with her would take a miracle.

It was close to late afternoon when Trevor returned. He had deliberately stayed away all day, needing time to deal with his newfound emotions. When he entered the cave, he stopped abruptly. Corinthians was sitting Indian style on the blanket with his small mirror in her hand, trying to brush the tangles out of her hair, and getting frustrated with the task. He stood there and watched her. His gaze wandered to the slender, shapely legs that showed from beneath his T-shirt, which she was wearing. Before entering the cave he had seen her jeans and shirt spread across a rock to dry. He had also seen her lingerie placed alongside them. Since he had not packed her any extra underthings, he could only assume she wasn't wearing anything under that T-shirt. That thought made his heart rate increase.

It took a few minutes before he could finally open his mouth to speak. "Having a bad hair day?" he asked her.

Corinthians stopped brushing her hair and turned quickly toward Trevor. She had not heard him enter the cave. "Yes. It got wet yesterday and I can barely do a thing with it."

She took a good look at Trevor. He had been gone most of the day. She had begun worrying about him, although she knew he could take care of himself. He was standing at the mouth of the cave, gazing at her with an intense look on his face. Behind him the afternoon sunlight was peeping through the waterfall, casting its fading rays upon him. That backdrop made him look more handsome, manlier and more desirable. She took a sharp intake of breath when he began walking toward her.

"Come here. I think I can help," he said when he stood in front of her. He held out his hand to her.

Corinthians lifted a brow as she took his hand and let him pull her to her feet. "You used to be a hairstylist in another life?"

"No, but I used to do Gina's hair all the time."

A sharp stab of jealousy went through Corinthians. "Who's Gina? An old girlfriend?" she asked, trying to downplay any envy in her voice.

"Not hardly," he said, laughing. He took the brush from her. "Gina's my sister. Her real name is Regina, but we call her Gina for short."

Corinthians stared at him in surprise. "Sister? I didn't know you had a sister. Why didn't you mention her when I asked you about your family?"

Trevor sat on a ledge that jutted out from the rocky wall like a shelf. "You never got around to the question of siblings. You asked me about a wife and children. Then you shifted your attention to the issue of why my parents are separated and not divorced."

"Oh."

"Yeah, oh."

"How old is she?" Corinthians asked curiously moments later.

"Gina's twenty-seven. There's a ten-year difference in our ages," he said as he gently pulled her between his opened legs with her back to him. He began brushing her hair.

At first Corinthians tensed at the feel of her hips cradled between Trevor's thighs. Then she allowed herself to relax against the hard, masculine chest that supported her back, and the hard thighs encasing her hips. The only barrier between them was the denim of his jeans and the cotton of the T-shirt she wore.

The feel of him brushing her hair felt wonderful. She almost groaned with every stroke the brush made through her hair. There was something soothing about the movements. Each stroke was measured. Each stroke was a caress. Then moments later, he placed the brush aside and began combing through her hair with his hands. His callused fingers gently massaged her scalp all the way down to the root. It became more difficult to stay still, so she automatically leaned her body back against him, fitting snug against his front. When she did, she felt his hard arousal pressing against her rear end.

She took a deep breath when he picked up the brush again and began brushing her hair, before taking his hands and gathering her hair and forming it into a single, neat braid. She knew the moment he had finished, but for the life of her, she could not make herself leave the comfort of being in such an intimate position with him.

Trevor inhaled deeply as Corinthians's scent floated all around him. As with a will of their own, his hands began stroking her back, and then cupped the back of her neck in the palm of his hand as enormous emotions washed through him. No matter who she was in love with, as far as he was concerned, she was his. She was *his* woman.

He loved her and if he could not have her heart, then he wanted to make her his, body and soul. He pulled her braid, tilting her head back as his mouth began placing warm butterfly kisses across her cheek, down her neck and the deep hollow of her throat. With his other hand, he began caressing her thighs. His body ached with the feel of touching her smooth skin. The soft moans that parted her lips were like an open invitation, begging him to come inside her mouth and taste her.

And so he did.

He turned her around to claim her lips. With all the love in his heart, he kissed her. When he did, passion tore at him, making him feed greedily off her mouth, making him mate hotly with her tongue. His hunger for her intensified. His craving for her increased. He was driven by need, but mainly by love.

Fire ignited his hands as he reached down and lifted the hem of the T-shirt she wore to explore the places underneath. He allowed his knuckles to brush between her thighs as his mouth continued to be hot and demanding on her lips. He caught her groan in his mouth when she felt his intimate touch.

Pleasure, the likes of which he had never experienced before, swept through his body. For one crazed moment, he wanted to believe she felt all the things for him that he felt for her. But if nothing else, at least he knew that she wanted him. That was evident in the way she was returning his kiss, molding her mouth ardently to the shape of his. She was kissing him with fervency born of hunger and desperation. The yearning and the wanting that raged inside of him demanded relief.

Trevor broke off the kiss and whispered hotly in her ear. "I want you, baby."

A knot suddenly tightened within Corinthians. Those weren't the words she had wanted to hear. She didn't want him to just want her. She wanted him to love her. There was a big difference in the two. If only he knew how desperately she wanted him, too. But she loved him just as much as she wanted him.

She pulled herself out of his arms. "I can't, Trevor. I can't sleep with someone without love."

Trevor flinched. She had just reminded him that she didn't love him. Suddenly, a deeper emotion, anger, raised its ugly head and his lips twisted into a bitter smile.

"Love? If that's true, why did you plan Dex's seduction that night? He sure didn't love you. Yet, you were going to give yourself to him without love. You were prepared to sleep with him that night just to get him interested. So don't pretend love makes such a big difference to you," he snapped. "You'll never convince me that it does."

Corinthians was hurt by Trevor's words, but she felt compelled to make him understand. She wanted to tell him she never loved Dex and had only thought that she did. She wanted to tell him that he was the man she knew within her heart that she loved. "I made a mistake that night. I—"

"Tell me something I don't know. Your biggest mistake is wanting a man you'll never have."

A part of her knew his words were true. She would never have Trevor. "Probably not, but that won't stop me from loving him," she said quietly, knowing he thought she was referring to her feelings for Dex. But the truth was, she was referring to what she felt for him. However, she would never tell him that now, especially after what he had just said. He would never know that he was the man she loved.

Trevor stared at her, long and hard. He then turned and walked out of the cave.

Regina Grant Farrell sipped her coffee and watched her parents closely. She had been surprised when she had come to her mother's home straight from the airport and her father had opened the door. She had known immediately after walking into the living room that he had spent the night. Blankets had been thrown all over the sofa.

She knew if Trevor were here, he would caution her to not make a big deal about it, but there was no way she could not. This was the first time she had seen her parents in such close quarters together in years. Although they had remained on relatively civil terms for her and Trevor's sake, she knew that over the years they had pretty much avoided each other.

She couldn't help but study her mother. It seemed that this morning she had gone an extra length in making herself look radiant, which wasn't hard to do. As far as she was concerned, her mother was still a beautiful woman who wore her age of fifty-six rather well. She could easily pass for a woman in her early forties. She was glad her mother had kept herself looking good over the years.

She inwardly smiled. From the looks her father was giving her mother, when he thought it wasn't obvious to anyone, he apparently noticed how good her mother looked, too.

Trevor had been sixteen when their parents had separated, and Regina had been six. Although, after the separation, her father had still spent a lot of time with her, it hadn't been the same as when they had lived together. She had missed that family unity.

She had a close relationship with both of her parents and unlike Trevor, she was still holding out and hoping that one day they would put the past behind them and get back together. No one could convince her they didn't still care something for each other. Even this morning she noted her mother had cooked a huge breakfast that had included all the things she knew her father liked.

Regina smiled and made a mental note to share that bit of info with Trevor when he got home.

Trevor.

No sister could ask for a more caring brother. Unlike most guys with younger sisters, he never made her feel like she was a pain in the rear end. He'd always treated her with love and adoration. And when her marriage after college had ended in divorce less than four years later, he had been there for her.

She hoped that wherever Trevor was, he was safe.

Ennis, Texas

Justin Madaris stood embracing his wife. His breath was warm against the top of her head and his hands were wrapped around her waist. "Are you sure about that, Lorren?"

Lorren Madaris tilted her head back and looked up at her husband. "I'm positive. There's no way I can let you plan a birthday party for me knowing Trevor won't be here. When he comes home we can celebrate then." She smiled. "Besides, what woman in her right mind would want to celebrate turning thirty?"

Justin tightened his arms around her. "A very beautiful one." It didn't seem like four years had passed since he had first laid eyes on her at a birthday party that had been given for her foster mother. But four years had passed, and they had been very special.

Lorren was everything he needed and desired. She was still the love of his life. July 19 was her birthday, and as he had always done in the past, he was planning a huge cookout to celebrate the event and would invite all their family and friends. The bash usually lasted through the weekend with everyone staying over and spending the night. Now, there wouldn't be a party until Trevor returned.

He led Lorren over to the sofa and sat down and pulled her into his lap. "At least there's a strong possibility Trevor will be coming home. I was scared there for a while. You don't know how relieved I was to receive that call from Dex saying Trevor had eluded the terrorists and had escaped into the jungle."

He chuckled. "And with a good-looking woman at that. How lucky can you get?"

"So you think the woman he took in the jungle with him is really Corinthians Avery?"

Justin gave his wife a slow, lazy grin. "Yes, but we'll know for sure sometime today. According to Dex, the families of the hostages have all been notified so the media will probably release their names soon. I think it will be a sure bet Corinthians Avery's name won't be on that list."

"I'm glad. I'd much rather see her with Trevor than in the hands of those terrorists."

Justin couldn't help but agree. "I'm sure Corinthians's family feels the same way. Dex talked to her parents this morning and assured them that Trevor was capable of keeping their daughter safe. I think they were relieved to hear it."

"That was thoughtful of Dex to do that. I'm sure that was reassuring news to them."

"Dex thought so, until he talked to Joshua Avery, Corinthians's brother."

Lorren lifted an arched eyebrow. "The senator?"

"Yes, the senator now, the governor of Texas later, if Avery has his way. It seems that although he's glad his sister is safe from the terrorists, he's concerned with how it looks for her to be spending days and nights alone in the jungle with a man. He had the nerve to question Dex on Trevor's character. I don't want to think about what Dex might have told him. He asked the wrong person."

Lorren couldn't help but laugh. She totally agreed with her husband. Of the three Madaris brothers, Dex was *not* the one to cross. He was a real no-nonsense man. "I can't believe Senator Avery would actually be concerned about such a thing. Corinthians and Trevor were staying at the same hotel with rooms that were apparently close enough to each other for Trevor to have gotten her out of the hotel that time of night with him."

"I agree, and I think that's what is bothering Avery. No doubt he's wondering just how close their rooms were and if there's a possibility something is going on between them."

"Why would that concern him? Corinthians is a grown woman."

Justin inwardly smiled. He decided now was not the time to remind her she had taken a similar stand upon discovering something was going on between his brother Clayton and her best friend Syneda.

"Avery is a politician, straight to the bone. And he doesn't want anyone, family or otherwise, screwing up his future political plans by letting their behavior and actions reflect negatively on him," he said. "According to Dex, Avery mentioned that there's some sheikh's son in Washington who's interested in Corinthians. He was the one who took her to that dinner in Senator Nedwyn Lansing's honor a few weeks back. Avery is pushing the relationship for his gain."

Lorren frowned in deep concentration. "Oh, I remember seeing Corinthians with her date that night. And I have to admit the guy was quite a looker, a real hunk. Syneda saw him first, then she showed him to me. I showed him to Caitlin."

Justin raised a dark brow. "Oh, really? I wonder what Dex and Clayton would think if they knew our wives were at that dinner checking out other men."

Lorren smiled sweetly. She turned in Justin's lap and wrapped her arms around his neck. "They wouldn't think anything about it. Although we did give the man a little more than a cursory glance, the three of us concluded the Madaris brothers were the best-looking men there that night. Hands down."

Justin chuckled as he tilted Lorren's mouth close to his. "I see you cleaned that one up rather quickly."

He pulled Lorren closer to him. "You're too beautiful for your own good," he said as he placed a kiss on her lips.

"Even though I'm fast approaching thirty?"

"The older you get, the better you get. I can prove it to you."

A smile curved Lorren's lips. "Then prove it."

Justin stood with her in his arms. He was through seeing

patients today, and he had a couple of hours before he had to go into town to pick up their eight-year-old son, Vincent, from school. He also knew that Lorren had just put their two-year-old daughter, Justina, to bed for a nap, and had done likewise to their seven-month-old son, Christopher.

"Your wish is my command, sweetheart," he said as he headed upstairs to their bedroom, carrying her in his arms.

Chapter 16

For the first time in his life, Trevor felt he was about to snap. Intense fury mounted within him. Never before had any woman driven him to anger so deeply and so quickly. He forced himself to take a deep breath and let it out slowly.

He was tempted to go back inside the cave and have it out with Corinthians once and for all, and tell her exactly how he felt. But he couldn't do that. Although she was stripping bare his needs, emotions and control, he still had his pride. He refused to let her strip him of that.

He had forced himself to accept that although he loved her, she was in love with someone else. He had not wanted to fall in love with her; he had fought it to the very end, until he could not do anything else but admit those feelings to himself. And knowing she loved Dex, he had decided to be a patient man and wait for her to get over it. But the words she had just spoken to him made him wonder if she ever would get over it. And if she didn't, where did that leave him?

He didn't want to think about that possibility. He loved her and was powerless to do anything but hang in there and use whatever means he had to to eventually win her love. He was not a person who gave up easily. One ace he held was the attraction they had for each other. She could not deny the fact that although she did not love him, she desired him as much as he desired her. That was evident each time he held her in his arms, and every time they kissed.

For once, he would not consider playing fair. The knowledge that her desire for him was just as great as his desire for her filled him with renewed determination.

Corinthians Avery would soon discover she had finally pushed him to his limit. And when pushed to the limit, he was a force to reckon with.

Corinthians angrily paced the confines of the cave. Okay, so she had made a bad call in planning Dex's seduction that night. She had tried admitting that to Trevor, but had he listened? No! He had not wanted to hear anything she had to say and had walked out on her.

Fine, she thought. *Let him be that way. I could care less. I can't wait until I'm rescued, and I hope I never see him again.*

Even as she thought those words, she knew she was lying to herself. As much as she was angry with him right now, she knew she still loved him.

Hours later, she heard him reenter the cave. It had gotten dark outside, but tonight the fire blazing in the center of the room seemed brighter. She could make out his features and could tell his mood hadn't changed. She watched as he walked over to his corner of the cave without even glancing her way. She glared across the room at him. As if he felt her glare, he looked at her, and his gaze seemed to pierce right through her. Turning, she decided to ignore him.

* * *

Trevor wondered how long it would be before the sexual bomb inside him exploded. He should have stayed outside. Being in such close quarters with Corinthians was going to drive him crazy, but for the life of him, he could not force himself to turn and walk out. He watched as she wandered around the room, trying to ignore him. But he did not intend to ignore her. He found a good spot in his corner of the cave where he could sit braced against the wall and blatantly stare at her. He put his arms behind his head and rested back against his hands. He didn't give a hoot if it bothered her or not. And from the glares she gave him, the attention he was giving her was bothering her.

Lengthy silence continued to ensue between them. Minutes seemed to become hours, and he couldn't help but wonder who would be the first to break it. He was adamant it would not be him. The heat from the fire and the heat he felt from watching Corinthians as she paraded around in his T-shirt made him begin to perspire. To find relief, he removed his shirt and tossed it aside. That helped some, but he still felt unbearably hot.

He lifted a brow when she began to hum. It seemed the more he stared at her, the louder she hummed. He watched her leave the cave and return moments later with her dry clothing. She then began folding the items in a neat stack. His brow lifted when she took the blanket and spread it on the floor. Her back was to him as she was bending over, attempting to bring some sort of order to the place where she would eventually bed down for the night. She was letting him know, in no uncertain terms, that no matter how cold it got tonight, she would not be sharing his heat again.

As he continued to watch her, the fire in his belly began to burn hotter, when the T-shirt she wore stretched tight across her hips with each and every movement she made. He blinked several times, took one long, shaky breath and held it. He was glad when she finally settled down on the blanket, retiring for the night.

Corinthians couldn't sleep and refused to pretend that she could. She sat up and immediately felt the icy blast of Trevor's stare from across the room. If he had nothing better to do than to sit there and stare at her all night, then let him. She was determined not to let him get next to her. When she heard him mutter a not so nice word, she turned to let her gaze fall upon him.

He had taken off his shirt, in deference to the heat. For the first time since he had entered the cave, he was no longer looking at her. He was gazing at the cave's opening. The look on his face appeared indecisive as to whether or not he should go out or stay in. A part of her wanted him to leave, but then another part wanted him to stay.

A piece of wood shifted on the fire in the quiet stillness of the room, startling them both. Trevor suddenly turned around and met Corinthians's eyes. Locked in his gaze, she watched as his nostrils flared and his breathing deepened. He then began walking toward her slowly, like a hunter stalking his prey.

She stood and started to take a few steps back, then decided against it. If he wanted a showdown, he was going to get it.

"Do you have any idea what I'm going through?" he asked in a steely voice when he stood directly in front of her.

"Whatever you're going through, you brought on yourself," she snapped.

"You think so?"

"Yes."

"Well, I don't. I think you know exactly what I'm going through, and you're deliberately trying to drive me out of my mind."

Tired, frustrated and having no idea what he was talking about, Corinthians stiffened her spine. "You're nuts to even think such a thing. The problem with you, Trevor Grant, is that you're used to having things your way. So don't try dishing out a load of bull to me."

"A load of bull?"

"Or a bunch of crap. Whichever terminology you prefer."

Trevor's laugh resembled a snort. He took a step closer to her. "Such words coming from a *lady?*"

Corinthians's temper snapped. She was sick and tired of him taking potshots at her character. She shouted at him, "You are the most infuriating man I know. Do you hear me?"

"Every living thing on this mountain can hear you. You're rather loud."

Loud? He wanted loud? She would give him loud. She screamed the next words at the top of her voice. "Forget you, Trevor Grant!"

Something snapped inside Trevor. An angry sound rumbled deep in his throat. "Forget me? The hell you will! And I'm going to make damn sure you don't!" he snarled moments before letting his mouth sweep down on hers.

At first Corinthians tried resisting his kiss by flattening her hands against his chest with the full intention of pushing him away. But she found herself locked tightly in his embrace as the strong hardness of his lips devoured hers. Then suddenly, her body stopped resisting him, and she responded to the seduction of his passion. She found herself parting her lips and demanding more of the taste he was giving her. The heat of her anger dissolved and was replaced with fire...red-hot fire. Passion inched through her veins and ignited full force. She returned Trevor's kiss with equal, reckless abandonment as he smothered her mouth with demanding mastery. He drew her hard against his groin to let her feel his need and his desire.

His tongue claimed hers as he continued to take her mouth with savage intensity. When she felt his hands move down the length of her back and press her even closer to him, she moaned aloud. Her entire being was enflamed with fire and flooded with desire. Her body became one aching need of flesh.

His kiss was possessive and made her whimper with a need she finally acknowledged and gave in to. When she felt him lift her off the floor and into his arms without breaking their kiss, her arms swept tight around his neck. And when she felt him place her down on the blanket, and felt the hard floor pressed against her back, she knew there was no turning back.

A part of her wanted to deny what she was feeling. It wanted to convince her that this was not the way to his heart. But she could not resist him any longer. Someday she may regret her actions, but not now, not today. She loved him and all the reasons for not making love to him suddenly vanished. She wanted this time with him, and then after they were rescued, she would be left with memories.

She continued to return his kisses with the same fervor as he was kissing her. She felt his hands reach beneath her T-shirt and trace a path down her skin, gliding from her breasts and waist, and sliding downward to her hips and thighs to settle in the warmth of her feminine core. His intimate touch sent shock waves of exquisite pleasure through her. And like fire, it grew hotter and hotter.

Trevor suddenly ended the kiss and buried his face in her hair. His breathing came out in short gasps. He fought violently to catch his breath.

Corinthians's breathing was just as sporadic, coming out in deep gulps. She wondered if her heart would ever settle back to its natural rhythm as she felt it hammering in her chest. She looked up into Trevor's dark eyes. He was crouching over her with an intense look in them. For a moment, they just stared at each other, trying to catch their breaths, and at the same time, pausing...waiting for one of them to make the next move.

"You bring out the worst in me, Trevor," Corinthians finally whispered softly. She became lost in the mesmerizing darkness of his eyes.

Trevor gazed deeply into her eyes, seeing the same longing and desire he knew were in his. "Then maybe it's time that I bring out your best," he replied huskily before leaning forward and claiming her lips again.

As always, whenever he kissed her, a ravenous need shot through him, drugging him with desire. She opened her lips to him and at that moment all reason was lost.

Corinthians felt the T-shirt being stripped from her sensitive skin and quivered from head to toe as she felt his hands trace a sensuous path over her bare body. Then his mouth replaced his hands and with every touch of his lips, fire flickered through her.

"You're beautiful, Corinthians," he rasped against the warmth of her ear. Then he whispered some more words to her, this time in Portuguese.

She wondered their meaning, but the throbbing need pulsing through her body tossed her into another world where the only thing that mattered was the fevered intensity Trevor was making her feel. She reached out with trembling fingers and tugged at the fastening of his jeans, then molded her fingers over him. She wanted to say something, to tell him just how she felt, but she couldn't emit a sound because he was kissing her again.

She had never known passion like this before. All the love she felt for him poured forth. And she knew that she wanted him to make love to her.

He shifted his body to quickly slip out of his jeans. When that was done, he crouched back down over her. He was naked, and large amounts of sweat beaded the top part of his body, making his dark skin glisten from the light of the fire.

Their eyes met and held as he covered her slender body with his muscular one. He shifted the lower part of his body, and eased down to her. Reaching under her, he cupped her hips in his hands, lifting her off the hard floor as he slid inside her.

He went still, frowning when he encountered resistance. He withdrew a little and was about to say something. But she arched her back and wrapped her legs around him, gripping him tighter inside her, and when she pulled his mouth down to hers and kissed him, the only thing he could do was to press deeper inside her. He wanted to make her his. He wanted to mate with the woman he loved.

And so he did.

He made love to her like he had never made love to a woman before. Loving her with all his being, his muscles flexed over her body each time he pressed deeper and deeper into her. A rhythm filled with passion and pleasure continued to consume the both of them with searing need. Their bodies locked together, rocking and reeling, enflaming and engulfing, consuming and being consumed.

Trevor's movements became faster, harder, more powerful. And Corinthians was right there with him, taking what he was giving, then giving her own, proving that she wanted him just as much as he wanted her as he pushed her closer and closer to the edge. It seemed they could not get enough of each other. So he continued to love her in the only way he knew how, and knowing on this level they were a part of each other. They were as one.

Corinthians's breath was choppy and restrained. She breathed lightly between parted lips, releasing whispered moans of ecstasy. Her emotions were wired, her passion roused and strong as the epitome of pleasure radiated throughout her body with every movement Trevor made inside of her. She could feel the heat of him mate deep inside with the heat of her, pushing her closer to the peak of total and complete fulfillment.

"Ye-esss!" she cried out, sobbing her pleasure as her world shattered into a billion passionate pieces.

Trevor followed and the deep guttural sound he made echoed off the walls as he clutched Corinthians closer, driving into her deeper. Shivers of sexual delight tore through both of them.

Their bodies shone with sweat, shuddered uncontrollably as they both found the shattering release they sought. Afterward, they collapsed in each other's arms.

Chapter 17

Trevor knew he had made a mistake the moment the last ripple of pleasure passed through his body, and the last passionate spasm had subsided. There had been nothing to hold his ferocious and turbulent hunger for Corinthians in check. When she had parted her lips, welcomed his kiss and released that sensuous moan from deep within her throat, he had completely lost it.

He had made love to her with a wildness and desperation that were the result of two years of deep longing and heated desire. Not only had he been rough with her, but he had made love to her on the hard floor in a cave somewhere in the jungles of South America. There was no excuse for what he had done or the way he had treated her.

She had deserved better. She had deserved a romantic setting that included a bed covered with soft satin sheets in a room filled with lit candles, an assortment of beautiful flowers and low, sultry music. But he had not given her any of those things.

On a long breath he shifted his body off her. *Had he hurt her? Had he been too rough with her?* He supported himself on one arm and looked down at her. She was lying perfectly still with her eyes closed. He wished she would open them and say something. She could yell at him and call him all sorts of names, anything. He just wished she would say something.

Corinthians had felt Trevor separate his body from hers and immediately regretted losing the intimate contact. The pounding of her heart decreased as she slowly regained control of her mind and body. She didn't want to open her eyes just yet. She wanted to stay as she was and savor the moment, the glorious aftereffects of being made love to by him. He had done exactly what he claimed and brought out her best. It was a part of her she had not known existed. She had never known such fulfillment before in her life. She had not known anything could be so sensually gratifying.

He had made love to her with a fierceness that had incited her hunger, overfilled her with sexual greed and tantalized every nerve ending in her body. He had touched her on a level that had unlocked every single emotion she possessed. She had been ravaged with uncontrollable need, and he had satisfied each and every one of her desires. The real thing had been better than any dreams she'd ever had of them together this way.

From the first time she had met him, she had had this gut feeling that Trevor would be the one man to unlock the passionate side of her. She had known he would not handle her with kid gloves, nor would he treat her like she was some fine piece of china. She had known he would be the one to see beyond her polished manners, and her prim-and-proper persona. From the very beginning, he had treated her like an alluring woman more so than a well-bred lady. He had made her feel hot, sexy, sensual and desirable.

She wanted to lie in his arms for a while longer and wished

their bodies were still connected. She was basking in the after-glow of their unrestrained and undisciplined lovemaking. She wanted to give herself to him again, right now. She wanted to feel the fierce sensations of their bodies, sleek with sweat, pressed together in the most intimate way, bare skin against bare skin, as they moved at a steady, yet tempestuous rhythm, a rampant, sensuous beat, giving each other profound pleasure.

She wasn't ready for this time with him to end.

And she wasn't ready to open her eyes and look at him for fear of what she might see—regret, loathing, disappointment. She wouldn't be able to stand it if she saw any of those things in his eyes.

"Corinthians?" He said her name quietly, softly.

When she didn't respond, he called her name again, this time with a tinge of nervousness in his voice. "Corinthians? Are you all right? Was I too rough? Did I hurt you?"

She opened her eyes and looked up at him. His features were tense and worried. She thought it best to answer him now. "Yes, I'm all right. And no, you weren't rough."

Corinthians saw Trevor's features relax…at least at first. Then she saw the exact moment a thought occurred to him, and he reached out and gently caressed the curve of her cheek with his knuckles. The deep darkness of his eyes was compelling and at the same time compassionate, filled with deep concern. "You didn't answer my question as to whether or not I hurt you. Did I hurt you, Corinthians?"

She shifted her eyes from his to let her gaze settle on something other than his face. She chose the cracks in the wall. Dawn was breaking, and daylight was filtering through them. "No, you didn't hurt me, Trevor," she answered quietly. *The truth of the matter,* she thought to herself, *is that I've hurt myself by destroying any chance of you ever loving me. In your eyes, I've proven you right. Now more so than ever, you believe I can love another man, yet sleep with you. You thought poorly of my character before. I don't want to know what you think of it now.* Pain settled in Corinthians's heart and she fought back a multitude of tears.

"Are you sure I didn't hurt you?"

She nodded, still avoiding his eyes. "I'm sure."

Trevor wanted to desperately to believe her, but now, he couldn't think straight. The only think he could think about was that just a while ago, he had been presented with undeniable proof that she had never slept with another man before him. It was hard to believe a woman her age had not engaged in some sort of sexual activity before now. Then he painfully remembered that on a night two years ago, she had been prepared to rid herself of her virginity for Dex. It hurt him to know that he had not been the intended recipient of such a precious gift from her. He had not been her chosen one. But he had been the one to receive it nonetheless. And the sad thing was that a part of him was glad it had been him.

"I'm sorry, Corinthians," he said quietly. "I know it's too late for those words, but I'm saying them anyway. I'm sorry I lost control like that."

He knew his words were no excuse for his actions, and wished he was sincere in saying them, but he wasn't. He had no regrets for making love to her. Until the day he died, he would never regret that.

The last thing Corinthians wanted to hear was that Trevor was sorry for making love to her, and that he was sorry for touching her. She didn't want to hear that he regretted making her feel things she had never felt before, and for a little while, making her believe there was a chance for them, and that one day he could grow to love her as much as she loved him.

But now that would never happen. There was too much mistrust and misunderstanding between them. She met his gaze. "Why are you sorry?" she asked softly. "You've accomplished what you wanted to do and that was to settle a score." Then she turned her head and rolled away from him.

Trevor opened his mouth to refute her statement, then

decided not to. What good would it do? He moved away from her, reached for his clothes and began putting them on.

After getting dressed, he looked down at her. She lay wrapped in the blanket with her back to him. He knew he could not leave things this way between them. Knowing she probably hated his guts right now, he wanted to set the record straight. He did not want her to think what they'd shared had meant nothing to him.

He crouched back down and gently turned her face to him. He saw the tears swimming in her eyes. The sight of them tore through him, crumbled his defenses and pulled at his heart— the one she unknowingly owned.

He *had* hurt her. If not physically, he had hurt her mentally by taking something from her than she had not intended for him to have.

He reached out and took her chin in one hand, holding it until her eyes finally met his. All the love he felt for her came rushing through. And with that feeling came the need to tell her how much he loved her. He leaned forward. His lips brushed along her cheekbone and eyes before his mouth touched hers in a tender and sweet caress. Gone was the urgency and desperation of before. The kiss he bestowed upon her now was gentle and smooth. With painstaking care, he tried kissing her hurt away. A few moments later, he pulled back and rested his forehead against hers.

"There's something I have to tell you, Corinthians. It's something I should have told you before making love to you. It doesn't excuse my behavior or my actions, but maybe it will explain the reason why I wanted you so much."

Corinthians's breath was unsteady when she asked, "What do you have to tell me?"

Trevor opened his mouth to speak but closed it suddenly when his ears picked up a sound outside of the cave. His features were immediately put on alert.

Corinthians noticed it. "Trevor, what is it? What's wrong?"

He let out a deep sigh. It was more of disappointment than relief. There was no mistaking the soft cooing call he had just heard. He would recognize it anywhere. As much as he wanted them to be rescued, Ashton's timing was off. He had found them at the worst possible time. Now, more so than ever, he and Corinthians needed additional time alone to talk things out.

"We have to finish this conversation later," he said gently, rising to his feet. "You need to get up and get dressed. The cavalry has arrived."

Chapter 18

"If I didn't know better, I'd think you weren't glad to see me, Captain."

Ashton Sinclair spoke those words as he stood with his muscular body casually braced against a huge boulder. His keenly observant gaze was intrigued with the look he saw on Trevor's face the moment he had walked out of the cave. The dark of Ashton's eyes flickered with interest as he watched Trevor walk toward him. He took another puff from his cigar, causing a billow of smoke to curl around his head like a halo.

Trevor came and stood at Ashton's side. He accepted the lit cigar that his friend handed to him. "On the contrary, Colonel. I am glad to see you. It's just your timing is lousy."

Ashton caught a particular look in Trevor's eyes. "Oh, that's the way it is, huh?"

Trevor took two slow puffs off the cigar before answering, "The way what is?"

"You and Corinthians Avery. Ever since the names of the

hostages were released to the media yesterday, everyone assumed the two of you escaped into the jungle together."

"They assumed right."

Ashton finished off his cigar and tossed it to the ground. Then he ground the remains into the earth with his military boot. "There are some people who are doing more than just assuming. They're also speculating that you and Miss Avery got a thing going on. Otherwise, how would you have gotten her out of the hotel with you as quickly as you did. Unless, of course, the two of you just happened to be sharing a room that night."

Trevor stopped smoking. His brows lifted in surprise just seconds before his gaze darkened. All traces of humor left his eyes. "For crying out loud, Ashton, who in their right mind would even care about something like that under the circumstances?"

"Oh, you'd be surprised. She's the sister of a United States senator. You and Corinthians Avery's daring escape from the clutches of the terrorists made headline news."

Trevor gave Ashton a sidelong glance before asking, "What did the media have to say about it?"

"Mostly about how the two of you were able to escape the terrorists. But you know how they are. They're always looking for a story. And with her brother being a senator, especially one who, from what I hear, is dead-set on becoming Texas's first black governor, and added to the fact he's not particularly popular with some folks, that makes any of Miss Avery's activities that much more interesting to some people."

Trevor's eyes darkened. The last thing he needed was anyone sticking their noses in his and Corinthians's business. What was between him and Corinthians was just that— between him and Corinthians. "Well, whoever is interested needs to get uninterested."

"I agree, but just a warning. You may have to deal with her brother. Ever since this entire hostage incident, he's been throwing his weight around Washington big-time. He's been a monumental pain in the rear end."

Trevor nodded. He had never met Joshua Avery, and if the truth were known, he never wanted to, either. He did not agree with any of Avery's political views. In fact, he thought Avery was a prime example of a brother who had forgotten where he'd come from. He had no intentions of supporting Avery for governor of Texas or anything else for that matter.

"Any word on the hostages?" he asked Ashton after tossing down his unfinished cigar and stomping it out.

"The United States military is on top of it. The oil companies are prepared to pay ransom, but the president is discouraging them."

"Does anyone know who's behind it?"

"Yeah, a man by the name of Araque. He will be dealt with severely when he's captured. Our main concern right now is the hostages' safety."

Trevor released a deep sigh. "There's a number of things about this entire situation that don't add up, Ashton. I need to go over them with you in detail when we get back to the embassy."

Ashton turned and looked directly at Trevor. "We're not going to the embassy. I have direct orders to fly you and Miss Avery to the nearest military base on United States soil. So, you're on your way to Key West, Florida."

Trevor frowned. He knew that was not the usual military procedure. "On whose orders?"

"Like I said, Senator Joshua Avery has been throwing his weight around. I think the people at the Pentagon went along with his request just to shut him up and get him out of their faces. Needless to say, a military aircraft should be waiting for us below in the clearing. There's no doubt in my mind that Avery will be in Florida waiting for his sister as soon as the plane lands. So be prepared. Like I said, he's a pain in the rear end. And he probably feels you've done enough to ruin his sister's reputation."

"Ruin her reputation? He should be grateful I saw to it she wasn't taken as a hostage."

Ashton let his smile widen. His dark eyes reflected glimmers of humor. But the tone of his voice was controlled when he said, "I suggest you tell him that when you see him."

Trevor only grunted. He had other things on his mind than worrying about Joshua Avery's apparent stupidity. He glanced around the mountainside. "You came alone?"

"Yes, you know me. I work better that way. I called in my men once I was sure of your location. Tracking you wasn't hard."

Trevor lifted his broad shoulder in a shrug. "For you I'm sure it wasn't, but for anyone else it would have been. Did you stumble across the present I left for you?"

"Yeah, I found him, all neatly wrapped. Unfortunately, he refused to do any talking. When I get back, I'm going to have to be more persuasive."

One corner of Trevor's mouth twisted upward. He knew just how persuasive Ashton could be. He had seen his powers of persuasion at work. "What about the other two men?"

"I came upon them and caught them unawares. I convinced them to take long naps." An easy smile played at the corners of his mouth. "You can say I kind of insisted upon it. By now my men should have found them, and all three of them should be in military custody. The only person we don't have is their leader and the rest of his men. But I feel confident that in time, we'll have all of—"

Ashton stopped talking when he caught a movement in his peripheral vision. Turning, he saw Corinthians walk out of the cave dressed in her black jeans and top. His lips tilted in a huge leisurely smile. "I've always said if you have to escape into the jungles, do so with a beautiful woman. You, Captain, definitely took my advice."

* * *

Corinthians saw the tall, muscular, good-looking man who was dressed in military fatigues standing next to Trevor. She wondered if he was Trevor's friend, the one he'd been so sure would find them. He didn't look old enough to be a colonel. And with his striking good looks and his long black hair secured tight in a ponytail, he definitely did not fit the image of a top military commander.

She watched as he left Trevor's side and walked toward her. She nearly flushed at the intensity of his gaze. As he came closer, she saw that his eyes were as dark as Trevor's, and from his features, she immediately picked up on his mixed ancestry of African and Native American. He gave her a charming smile when he saluted her.

"Miss Avery, I'm Colonel Ashton Sinclair of the U.S. Marine Corps. You are now officially under the protection of the United States military."

Trevor's first impulse when he had seen Corinthians walk out of the cave was to go to her, and pull her into his arms and again tell her how sorry he was. But he knew he still would not be completely sincere in his apology, so he decided to leave well enough alone. The damage he'd done to her was irreparable.

They ate breakfast in silence, as well as packed up all of their things. It was close to noontime and he and Corinthians had not exchanged a single word since Ashton arrived.

"Are the two of you ready to go?" Ashton's words cut into the long moments of silence.

"Yeah, we're ready," Trevor answered for the both of them as he settled his overnight pack onto his back.

Ashton nodded. "For safety reasons, Miss Avery, I'll lead the way. I want you to follow me, and Trevor will bring up the rear. Be careful and watch your step. Yesterday's rain has left some places steeper than they were when you first came up here. Going back down will be even more strenuous. Do you think you'll be able to handle it?"

Corinthians nodded. "Yes, I'll be able to handle it."

Trevor knew she had every intention of doing just that. But they hadn't even started their downward journey before he noticed how the movement of her body appeared stiff and slow. Although she tried to hide it, he saw her features wince with certain movements she made. He immediately knew why. It was the result of his aggressive lovemaking. Added to that was the fact it had been the very first time she had been touched intimately by a man. He could just imagine how bruised, battered and sore her body felt.

"Hold up a minute, Ashton." Before Corinthians knew what Trevor was doing, he reached out and lifted her up into his arms.

"Just what do you think you're doing! Put me down, Trevor!"

"Take it easy, Corinthians, and don't waste your time trying to fight me on this. I'm carrying you the rest of the way down this mountain. It's obvious that you're sore. Don't try denying it, because I can tell by the way you're walking that you are. And we both know the reason why."

Corinthians felt her face tinting a darker brown. "Good grief, Trevor. Do you have to make an announcement?" she asked angrily under her breath as she flashed a quick glance in Ashton's direction. Luckily for her, Ashton Sinclair had the decency to pretend he was ardently studying the sky. Although she doubted he saw anything up there to hold his rapt attention that much.

"Put me down, Trevor. Haven't you done enough already?" The quiver in her voice was apparent, but she refused to let him see her tears again. "You don't have to carry me."

"Yes, I do," he responded. His voice was tenacious, unyielding. "I'm the reason you're hurting."

She looked up at him and saw the determined look on his face and the steadfast gaze in his eyes. A tight pain settled around her heart in knowing this man whom she loved so much would never love her back. She fought hard against the tears she refused to let fall.

"Physical pain I can handle, Trevor," she whispered softly, before allowing her face to relax against his hard, masculine chest. She knew he was not going to put her down no matter how much of a fuss she made, so she sought refuge from her heartache in the strong, protective arms holding her.

"You can stop counting the clouds now," Trevor called out to Ashton. "We'd better keep moving."

The aircraft was warmed and ready to go by the time they reached it.

"You can put me down now," Corinthians said softly to Trevor. She knew to have carried her all the way down the mountain and across the stretch of clearing to the plane must have been quite an ordeal for him. Ashton had been right. The path down the mountain had been rougher, which she knew required an increased amount of strenuous exertion on Trevor. She wouldn't consider herself a lightweight person by any means, and added to that was the fact he had also carried his overnight bag on his back.

When Trevor made no effort to place her on her feet, she repeated herself, thinking he must not have heard her. "You can put me down now."

He dropped his eyes momentarily to hers before adjusting his hold on her when one of the military men rushed over to relieve him of his overnight bag.

"Thanks, Major," Trevor said to the man.

"You're welcome, Captain."

Corinthians raised a brow. *Captain? Had Trevor been a captain in the Marines?*

All thoughts left Corinthians's mind when Trevor began climbing into the plane with her still cradled securely in his arms. Once inside, he walked down the aisle of the small military aircraft and lowered his body in a seat with her planted firmly in his lap. He didn't say anything as he secured the shoulder harness over them and fastened the seat belt around them.

"Aren't you going to put me down now?"

"No."

Corinthians frowned. "Why not?"

"Because I don't want to."

Corinthians felt her face heat up. Why was he treating her as if she were an invalid? Being sore wasn't that big of a deal. She was about to tell him that, then changed her mind. In all honesty, she actually liked being held by him. She enjoyed feeling the dormant strength in his body as his arms curved around her waist, holding her to him.

Cushioned against the solidness of his chest, she began feeling sleepy when she heard the plane's propellers beginning to turn.

"Get some rest, Corinthians," Trevor whispered to her softly over the noise of the plane's engine as it roared to life. He gently pressed her head against his chest and adjusted her more comfortably in his arms.

Corinthians suddenly felt extremely tired. Then she remembered that neither of them had actually slept last night. They had been too busy yelling and screaming at each other, then later they had been too busy making love.

She closed her eyes as the engine continued to roar to life. By the time the pilot had gone through all the start-up procedures, and the plane began moving for takeoff, she had fallen asleep in Trevor's arms.

Trevor tightened his arms around Corinthians, knowing that this would be the last time he would ever hold her like this. Sadly enough, their adventure was ending, but he would remember the time he had spent with her in the jungles of South America for the rest of his life.

Physical pain I can handle, Trevor.

Those words she had spoken to him earlier still consumed his thoughts. In so many words, she had let him know it was the mental anguish and pain of what he had done to her that would always remain with her.

Trevor took a deep, soul-searching breath. He then made a promise to himself that he would never hurt her again.

It took all the desperate strength he possessed to accept what he must do, what he had to do. He looked down at Corinthians and thought how adorable she looked sleeping peacefully. And he wanted her to retain that peace, always.

Until the day the last breath left his body he would love her. But in defeat, he acknowledged the fact that he would never have her. He knew that because of what he had done to her, and what he had taken away from her, the best thing to do was to give her up and walk away. For the rest of his life, his punishment would be to forever love a woman he would never have.

He closed his eyes briefly before looking back down at her. His heart felt heavy, and overflowed with the love he felt for her. He could no longer hold back saying the words to her. He *had* to say them to her, but this time he would say them in English. He had spoken them to her in Portuguese, when he'd been making love to her, knowing she hadn't understood what he was saying.

He reached down and lifted her chin with his fingers, waking her. When she looked up at him with sleep-filled eyes, he leaned down and placed a tender kiss on her lips.

"I love you," he whispered softly, quietly, intently.

She smiled faintly at him before drifting back off to sleep.

It was completely dark when the aircraft landed on the military base in Key West, Florida. Corinthians was still sleeping.

When the plane came to a complete standstill, unlike the others on board, Trevor didn't move. For just a little while longer, he just wanted to sit and hold her in his arms.

"Trevor, it's time to go."

Trevor's breath caught in his throat upon hearing the words Ashton directed at him. "All right. Just give me a minute," he responded quietly.

Out of the corner of his eye, he saw Ashton eyeing him closely. "You okay, man?" Ashton asked with deep concern in his voice.

"Yeah, I'm fine."

Ashton nodded then hesitated for a brief moment before turning to depart the plane along with the other military men onboard.

Through the aircraft's window Trevor saw a white military limo pull up beside the plane. A man he knew was probably Joshua Avery got out, along with a tall, broad-shouldered and powerfully built older man. There was something about him that conveyed his ability to inspire confidence and garner respect. In the bright lights lining the runway, Trevor was able to note some similarities in the older man's features to that of the woman he held in his arms. He quickly reached the conclusion that the man with Senator Avery was none other than Corinthians's father.

A part of Trevor inwardly applauded Joshua Avery's decision to have them flown here instead of being taken back to the embassy. Although he was sure the senator had done it for his own self-serving purpose, it had proven to be a rather good move. No doubt there were reporters waiting for them to arrive back at the embassy, but there were no reporters here. There would be no questions to answer, no speculations to defend and no explanations to give.

There were only goodbyes left to be said.

Knowing he could not delay getting off the plane any longer, Trevor unfastened the shoulder harness and seat belt from around them. Corinthians stirred in his arms and snuggled closer to his chest, turning her face into the curve of his neck as she continued to sleep. He stood with her in his arms and slowly began walking toward the front of the plane.

Trevor stood in the plane's doorway and looked down at the small group of men gathered below before descending the plane with a sleeping Corinthians still cradled in his arms.

He was sure he could give credit to the dark, hard stare he gave Joshua Avery that kept the senator from coming forward to take Corinthians from him. He watched as Corinthians's father walked toward him. When the older man came to a stop directly in front of him, he gazed into the other man's eyes and read deep relief and sincere appreciation in their depths. The man then glanced down at Corinthians, and Trevor read both love and joy in his eyes. He then looked up and met Trevor's intense gaze. "Thank you for keeping my daughter safe and bringing her back home to me, Mr. Grant."

Trevor tried to say something and couldn't. He glanced down at Corinthians. "She's been out like a light for quite a while," he finally felt compelled to say to the man who had fathered the woman he loved. "She's been a real trooper, sir. You would have been proud of her."

The older man nodded, but said nothing. He continued to look at Trevor intently.

"The last twenty-four hours were pretty hard on her. She deserves as much rest as she can get and will probably sleep throughout the night," Trevor added, not understanding why he found it necessary to ramble.

"Thank you for letting me know that," was Reverend Nathan Avery's soft reply.

Trevor nodded. Then he gently transferred a sleeping Corinthians into her father's arms. He felt he was losing a part of himself in the process.

Trevor blinked several times before meeting the man's gaze again. "Take care of her," he whispered hoarsely to the man.

"With God's help I will, Mr. Grant. And I pray God will continue to take care of you, as well."

Trevor nodded and without saying any more words, he turned and slowly began walking away into the darkness.

Chapter 19

"Would you care to explain what the devil went on back there, Trevor?"

Trevor released a long, deep sigh as he turned around to stare into Ashton's face. He should have known his friend would follow him inside the terminal with questions. Trevor's dark eyes narrowed slightly. He didn't care what questions Ashton had, he was in no mood to answer them.

"Nothing went on," he replied curtly. He watched as Ashton rolled his eyes and knew his response had not been good enough.

Ashton shook his head slowly before saying. "I know what I saw back there, man. It's plain to see you care a lot for Corinthians Avery. Why did you just give her up?"

"Is that what I was doing?"

"Looked that way to me."

Trevor let out a frustrated sigh as Ashton's statement slashed into him. He jammed his hands into his pockets and continued to meet Ashton's gaze. "You can't give up what you never had. She was never mine to begin with. I was the wrong man from the very beginning. She's in love with someone else." He didn't add that the man she was in love with was a man he considered as a brother.

Ashton's brow lifted, surprised at what Trevor had said. As far as he was concerned, there was no way Corinthians Avery was not in love with Trevor. He had seen the way she had looked at him. It was clear as glass that Trevor was the man who owned her heart.

"Well, I happen to see things differently," Ashton said slowly, wondering how two people could be in love with each other without the other knowing it. "I don't know what went on between you two before I arrived, but from what I can see, she *is* yours in every way a woman can belong to a man. I've never seen you display that much care and concern toward any woman before."

Trevor closed his eyes and lowered his head, fighting the pain he felt in his heart. Moments later when he opened his eyes and lifted his head, his gaze clearly showed the torment he felt. "I hurt her, Ashton." His deep voice shook with raw emotion.

Ashton frowned. "I don't know about all that, but I do know she's going to be hurt even more when she wakes up and finds you gone without having told her goodbye."

"It's better this way. Corinthians and I need time to put things back in perspective. Our paths will cross again since she works for Remington Oil," he said. *And hopefully when I do see her again, I'll be prepared for the pain,* he thought further.

With a heavy heart he walked across the room to gaze out of the huge window overlooking the runway. Only a few military personnel were still out there. Against his will, his eyes moved to the spot where the white limo had been parked moments earlier. It was gone.

"There's an old Indian saying my father shared with me on my sixteenth birthday," Ashton was saying behind him.

"What is it?" Trevor asked as he leaned over and pressed his forehead against his hand on the window.

"He said there are two things a man should never give up—his land and his woman. At least not without a fight. Tonight I saw you give up your woman, Trevor. And you gave her up without a fight."

Corinthians was in a state of deep sleep. She was completely drained of energy from her vigorous lovemaking with Trevor, combined with her lack of sleep the night before. She snuggled closer into the arms wrapped gently around her.

"Trevor." In sleep, the name was whispered like a soft caress from her lips as she continued to replay her dream over and over in her mind. In her dream, Trevor had told her that he loved her. "I love you, too," was her quiet, sleepy reply as she cuddled closer into the arms holding her.

The Reverend Nathan Avery pursed his lips thoughtfully after hearing his daughter's whispered declaration of affection for Trevor Grant. He was glad Joshua had gotten out of the car moments earlier to clear their departure at the gate. Joshua was the last person who should be privy to his sister's subconscious thoughts and inner feelings.

He gazed down at his daughter as she slept peacefully in his arms. So that's the way it was, he thought as he continued to gaze down at her. Physically she looked fine, but he had a feeling that there were scars he could not see. Scars of the heart.

As he shifted positions to hold his nestling daughter more comfortably, he was reminded of Proverbs 4:23. *Above all else, guard your affections. For they influence everything else in your life.* It seemed Corinthians had not guarded her affections and had fallen in love. He had a gut feeling that it would influence and change her life forever. He wondered if she was ready for those changes, the joys and happiness, as well as the heartbreak and disappointments. Love encompassed many things, and love was never easy, especially to someone who may not have been prepared for it.

He released a long, deep sigh. Corinthians was fast approaching thirty-one. For years her only love affair had been with her job. It was time for her to settle down, find a good man and become a wife and mother. He turned his thoughts to Trevor Grant. There was no doubt in his mind that the man cared deeply for Corinthians, but evidently there was some sort of problem between them.

Reverend Avery shook his head. He had a gut feeling Corinthians and Trevor Grant had a lot of things to work out. Something had happened between them in the jungles of South America that didn't go over well and needed repairing.

"Dang, she's still sleeping?" Joshua Avery asked in a whispered voice as he got back inside the car. "Maybe we ought to take her to the hospital and have a doctor look her over. There's no telling what Trevor Grant did to her."

Reverend Avery frowned at his son's statement. Since Joshua's emergence into the political arena, he had become the type of man that only parents could truly love. "What he *did* to your sister, young man, was to keep her alive, and don't you forget it." He leaned back against the seat. "Your mother is waiting for us at the hotel, and she'll take care of Corinthians. Besides, you and I know what a hard sleeper your sister is after working herself into a state of total exhaustion."

"But still, Dad, I—"

"Enough Joshua. The only place Corinthians is going is to the hotel. Then we'll take her home to Louisiana."

The man in the dark suit was angry. Extremely angry. Araque's men had not captured Corinthians Avery, and had gone so far as to get captured by the United States military. At least he didn't have to worry about them talking and implicating him. Only Araque knew his identity and he wouldn't talk. He had too much to lose if he did. As long as he continued to supply Araque money to help finance his illegal activities, he would keep quiet.

He threw down the newspaper he had just finished reading. He knew all about the political machinations going on between South America and the United States to capture Araque and release the hostages without any ransom being paid. He was not concerned with the hostages, only with Corinthians Avery.

Only yesterday, he had ordered that a special room at his secluded hideaway be decorated for her. He had ordered the finest and most expensive of furnishings. And the clothing he had purchased for her, all lingerie, handmade from the richest silk, was proof of her value to him; proof of how much he wanted her. And thinking that she would soon be within his reach had made his desire for her increase that much more. He couldn't get out of his mind how beautiful she had looked at the dinner party that night.

So much for depending on Araque, he seethed silently as rage covered his face and his hands tightened into fists at his side. Soon, he would have Corinthians Avery and he would personally pick someone he felt he could depend on to do the job. She may have escaped being captured once, but she wouldn't do it twice.

There were three happy people sitting around the dining-room table. It was almost three o'clock in the morning, but Stella Grant couldn't contain her happiness or excitement. Trevor had called and told her he had checked into a hotel in Key West, Florida, and had made arrangements to fly home to Texas sometime later that day. The thought that her son was coming home had returned a smile to her face and the sparkle to her eyes. Her nightmare was over. But her heart went out to the families whose loved ones were still being held as hostages in South America. She said as much to Maurice and Regina.

"I wish there was something we could do."

"There is," Maurice said, reaching across the table and taking her hand, squeezing it gently. "We'll continue to pray for their safe return."

Regina nodded in agreement. She had seen her father take her mother's hand and hold it a number of times since she had returned home from her business trip. The gesture seemed so automatic she doubted he realized he was doing it. Over the past few days she couldn't help but notice how close her parents seemed to have become.

She released a deep, satisfied sigh. Nothing would please her more than for them to get back together. When she noticed the sad silence around the table, she decided to switch the conversation to a more lighthearted note.

"I wonder if Sterling Hamilton came up with a good excuse for his wife as to why he was caught on camera leaving Diamond Swain's hotel room at three in the morning."

. Maurice Grant raised a brow. "Who?"

Regina shook her head, smiling. "Sterling Hamilton, Daddy, the movie star. According to this morning's paper, he was seen leaving his costar, Diamond Swain's, hotel room at three in the morning. And he just got married last month, which in itself was a shocker since he was a devout bachelor."

Regina took a sip of her coffee before continuing. "A reporter asked Sterling Hamilton's wife about the article. Her response was that she didn't believe it. Can you believe she would say that after seeing that picture of him holding Diamond Swain in his arms? That picture probably hit the front page of every newspaper in this country, as well as abroad."

"Yes, I can believe she would say that," Maurice said with a touch of coldness in his voice. He looked at his daughter before moving his gaze to his wife. He then disjoined their hands. "There are some wives who trust their husbands. There are some wives who are so secure in their love and marriage, that nothing, not even what's probably an innocent pose caught on camera, can destroy that security."

Silence stretched out painfully across the table. Regina immediately regretted bringing up the article about Sterling Hamilton. All it had done was dredge up painful memories for her parents as to the reason they weren't together.

"I have to go."

"Go where?" Regina asked her father when he stood. He had been staying with her mother ever since news of the hostages had broken. Although he had spent his nights sleeping on the sofa, he'd still been here, close at hand, providing her mother with comfort and support.

"I'm going home, Gina, to my place. I've stayed around here long enough. With Trevor on his way home, things can get back to normal."

Regina knew that to her father, getting back to normal meant once again putting distance between him and her mother. "But Daddy, I thought we'd all be here together when Trev got home, the three of us," Regina explained, not wanting him to leave, and feeling she was the cause of him doing so.

"No, I don't think that's a good idea," Maurice Grant said, placing his chair under the table. "Trevor will understand. When he gets here, tell him he knows where he can reach me. I'll see you two later." He turned and quickly walked out of the kitchen.

Regina looked at her mom and saw the sadness and pain etched in her face. She saw her shoulders slump at the sound of the front door clicking shut behind her father.

"Mom, I'm sorry. I shouldn't have—"

"No, Gina, don't worry about it. Your father is right. Trevor will understand. And he was right about something else, too. Some wives do trust their husbands. And I will regret for the rest of my life that I was not one of them. I admire Sterling Hamilton's wife for taking the position that she did."

Regina watched as her mother stood and quietly left the room.

* * *

Trevor lay in bed in total darkness, looking up at the ceiling. He missed Corinthians already. Ashton just didn't understand that things had to end the way they did between them. If he had known the whole story from the beginning, then he would know there was no other way for things to end.

What he had told Ashton had been the truth. Her love had never been his. When he had first laid eyes on her, he had been the wrong man. He had not been the man she had planned to seduce. Just like he had not been the man she had planned to give her virginity to. Again, he had been the wrong man.

He shifted positions in bed. With every fiber of his being, he ached to hold Corinthians in his arms once more. He ached to go to sleep with her beside him and to wake up with her in the mornings. And he ached to show her just how much she was loved. The only thing he had left were memories he would cherish forever.

Not being able to stay in bed any longer, Trevor got up and slipped into his jeans. He was about to pick up the phone to call downstairs to see if one of the restaurants in the hotel was still open when he heard the knock on his door.

His eyes narrowed. His late-night visitor could only be one person, and the last thing he wanted to hear was another Indian saying from Ashton. He went to the door and snatched it open. "Don't you ever give up?"

Ashton laughed. "Not too often," he drawled in an Oklahoma accent.

Trevor cocked his head and looked at Ashton. He had changed clothes. Gone were the military fatigues. Now he was dressed in a pair of well-worn jeans and a pullover shirt with a fringed cowboy vest over it. His hair was no longer secured in a ponytail, but hung loose around his shoulders. Even with the darkness of Ashton's skin, tonight he looked more Indian. Trevor glanced down at Ashton's feet. He even had on a pair of moccasins.

Trevor couldn't help the one corner of his mouth that lifted slightly into a smile. "Going to a powwow?"

"I wish." Although Ashton returned Trevor's smile, his eyes couldn't hide a host of painful childhood memories. And Trevor understood why. Ashton had once told him how hard it had been as a child to be torn between his Indian and his African American heritages. His summers had been spent with his father at the Cherokee nation in Oklahoma, and his school year had been spent with his mother's parents in Washington, D.C. His grandparents had spent those nine months of the year trying to de-Indianize him. They had never come to accept their daughter's marriage to an Indian, even though it had lasted less than a year thanks to their interference.

"What's up?" Trevor asked, moving aside to let Ashton enter the room.

"Figured you wouldn't be doing much sleeping tonight, so I thought we could use this time to talk. You mentioned something about having a bad feeling about this hostage thing. Would you care to enlighten me?" he asked, dropping down in the recliner in the room.

"I may as well," Trevor said, taking a seat in the chair at the desk. "First of all, that terrorist who managed to track me and Corinthians down in the jungles spoke Portuguese. I was surprised by that, since the two men who tried to abduct Corinthians in São Paulo spoke Spanish. And I've—"

"Whoa, wait a minute. Back up. Are you saying two men tried abducting Miss Avery in São Paulo? Before the terrorists' attack?"

"Yeah, the day before. She was in a McDonald's at the time, and had gone to use the ladies' room. I walked into the place just in time. Afterward, I thought it was just a case of an American tourist being set upon by a bunch of thieves, but now I'm sure that wasn't the case."

Ashton lifted a dark brow. "Why do you think that?"

"Because we ran into those same two men the night we

escaped into the jungle. We hid from them in the dense under-brush. And although they spoke in rapid, clipped Spanish, I was able to keep up with most of their conversation. One of them told the other that someone named Santini would not like having to tell someone named Monty that they had liter-ally screwed up again, and that someone else had gotten to the woman before they did. At the time, I thought they were part of the terrorist group, but now I'm not all that certain about that. I've never known any Spanish-speaking terrorist and any Portuguese-speaking terrorist to join forces on anything. In fact, you know as well as I that they usually oppose each other."

Ashton nodded. "And you're sure one of those Spanish-speaking men mentioned the name Monty?"

"I'm positive."

Ashton stood and began pacing the room. A prickle of unease flowed through Trevor's body as he watched him. "Is there something you need to tell me, Ashton?"

Ashton stopped his pacing and looked over at Trevor. "What you've just told me has raised my suspicion of who may have been behind the taking of those American hostages."

A deep frown covered Trevor's face. "Who?"

Ashton took a long, weary breath. "The CIA has been watching someone for the past six months. And although they haven't been able to come up with strong, concrete evidence, it's believed that this very wealthy individual is behind the recent increase in illegal contraband coming into South America. And you're right about the Spanish-speaking South Americans and the Portuguese-speaking South American terrorists not being able to work together; however, enough money can make anyone do just about anything."

"Who is this person?" Trevor asked again. He wanted a name. He wanted to know the identity of the person who had placed his and Corinthians's life in danger for four days.

"I want a name, Ashton," Trevor said upon sensing Ashton's reluctance to give him one. "And don't try pulling that military security stuff on me. Don't forget I've been there and I've done that. After all I've been through, I think I deserve a name."

Ashton stared long and hard at the man whom he considered a very close friend; a man who had once risked his life saving his. "The man is Armond Thetas. Known as Monty to his friends."

Trevor immediately went into shock. "Armond Thetas?" Nothing in his voice even hinted at the deep rage he felt, just the shock. If the CIA had Thetas under suspicion, there was a good reason for it. "And you think he's behind the attack?"

"Yes, we have our suspicions although we can't prove it right now."

"What makes you think he's involved?"

"The CIA had an inside informer who worked inside Thetas' villa. He kept the CIA pretty much informed as to Thetas' activities, which seemed to be operating more than an oil company in South America. Large amounts of money were withdrawn from his bank account just weeks before a huge weapon shipment found its way to South America undetected. The last time the CIA heard from their informer, he warned them about something big going down, but didn't give any specifics. We think the kidnapping of the American hostages could be it, but we aren't absolutely sure."

Trevor nodded. "What about the informer? Wasn't he able to—"

"No," Ashton cut in. "He had to be pulled out of there immediately. Somehow Thetas found out someone from the inside was a traitor. Plans were in motion to find out who he was and to have him eliminated." He stuck his hands into his pockets and met Trevor's gaze. "You may as well know that Drake was the informer."

Trevor flinched and sucked in his breath. Drake Warren

was a good friend of theirs and a former member of the Force Recon where they had fondly tagged him "Sir Drake." Now he worked for the CIA doing various things for the American government. They were things Trevor didn't even want to think about and knew better than to ask about. No doubt Drake was taking chances he shouldn't be taking. Their friend lived dangerously on the edge. As far as Drake was concerned, his life had pretty much ended when the woman he loved was murdered by a group of revolutionaries out to overthrow the Haitian government nearly three years ago.

"Where's Drake now?"

"Who knows, man. The CIA forced him to take time off to rest, but you know Sir Drake. The word *rest* is not in his vocabulary."

Trevor nodded. He then returned his thoughts to Armond Thetas. The man had been in Rio de Janeiro with them, attending the summit. He had also been the one to personally invite him and Corinthians to the dinner party that night at the hotel and then to his villa for rest and relaxation in Buzios the next day. As Trevor thought further, he remembered that Thetas had left the dinner party early claiming an emergency had come up. How convenient. A dark frown covered Trevor's face when he remembered how Thetas had looked at Corinthians that night when she had first entered the ballroom for dinner. Like the other men present, he had been entranced by her beauty.

Trevor's fingers tightened around the pen he had picked up off the desk. If Corinthians had been taken as a hostage, and with her being the only female geologist in the group— and a desirable one at that—he had a gut feeling she would not have returned unharmed. He thanked God that he had gotten her out in time.

"So what's the CIA's next move regarding Thetas?" Trevor asked.

"Right now, they're being cautious. The information Drake

provided proves he's into something illegal, but we have nothing to tie him to the hostages yet. As you know, Thetas left the hotel early that night, but our man who followed him said he went straight home and stayed there all night after receiving word that his young son of five had taken ill."

"He has a son that young?"

"Yes, from one of his mistresses. I understand he had several. He loves women just as much as he loves money."

Trevor didn't doubt that. "But there's one thing that still puzzles me, Ashton. Why did someone try to abduct Corinthians the day before the terrorist attack? Had they been successful in their attempt, I doubt that same group would have been stupid enough to turn around the next night and kidnap other hostages. It just doesn't make sense. And there's something else you should know."

"What?"

"Corinthians told me she got detained for hours at the airport by Customs when she entered Brazil. Even after all you've told me, I still have a bad feeling about this one. If I didn't know any better, I'd think we were dealing with two different groups here."

Ashton nodded, following Trevor's line of thinking. "As soon as I get back to the embassy, I'm going to check further into some things, like that incident in McDonald's and what happened at Customs. At least you've provided us with another name. I'm curious as to who Santini is. I'll pass his name on to the CIA for them to check out. I'll keep you informed if I hear anything." He smiled. "I have some leave time coming up. I just might come to Texas and pay you a visit in a few weeks."

Trevor shook his head. He knew if Ashton had plans to come to Texas, the main reason was not to see him, but to see Netherland Brooms.

Netherland, called Nettie by her friends, was the owner of Sisters, a popular restaurant and hangout in Houston. Ashton and Netherland had met a few years ago when Ashton had paid him a visit. He had taken him to dinner at Sisters and had introduced them.

"Yeah, you do that," Trevor said, smiling. "And before you ask, the answer is yes, Nettie is still single. But I thought she made it clear to you that she doesn't date military men."

A slow grin appeared under Ashton's eyes. "Then I guess I'll have to work at changing her mind about that, won't I?"

Trevor shrugged. Even with Ashton's art of persuasion, he had a feeling Nettie would not budge. But he would let Ashton find that out for himself.

"Oh, by the way, I think you might want this back," Ashton said.

Trevor took the ring Ashton handed him and returned it to his finger. "Thanks, for everything."

"Don't mention it. You would have done the same for me. In fact, you already have." Ashton looked down at his watch. "It's almost morning. We may as well go someplace and grab breakfast. I'm returning to South America in a few hours. When will your flight leave for Texas?"

"Not soon enough," was Trevor's reply as he grabbed his jacket off the table and followed Ashton out of the door.

Deep in the recesses of her sleep-induced mind, Corinthians faintly heard her mother calling her name. She frowned. Why was her mother out here in the jungle with her and Trevor? The last thing she wanted was her mother to find her naked in Trevor's arms, and especially not before he made love to her again. "No, go away. I want Trevor," she mumbled still deep in sleep.

"Corinthians, sweetheart, I'm here, and I'm going to take care of you."

"Trevor," was Corinthians's reply. She said the name in such a way that Maudlin Avery could not help but lift a brow.

"Corinthians, wake up, honey. You're having a dream," she

whispered softly in her daughter's ear. The last time Corinthians had slept this hard had been after working herself into a state of total exhaustion on that special project at Remington Oil a little more than a year ago. She had come home for two weeks to get some much-needed rest, sleeping twelve hours straight her first day home.

Maudlin Avery had always been concerned Corinthians was working too hard and that she didn't have much of a social life. She and her husband were yet to meet any man she dated unless it was someone Joshua managed to fix her up with. Heaven help them if she ever became seriously involved with anyone Joshua considered suitable. Suitable to Joshua meant just the opposite to them. She wanted her daughter to be the object of some man's deep affection and undying love, and not a way for him to advance his career or social status.

Maudlin Avery brought her thoughts back to the present when her daughter let out a deep, guttural moan. She frowned, wondering just what kind of dream Corinthians was having. "Corinthians, wake up," she said, shaking her awake.

Corinthians snatched her eyes open although they were still groggy from sleep. She tried focusing her gaze on the figure of the person leaning over her. "Mom!" she squeaked when her focus became clearer. She suddenly sat up in bed and glanced around the room.

"Mom? What are you doing here? Where am I?" she asked as she tried to clear sleep from her brain.

"You're at a hotel in Key West, Florida. The military brought you here after you were rescued from the jungles of South America."

"But how? When? I don't remember anything," Corinthians said flustered. "The last thing I remember is getting on that plane and going to sleep in Trevor's—"

She suddenly stopped talking midsentence and quickly glanced around the room. Had Corinthians taken the time to notice, she would have felt, like her mother saw, the look of sheer panic in her face. And she would have heard, like her mother did, the frantic tone of her voice when she asked, "Where's Trevor?"

Chapter 20

"Mr. Grant isn't here, Corinthians."

"What do you mean he isn't here?"

To Maudlin Avery's surprise, her fiercely independent daughter seemed quite upset to discover that Trevor Grant was not there. Corinthians had never been one to get worked up over a man. Her daughter's new attitude stunned her. Four days in the jungle could not have changed her that much, could it? But the look on Corinthians's face clearly showed she was not a happy camper.

Evidently Nathan had not told her everything she needed to know about Trevor Grant. The only thing he had told her was that the man had actually made Joshua's knees shake. She inwardly smiled at that. Any man who could put Joshua in his place was worth checking out. Now it seemed she needed to check Mr. Grant out for other reasons, as well.

"Mom, where is he?"

Corinthians's question interrupted Maudlin Avery's

thoughts. "I assume you're still asking about Trevor Grant?"

Corinthians looked puzzled. "Of course. Who else would I be asking about?"

Maudlin Avery's voice contained a faint hint of humor when she said, "I was just wondering since you've never shown much interest in a man before, and definitely not with so much distress in your voice."

"I'm not distressed," Corinthians replied in a voice that clearly showed otherwise. "I just want to know where he is. I need to talk to him about something."

Maudlin looked at Corinthians curiously. There was something about her that was different, although at the moment, she couldn't put a finger on exactly just what that difference was.

Corinthians was not paying any attention to her mother's close study of her. The only thing she could think about was the fact that Trevor had gone. He had left her without even saying goodbye. Had he been that anxious to get rid of her? Had he regretted making love to her? Her insides churned at the thought. She knew he didn't love her, but she had hoped what they had shared meant something to him like it had to her. Evidently it had not.

Tears she couldn't control misted her eyes. The next thing she knew, she was being pulled into her mother's arms. "It's all right, baby. Shhh, don't cry. Your father and I are taking you home with us to Louisiana. We'll take care of you and everything will be all right."

Corinthians pulled herself out of her mother's embrace and gazed up at her with tear-filled eyes. "No, nothing's going to be all right. Not ever again. He's gone and I didn't tell him. I should have told him anyway."

Maudlin reached up and soothingly stroked the single braid that hung over her daughter's shoulder. "You should have told him what?"

Corinthians opened her mouth to say she should have told Trevor that she loved him, but didn't say the words. She could not confess her love for him to anyone before first letting him know. When she thought about all the things he had done for her in South America, she couldn't help but be filled with love for him. He had placed her life before his own, he had fed her, kept her safe and warm and had made love to her in a way every woman should be made love to at least once in her life, with all-consuming fire and passion.

"Corinthians?"

Her mother's soft, gentle voice pulled at her and like a small child she went back into her mother's arms, seeking comfort. She sighed and relaxed in the warmth her mother offered.

"You're thinking that you should have told him how much you care for him, aren't you?"

A shudder of surprise touched Corinthians at her mother's question. But then it really shouldn't have. She had discovered a long time ago that God had given mothers special powers to read their children like a book at times, and Maudlin Avery was no exception. Her mother had read her feelings for Trevor loud and clear.

"Yes. I'm thinking that I should have told him."

For a long while her mother just held her and said nothing. When she did speak again moments later she said, "I'm glad you've finally come to terms with what you thought you felt for Dex Madaris."

Corinthians pulled back from her mother's arms and gazed up into her face curiously. "How did you know I thought I loved Dex?"

"How could we not know? When you first began working at Remington Oil, he was all you ever talked about. Your father and I knew you thought you were in love with him, but I always knew that you weren't."

"How did you know that?"

"Because, you were too cool and calm with your feelings, which to me indicated they were more like a crush and hero worship than anything. You've always been too tied down to your job to ever become involved with a man. Convincing yourself that you loved Dex Madaris was convenient for you. He was safe, and he wasn't any competition for what you were really committed to, which was to move up in your career at Remington Oil. And Dex Madaris made it easy for you to convince yourself that you loved him by being all the things you thought a decent man should be. But you were too easy in accepting the fact that he never returned your affection. I think if he had made one move that indicated he was the least bit interested in you, too, you would have panicked and lost interest. He would no longer have been safe. You were not ready to truly love a man…until now."

Corinthians considered her mother's words for a moment and knew they were true. She had often wondered why she had never pushed her and Dex's relationship to a higher level than friendship. She had always been satisfied with it until she had heard he had returned from Australia, and they would be working together on a project for Remington Oil. She had made the decision then to let him know her true feelings. Why?

"But I did try to push for more, Mom, around two years ago after he returned from Australia."

"And?"

Corinthians did not intend to tell her mother the full story of how she had made a fool of herself in that hotel room. "And I made a mistake by trying. That's when I found out he had gotten a wife and child since I'd seen him last."

"And what did you do after you found that out? Did you lock yourself in your condo and cry for days? Did you lose your appetite and stop eating? Were your insides ripped apart by the news? Did you rant and rave over losing the man you loved? I doubt you did any of those things. To be quite honest with you, I doubt very seriously you lost any sleep over it."

Corinthians sighed. Oh, she had lost plenty of sleep that night all right. But her loss of sleep had not been because of Dex. Trevor had consumed her every waking thought and had managed to invade her sleep, as well. That night when she had met him, he had stirred emotions within her so intense and fiery that for the longest time she had convinced herself it was only anger. But now she knew that wasn't the case.

She looked up at her mom. "But I want to do all those things now, Mom, because of Trevor. I want to lock myself in my condo and have a good cry. I don't care if I never eat again. I want to rant and rave, and I feel my insides have been ripped apart knowing he doesn't care."

"Are you sure he doesn't care?"

"Yes."

"How do you know that? Did he say he didn't care?"

"No, but he didn't have to. There's a lot about Trevor and my relationship you don't know."

Maudlin Avery nodded, knowing that was an understatement. "What I do know is that thanks to him, we have you back home with us." She hugged her daughter again. "And we're glad you're back."

She then stood. "Your father and brother will want to see you now that you're awake." She crossed the room to open the door. Before doing so, she turned back around to her daughter.

"Oh, and Corinthians, that must have been some dream you were having before I had to wake you." Maudlin Avery inwardly smiled when a dark flush came over her daughter's cheeks.

Rasheed sat across the breakfast table, studying his father. Wearing the customary clothing of their native land, the burnoose and kaffiyeh appeared a startling white against the sheikh's brown skin.

Sheikh Amin Valdemon had always been considered by many to be a good-looking man. He had a smooth, matured face, a full mouth and an aquiline nose. His eye coloring, dark as a starless night, made his gaze sharp and assessing. And his straight, black hair was flecked with a small amount of gray at the temples. At the age of sixty, he had always possessed a vitality that seemed endless. But lately, Rasheed had noticed his father always appeared tired and subdued. He looked nothing like the man who was one of the most influential sheikhs in the world. His influence had nothing to do with him being the ruler of a productive country because Mowaiti was not one. His influence and respect came as a result of being a successful, peaceful negotiator. More than once he had kept many oil-producing Arab nations from warring with one another. He had the ability to head off a confrontation between two countries better than anyone. For that reason, OPEC had chosen him as negotiator in their dealings with the United States. For the past three months, he had spent more time in this country than he had in his own. And that was what concerned Rasheed the most. His father was losing touch with the people who depended on him for their survival. But today, Rasheed had another concern as he looked at his father's plate. He had barely touched his meal.

"Father, are you all right?"

Rasheed saw the surprise dart through the sheikh's eyes before waving off the question with a hand that trembled slightly. "Of course I'm fine, Rasheed. Why wouldn't I be?"

Since he had asked, Rasheed decided to tell him the obvious. He leaned forward when he said, "I happen to notice you seem rather tired lately. Today especially."

Sheikh Valdemon pushed his plate aside. "If I appear that way, there's a good reason for it."

Rasheed knew of only one reason that could be blamed for his father's fatigue. He had never discussed with his father the issue of his overactive sex life. But he would never forget his surprise visit to the estate a few months ago. He had found his father passed out in his bedroom with as many as five naked women littering the living room floor. It had been obvious as to what had gone on earlier, before his arrival.

Rasheed had been disheartened at the sight. Up until that night, he had assumed that although his father, at the age of twenty-seven, had been forced by his father, the old sheikh, to marry his mother to form an allegiance between the Middle East and Egypt, sometime over the years they had fallen in love. In all the years he had known him, his father had never summoned a woman from his harem to share his bed. His mother had been the only woman his father had ever appeared to want. At least it had been that way until three months ago. Now he seemed obsessed with seeking out other feminine pleasures. Although he had never discussed that night with his father, he had discussed it with Yasir, who had shrugged it off and simply said that his father had begun developing special needs. They were needs one woman could no longer satisfy.

"I assume you had quite a night, Father."

The sheikh lifted a dark brow. "My nights are no concern of yours, Rasheed."

Anger flared within Rasheed. He was about to retort that he hoped his father's nights would not place his mother's health in any danger, when Yasir entered the room. The surprised look on his face indicated he had not expected to see Rasheed.

"I did not know you would be joining your father for breakfast, Prince Rasheed."

Rasheed looked at the man who was now standing beside his father's chair. He knew it angered Yasir not to know everything that concerned the sheikh. "I had an important matter to discuss with Father."

The sheikh gave his son his full attention. "What is it, Rasheed? Are you all right?"

Rasheed heard genuine concern in his father's voice. No matter what their differences were—and lately there seemed to be many—he knew his father loved him deeply.

"Yes, Father, I'm fine. I just wanted to let you know I will be returning to Mowaiti next week. I came to see if you wanted to return home with me, if only for a little while. The people of Mowaiti need to see you. And you haven't seen Mother for nearly three months."

Sheikh Valdemon's features appeared to soften at the mention of his wife. He opened his mouth to speak, but before he could do so Yasir's words cut him off. "Now is not a good time to leave here, your highness. Have you forgotten the President of this country has asked to meet with you next week?"

It was apparent from the disappointed look that settled in the sheikh's features that he had. "Yes, I had forgotten. Yasir is right. I should stay here to meet with the President. Tell your mother I'm still needed here and—"

Rasheed stood and faced his father. "What about Mowaiti, Father? Don't you think you're needed there, too? Your people need you. Have you forgotten about them?"

"Of course not! What I'm doing in this country will benefit our people, Rasheed. When will you see that? You are my heir and one day you will take my place. What I am doing is assuring that the United States will always be an ally to Mowaiti."

Rasheed's face hardened. "All your work won't mean a thing if Mowaiti does not survive as a country. All your diplomatic efforts would have been wasted, Father." He turned on his heel and angrily strode out of the room.

Trevor was scowling at the incessant knocking on his hotel door. He had just lain down to grab a few hours of sleep before checking out of the hotel.

He and Ashton had spent most of the early-morning hours in one of the restaurants downstairs. Since he knew Ashton had caught a military plane back to South America, he couldn't help but wonder who his visitor could be. When the knocking on the door became more persistent, he gritted his teeth as he slipped into his jeans. He angrily stalked over to the door and snatched it open.

A huge smile suddenly covered Trevor's face as his gaze lit upon the three men standing in the doorway—Justin, Dex and Clayton Madaris. Before he could open his mouth to say anything, Justin Madaris's deep voice spoke with broken calmness.

"We flew down in Uncle Jake's private plane. We're here to take you home, Trev."

Chapter 21

Three weeks later

Corinthians slowly opened her eyes to face another day. Sunlight filtered through the curtains in her bedroom, bathing it in a soft, golden glow. She yawned, then stretched. She started to get out of bed when suddenly a moment of dizziness and a feeling of nausea hit her, making her lie back down. She frowned. The same thing had happened to her yesterday morning, as well. Maybe her mother had been right in saying her resistance was probably low and that she was coming down with the flu or something.

It had been three weeks since she had flown to Louisiana from Key West with her parents and Josh. A lot of good things had happened since then. The Navy SEALs had infiltrated the terrorists' hideout and had overpowered them without harming any of the hostages. It had been a happy ending, although the leader of the terrorist group had managed to get away without being captured.

Her boss, Adam Flynn, as well as S. T. Remington, the president and CEO of Remington Oil, had flown to her parents' home to see her. S. T. Remington had ordered that she take some additional time off work with pay, four weeks to be exact, and that if she felt she needed more to let him know.

Dex and Caitlin had also flown to Louisiana to see her, and the flowers she had received from a number of people, including Rasheed Valdemon, had certainly lifted her spirits. Brenna had come to stay with her during her first week back. She had enjoyed the company of her best friend.

Corinthians slumped under the covers when she thought about the one thing that had bothered her over the past three weeks. Not once had Trevor called her. A part of her had not believed he would dismiss her from his life like he had, but he had proven her wrong. Each day she promised herself she would not think of him and that she would not care, but she ended up doing both of those things anyway.

When Corinthians heard the soft knock that sounded on her bedroom door, she sat up again, willing her bout of dizziness and nausea to pass. "Yes?" she called out through the door. "Come in."

She was surprised when Joshua walked in. "Josh, I didn't know you were home."

His frown was automatic. "I'm not home. I've told you more than once that this place can never be home to me. Home is Texas."

Corinthians raised her eyes to the ceiling. Her parents' move from Texas to Louisiana had always been a sore spot with Joshua. She had been in her freshman year of high school and Josh had been attending college at the University of Texas, when their parents had announced her father's acceptance to pastor a church in Alexandria, Louisiana. Josh had been furious and could not believe their parents would consider moving away from their beloved native state of Texas. He remained in Texas and refused to consider her parents' beautiful home as his, although he visited their parents occasionally. She had had no problem with the move although it had meant leaving Brenna. But the two of them had decided to keep in touch and hook back up when they attended college at Grambling State University near Shreveport.

"Sorry, I forgot. My mistake," she said. "When did you get in?"

"Late last night, but you had already gone to bed so I decided not to bother you. I'm only going to be here today. I'm flying out first thing in the morning." He came and sat on the edge of her bed. "How have things been going?"

"Fine, but I may be coming down with the flu. For the past few days I've been unable to keep anything in my stomach."

Joshua stood and immediately backed away. "Thanks for telling me. I can't afford to be sick."

"Why? Haven't you and your GOP friends cut enough social programs yet?"

It was evident Joshua did not appreciate her comment, but Corinthians didn't care. There was no way she would ever endorse her brother's political views.

"Let's change the subject, shall we?" Joshua said, taking a seat in the chair in what he considered to be a safe distance from her.

"It's your call," she said, smiling. "One day you'll realize your mistake."

"And one day you'll realize yours. Speaking of mistakes, I'm glad you didn't let anything develop between you and Trevor Grant while the two of you were on the run in the jungle."

Corinthians raised a brow and looked pointedly at her brother. "What are you talking about?"

Joshua shrugged. "I did mention the article that appeared

in the newspapers right before you and Grant were rescued, didn't I?"

"No. What article?"

"Nothing I was concerned about, of course, but a certain reporter who I've rubbed the wrong way one time or another took advantage of your escape into the jungle with Grant to get back at me. He wrote an article that insinuated you and Grant had a thing going on, and that's the reason he went to such extremes to protect you. But I assured anyone who asked that it wasn't true." Joshua shifted in his seat so he could look at her intently. "I was right, wasn't I, Corinthians?"

For the longest time, Corinthians didn't answer as pain sliced through her. The only thing she and Trevor had going on was in her mind...and her heart. "Yes, you were right, Joshua."

Joshua let out a deep sigh of relief, not noticing the mist forming in his sister's eyes. "I'm glad because it would have been a big mistake. The two of you aren't suited. You have everything going for you, and Grant has nothing. He's a laborer and not a professional person. He probably just barely finished high school. That's usually the case when men leave school and go directly into the military, and..."

Total anger consumed Corinthians. How dare Joshua put Trevor down. He sounded like a downright snob. "Shut up, Josh, and listen to me for just one minute, if that pea brain of yours can handle it. Trevor Grant is more of a man than you or your GOP friends will ever be. He's a professional in every sense of the word. He knows the meaning of hard work. I mean *real* work and not the paper-pushing kind you're accustomed to doing. Nor does Trevor spend his time each day skinning and grinning in someone's face trying to earn political points."

Fit to be tied, she got out of bed and walked over to where Joshua sat. She was boiling mad. "And as far as an education, he has a college degree, which he earned while working his butt off in the military in a special military unit. But above that, he has something you don't have—common sense and integrity, and plenty of it. Don't you ever put Trevor down in my presence again."

"What the devil is wrong with you, Corinthians?" Joshua asked, taken aback by the way she had gone off on him. He had never seen his sister this out of control before. "I didn't know the subject of Trevor Grant was such a touchy one with you. All I did was make a few observations."

"No, Josh, what you did was a total put-down of a man you know nothing about. And that's not fair. I won't tolerate you doing that to the man who saved my life." *The man that I love,* she thought further. "Now if you don't mind, I'd like you to leave."

Without wasting any time, Joshua quickly stood and angrily walked out of the room.

Trevor looked up from his meal when Dex and Clayton approached the table. "I was beginning to think the two of you weren't coming."

"Sorry we're late," Clayton said after he and Dex sat down. "Gramma's visiting the folks, and you know her. She's dreamed about fish for the past couple of nights and had to question all of us about it."

Trevor lifted a dark brow as he picked up a bottle of hot sauce and poured it over the huge piece of fried fish on his plate. "She had to question you about *her* dream? Why?"

"Because it was a fish dream," Dex said as a way of an explanation. "You know what it supposedly means when someone dreams about fish, don't you?"

"Nope," Trevor said, taking a huge swallow of Pepsi. "What does it mean?"

Dex shook his head. "According to her, it means someone's pregnant. I know for a fact it's not Caitlin. Clayton claims it's not Syneda and I talked to Justin to confirm it's not Lorren. Daniel and Raymond both swear it's not Tracy or Kattie, and we know it better not be Christy," he said of their baby sister, who would be entering her junior year of college in the fall. "So I guess this time Gramma's dream is a false alarm."

A chill of unease crept up Trevor's spine when it suddenly occurred to him that the one time he and Corinthians had made love, he had not used any protection. He put his fork aside, stopped eating and stared down at the piece of fried fish on his plate. "Has your grandmother ever had dreams like this before?"

"Yeah, lots of time," Clayton said, flipping through the menu the waiter had just handed to him. "And usually she's right on the money." He frowned and turned to Dex. "And that's what worries me. Do you think we ought to have a talk with Christy, just in case?"

Dex's charcoal-gray eyes darkened. "Don't even think it, Clayton. I don't feel like murdering somebody today."

Clayton nodded. "Yeah, you're probably right. Besides, Christy and I had a long talk earlier this year about safe sex."

"You did what!" Dex exploded. "Heaven help us all if *you* talked to her about safe sex. You should have been talking to her about 'no sex,' Clayton, not 'safe sex.' If I ever find out some mother's son has touched her, I will personally take him apart piece by piece."

"Yeah, and I'll be there to rearrange his body parts. All of them," Clayton added.

Trevor had tuned out Clayton's and Dex's conversation. His mind was in total chaos. Surely if Corinthians had gotten pregnant she would have called and told him, wouldn't she? He knew she was still at her parents' home in Louisiana. He had picked up the phone to call her several times, but had changed his mind. He was probably the last person she would have wanted to hear from.

"Tell me some more about your grandmother's dream," he said, interrupting Clayton's and Dex's conversation.

Dex and Clayton stopped talking. Their eyes centered on Trevor curiously. "What is it you want to know?" Dex asked.

"Whatever you can tell me. Is there a certain type of fish that she dreams about? Is it one large fish or a bunch of little ones?"

Clayton shifted his shoulders with uncertainty. "I don't know, man. It could be a piece of fish like the one you're eating, or one that's out there kicking around in the middle of the ocean. I don't really know. All I do know is that if it makes its way into her dream, it usually means someone's pregnant."

Trevor nodded. "Someone in your immediate family?"

"No, it doesn't have to be a family member. It could mean someone she knows is pregnant or someone she knows has gotten someone pregnant."

Dex had been sitting quietly listening to Clayton's explanation and studying Trevor at the same time. The way Trevor was absorbing Clayton's words pushed Dex to ask the question. "So what do you think, Trev? Do *you* know anyone who could be pregnant?"

Without answering, Trevor jumped up from the table. "I need some time off work, Dex."

Dex lifted a brow. "Sure. How much time do you need?"

"A few days."

"Beginning when?"

"Now," Trevor replied throwing more than enough money on the table to pay for his unfinished meal. "I'll see you guys later." He then quickly walked out of the restaurant.

Clayton frowned. "I wonder what that was all about."

Dex couldn't hold back his smile. "I might be wrong, but I think Gramma may be right on the money again."

Stella Grant paused briefly, building her courage, before she took a deep breath and rang the doorbell. When the door was opened, Maurice looked at her with surprise in his eyes. "Stella? What are you doing here? Is everything all right?"

She took another deep breath. There was no need to back out now. "Yes, everything is fine, Maurice, but I do need to talk with you about something. Do you think that you could spare me a few minutes of your time?"

He stepped aside. "Sure, come in."

Stella entered Maurice's home for the very first time. She glanced around. He had a nice place and she told him so.

"Thanks. Can I offer you something to drink? I have a few cans of Coke in the fridge if you're interested."

"Thank you, I'd like one."

"All right. I'll be back in a few minutes. Just make yourself at home."

Stella nodded, wondering how a woman could make herself at home in her husband's house. A house she had never been inside before. However, she decided to do what he had said and make herself at home. She sat down, kicked off her shoes and relaxed against the sofa. When he returned from the kitchen moments later with her drink, she was sitting on the sofa with her feet tucked under her.

Maurice couldn't help but smile. That had always been Stella's most comfortable position whenever she sat on a sofa. "Here we are. It's good and cold just the way I know you like it."

She took the drink he offered. "Thanks. How long have you been living here?"

Maurice shrugged. "Pretty close to fifteen years now. At first I lived in one of those apartments on Helena Street. That was all right for Trevor since he was older, but I wanted more for Gina. I knew she had a nice yard at home with you, but I wanted her to have a nice yard whenever she came to visit me, too."

Stella nodded. She then took a sip of her drink. "I don't think I've ever told you this, Maurice, but I appreciate how much you tried to work with me on making our separation as painless as possible for Trevor and Gina back then. Divorce can be real hard on children. In some cases devastating."

Maurice decided to remain standing. He walked over to the fireplace and leaned against the mantel. "We didn't get a divorce."

Stella turned away from looking at Maurice, her throat tightening. "Yes, I know and that's what I came to talk to you about." Finding strength, she turned and looked at him. She gnawed nervously on her bottom lip before saying, "I came to talk to you about a divorce."

A shaft of pain tore through Maurice with Stella's words. During all the years they had been separated, the issue of a divorce had never come up. When he had married her, he had intended for it to be forever. His mind couldn't help but conjure up memories of him and Stella the first day they had met. He had been a bus driver for the city transit system, and she had worked as a clerk for the library. Back then, taking a bus to work had been her only means of transportation. The highlight of his day had been picking her up from her bus stops every morning and evening.

"Maurice?"

"Yes?"

"I thought that maybe you didn't hear me. I said I came to talk to you about—"

"I know what you said, Stella. I heard you. Now hear me. There will never be a divorce between us."

A hushed silence fell in the room after Maurice's statement. Neither he nor Stella said anything else for the longest moment. Then he noticed the tears gathering in her eyes, and another shaft of pain tore through him. "Does a divorce from me mean that much to you, Stella?"

Stella wiped away her tears. "No, but I can't live like this anymore, Maurice. I can't live day after day knowing how much you hate me and how much you despise me for not trusting you enough and for not believing in you when I should have."

"I have never given you a reason not to trust me, Stella."

"I know, and I made a mistake. It was a costly mistake, and one I'll regret for the rest of my life. All I can offer you is an apology. But you have to let me get on with my life. Both Trevor and Gina have lives of their own now. They aren't children anymore for us to protect. It's time to put an end to what never will be again. You've gone to great lengths to make sure I know that."

"I have not," Maurice answered defensively.

Stella put her glass on the table and stood. Her eyes filled with more tears. "Yes, you have. I don't want to be a choke around your neck any longer, Maurice. You have to let me go."

Maurice pushed back from the mantel and walked over to where Stella stood. A mirage of hurt, pain and mistakes flashed before him. Then just as quickly it was replaced by memories: good memories of their wedding day, memories of the day they had brought a newborn Trevor home from the hospital, then years later, Gina. There were more good memories than there were hurts, pains and mistakes. Over the years they had both suffered. His pride had always kept him from completely forgiving her. His inability to put the past behind him had always kept a reconciliation from ever happening between them.

Now it was time move on or stay put. Maurice knew which he preferred doing. When he came to stand directly in front of her, he said in a deep, clear voice, "I can't give you a divorce, Stella, because I still love you, and I will always love you. I know there's a lot of healing left to do between us, and it will take time and love to get through it. But I'm willing to try if you are. We've wasted too many precious years already, Stel, and I don't want to waste any more living apart from you. If you'll take me back as your husband, I promise that the two of us will live the rest of our lives together happy, spoiling any grandchildren Trevor and Gina will give us one day. I promise to bring sunshine back into your eyes or die trying."

When Stella realized just what Maurice was saying, and

what he was offering, she reached out for him. "Oh, Maurice, I love you, too," she said before he pulled her into his arms.

Maudlin Avery checked the thermometer she had just taken out of Corinthians's mouth. "You don't have a fever, sweetheart. How about explaining those symptoms of yours to me again."

Corinthians nodded. "I sometimes feel dizzy and nauseated first thing in the mornings, and I can't keep any of my breakfast down. I usually start feeling better around lunchtime."

Maudlin eyed her daughter thoughtfully. "And just how long have you had these symptoms?"

Corinthians shrugged. "For the past couple of days or so. What do you think it might be?"

Maudlin doubted Corinthians was ready to hear what she thought was a possibility. Maybe it was time to drop a hint. "I'm not sure, dear. When was your last period?"

Corinthians frowned, wondering why her mother would ask her that. She thought back. When it occurred to her that the last time had been a couple of weeks before her trip to South America, she felt a sense of panic. Her body was extremely regular. She could not remember it ever being late. She and Trevor had not used any protection when they had made love. How on earth could something like that slip her mind!

"Corinthians?"

"Ahh, I need to go out."

Maudlin raised a brow. "Go out where?"

But Corinthians did not answer. She was already rushing out the door.

Chapter 22

Corinthians stared at the pregnancy kit sitting on the counter in her bathroom. She studied it with as much intensity as she would a geological core sample that had been taken from the earth's center.

She had analyzed the kit several times after she'd purchased it yesterday, and had read the directions so many times she had them memorized. According to what it said, the best time to get results was in the mornings. And it was morning. But she couldn't make herself take the next step, although it would take less than a minute and her worries would be over…or just beginning.

During the night, all she could think about was the possibility that she was carrying Trevor's child. She had berated herself a thousand times for engaging in unprotected sex; however, she knew if she were pregnant she wanted his child more than anything.

Corinthians rubbed a hand across her forehead, not

wanting to think about what her parents would say, especially her father. He had always drilled into her and Joshua the moral teachings of the Bible—sexual activity outside of marriage, protected or otherwise, was wrong. On the other hand, he had also taught them that a person was responsible for whatever decisions they chose to make in life. It had been her decision to make love with Trevor, and the outcome of that decision would be her responsibility.

She took a long, deep breath. Her parents had left to visit a sick church member at the hospital right after breakfast. It was a breakfast she couldn't stand to look at, much less eat, without getting a queasy stomach.

She had settled on having a piece of dry toast and a glass of orange juice. However, as soon as her parents had left, she'd rushed to the nearest bathroom when her stomach had refused to cooperate to keep what she had eaten down. Although she was alone in the house, a part of her wanted to wait and take the pregnancy test in the privacy of her own place when she returned to Texas in a few days. That would give her time to sort things through before announcing to her parents that they would be grandparents.

And before letting Trevor know he would be a father.

Corinthians wondered how he would handle the news. She gave herself a mental shake. Why should she concern herself with how he would handle it? Trevor Grant was the least of her worries right now. His failure to call had pretty much told her just what she meant to him. Nothing.

She would eventually tell him about her pregnancy—if she was actually pregnant—but she would let him know from the jump that he was under no obligation to do anything for her or her child. She would handle things without his help.

Her thoughts were interrupted by the ringing of the doorbell. She left the confines of the bathroom and headed toward the door, wondering who would be visiting this early in the morning. It wasn't even nine o'clock. Without thinking twice, she opened the door before checking to see whom her visitor was.

Intense surprise hit her full force and a soft gasp escaped her when she saw Trevor standing in the doorway. She was immediately consumed by a mixture of feelings—joy at seeing him again, puzzlement as to why he had come and anger at herself for still loving him so much.

"Trevor, what are you doing here?" The shock of seeing him caused the words to wedge in her throat.

Trevor gazed down at the woman who was the object of his fire, his desire and his complete love. He felt a tightness in his throat when he thought further that there was a possibility she would one day become the mother of his child. He studied her to see if he could detect any change over the past three weeks and found none. She still possessed the same startling beauty, the same refined yet fiery class that could make her a well-bred lady one minute, and a sensual hellion the next.

Today, standing in the door wearing a floral print sundress, she looked cool and composed, as if the hot, scorching Louisiana heat of summer had no effect on her. He knew at that moment he would love her forever and that if she was carrying his child, it was just an added bonus.

"Trevor, I asked what are you doing here?"

Her words broke into his thoughts. "I need to talk with you about something, Corinthians."

Trevor's voice, deep and smooth, shimmered in the air and sent a ripple of awareness through her. An image suddenly flashed through her mind; the memory of her naked in his arms while he made unadulterated, passionate love to her. Then, just as quickly, another visage came into play. It was the one of her waking up in that hotel room in Key West to discover he had left her without having said goodbye. That, coupled with the fact that he had not contacted her since their return to the States, hurt more than anything.

"I can't imagine anything we have to talk about."

Trevor stared at her a long time before saying. "I can." He pushed himself away from the doorjamb and walked past her into the house.

Corinthians took a sharp intake of breath when their bodies accidentally touched when he passed. When he turned around to face her, she stared at him, angered that he thought he could do whatever pleased him. "I didn't invite you in."

"I promise not to take up much of your time."

Corinthians tried not to focus on what he was wearing, but couldn't help herself. The open V of his shirt exposed a portion of his dark, hairy chest. It was the same chest she could barely keep her eyes off during the times he'd walked around in the jungle shirtless.

She shook her head, trying to clear the thoughts clouding it. She needed to get her mind back on track. Closing the door, she walked into the room to face him. "What do you want?"

Trevor took a deep breath. When he had arrived, he had had every intention of just coming right out and asking her if she was pregnant. But when she had answered the door, he'd almost reached out and taken her into his arms and kissed her, wanting to experience the taste of her again. He wanted the feel of her in his arms.

"Trevor, I asked why—"

Corinthians stopped talking when suddenly the queasiness in her stomach returned. Muttering a barely audible "excuse me," she dashed down the hall to her bedroom.

That was where Trevor found her moments later stretched out across the bed. When she heard the sound of him entering the room, she tried to pull herself together and sit up, but couldn't. She was too weak to move. What she was experiencing this morning was worse than ever. Coupled with her nausea, she felt unusually weak and dizzy.

"Corinthians?"

She forced herself to turn toward the soft sound of Trevor's voice. He was kneeling beside the bed. "Are you all right?" His voice was filled with deep concern.

Although she answered with a slight nod, the truth of the matter was that she was not all right. She no longer needed a pregnancy test to tell her what her body was forcing her to accept.

"Stay put, I'll be right back."

She watched him walk into the connecting bathroom and return moments later with a warm, damp washcloth. He sat on the side of the bed and gently slipped his arms around her. Lifting her into his lap, he began to lightly wipe her face. After he had finished, he tenderly stroked her cheek with his knuckles, gazing down at her intently.

"You know, don't you?" Corinthians managed to get out her words in a shaky whisper. There was no way he could not have seen the pregnancy kit sitting big as day on the counter in her bathroom.

His dark eyes held hers. "Yeah, I know. I had a gut feeling about it. That's why I came," he said quietly.

"But how?" she asked with wonder in her voice.

"It doesn't matter." He gently eased her out of his arms and placed her on her back in the center of the bed. Kicking off his shoes, he lay down beside her and cuddled her in his arms, placing his hand on her unsettled stomach. He began rubbing it soothingly. Through the cotton material of her dress, she felt him trail his fingers across her belly and around her navel, the place where his child nested inside of her.

A lump formed in Corinthians's throat. Although Trevor didn't love her, he had always been there to take care of her when she needed taking care of. And in his own way, he was taking care of her now. She tried to stifle a yawn or two, then gave up. She slowly drifted off to sleep with Trevor holding her in his arms.

Trevor continued to softly massage Corinthians's stomach long after he knew she had gone to sleep. He knew he should get up, leave and come back later so the two of them could talk. But the rough airplane ride into Louisiana, combined with a number of sleepless nights, made his eyes flutter a few times. Then like Corinthians, he, too, drifted off to sleep.

Gina pulled her car up in front of the quaint oceanside inn. It was a beautiful Spanish-style structure that overlooked the Gulf of Mexico. She wondered why her mother had asked that she join her for brunch there. Her mother's voice on the phone had been rushed, almost anxious. And the only thing she had said was to join her for brunch at this place. She had a surprise for her.

Taking a deep sigh, she looked out over the ocean, watching the waves repeatedly hit against the rocks just offshore. The view was breathtaking. She wondered what had made her mother select such a charming and enchanting place to eat. The setting was too beautiful to just eat and leave. It was a place a person would want to stay awhile to enjoy and appreciate the surrounding beauty, savor the moments and cherish the memories. It would be a perfect place for lovers.

After entering the building, she glanced around the restaurant, searching for her mother. She saw her waving at her from across the room, trying to get her attention.

Gina smiled and began walking in that direction. When she got closer, she slowed her pace when she recognized her father sitting next to her mother. A number of questions flooded her mind.

"Mom? Dad? What's going on?" she asked, pulling out a chair and joining them at the table.

Stella Grant smiled brightly. "Your father and I have something to tell you. We wish Trevor could be here, but he left a message on my answering machine saying he had to go away unexpectedly on business."

Gina nodded. She then looked at her parents, waiting. "Well? What is it you and Dad have to tell me?"

Gina watched as her father reached across the table and took her mother's hand in his. She then watched her mother's face light up with a beautiful, peaceful glow, one she had never seen before. And her father, she thought, seemed more relaxed, at ease and also at peace.

She glanced from one to the other. "Mom? Dad? What's going on?"

It was Maurice Grant who finally spoke. "Gina, your mother and I have decided to renew our vows and live the rest of our lives together as man and wife. We love each other very much and don't want to waste any more years apart."

Gina closed her eyes. It had been nearly twenty years since a little girl had gotten on her knees and asked God to bring her parents back together. It had been a request she had continued to pray for over the years. The answer had been a long time coming, but He had come through for her.

"Gina, are you all right?"

Her mother's soft voice was filled with concern. Gina opened her eyes, not ashamed of the tears that filled them. The smile she gave her parents was full, happy and, most of all, thankful. "I'm fine, Mom. It's just that I'm filled with so much happiness for the two of you. I just had to take a moment to thank God for everything. He has truly answered my prayer."

"Corinthians Elizabeth Avery, wake up!"

As the sharp, loud voice of her father suddenly demanded, Corinthians came awake immediately. Her sudden movement also made Trevor open his eyes. He wiped the sleep from his face and found himself staring up into Reverend Avery's deep, dark frown. Next to the man's side was a nice-looking older woman Trevor could only assume was Corinthians's mother.

"Dad! Mom!" Corinthians was saying, scrambling off the bed. "When did you get back?"

"Never mind when we got back. I want to know what's going on here?" her father asked. The tone of his voice did not hide the fact that he was upset.

"It's not what you think, Dad. See, we still have our clothes on."

Reverend Avery's frown deepened. "Is that supposed to assure me of anything, young lady? You better have a good reason why you and Mr. Grant are sharing a bed in my house. I want to see the both of you in my study in less than five minutes."

Without saying anything else, he turned and walked out of the bedroom.

Corinthians wished there were some place where she could go and hide. She turned pleading eyes to her mother who was still standing next to the bed. "Mom, please, talk to him."

Her mother shook her head. "No, sweetheart, this is one you'll have to handle on your own."

Maudlin Avery then turned her full attention to the man who had not made an effort to get up out of her daughter's bed. So this was Trevor Grant, the man who had made her son's knees shake and had put her daughter in a tizzy when she had awakened in Key West to discover him gone. He was also the man—if her guess was right—who had fathered her first grandchild.

"Mr. Trevor Grant, I assume," she said, extending her hand out to him. "I'm glad to meet you."

Trevor relaxed somewhat. The smile on Mrs. Avery's face was friendly. He couldn't help but return the smile. "Yes, ma'am. I'm glad to meet you, too," he said, sitting up and accepting her handshake.

"I'll give you fair warning, Mr. Grant. My husband gave you and Corinthians less than five minutes. If I were you two, I'd make it even less than that." Smiling brightly, Maudlin Avery turned and walked out of the room.

Corinthians closed her eyes, feeling a headache coming on. She knew her father was livid. It didn't matter that she and

Trevor were fully clothed. All that mattered to him was that he had found them in bed together…under his roof.

"Corinthians?"

Corinthians eyes flew open and she gave Trevor a look that could have melted steel. Why did she always manage to find herself in some of the most embarrassing situations with this man?

"You have to go so I can smooth things over with my father. I appreciate your being here when I wasn't feeling well, but I'm fine now. It'll be best if you go."

Trevor looked at Corinthians, totally lacking an understanding of where she was coming from. "Go? And just where do you expect me to go? You heard your father. He wants to see the both of us in his study."

"Let me handle Dad. I'll—"

"I'm not letting you handle anything. There's a lot your father and I have to talk about and it's best we do it now. I want him to know that I plan on upholding my responsibility as your baby's father."

"What! Are you nuts? Dad doesn't even know I might be pregnant. Even with these symptoms I've been having lately, there's a chance something else might be wrong with me. Let's not get carried away and blow things out of proportion. Just leave and let me handle things with my father."

Trevor gave Corinthians a hard look. "I'm not leaving. If you don't tell your father you're pregnant, then I will. I won't let him think I'm not man enough to take responsibility for what I did."

Corinthians sucked in a furious breath. She had heard what he'd said earlier, before they had fallen asleep on her bed. The only reason he had come was because he'd had a gut feeling she was pregnant. He had not come because he loved her and wanted to be with her. The last thing she wanted was Trevor in her life because of any sense of responsibility he felt.

"I don't need for you to take responsibility for anything, Trevor Grant. Even if I am pregnant, I won't need your help.

I will raise my child alone. I'll be fair and allow you visitation rights, but—"

"Don't even go there, Corinthians. I won't be just some visitor in my child's life. I refuse to be a part-time dad. So you may as well get used to the idea that we're getting married."

"Married?"

"Yeah, married. I suggest you go ahead and take that pregnancy test because if you are carrying my child, we will be getting married."

Corinthians gave him a look that told him just what she thought, but for good measure and to make sure there wasn't any misunderstanding, she stated it anyway as she glared up at him. "I am *not* marrying you."

Trevor's eyes narrowed and he glared back at her. "Yes, you are."

Corinthians was completely livid. She tipped her head to look up at him, with hands on both of her hips and her dark brown eyes flashing. "I am not!"

"We'll see, won't we? If you're pregnant, we get married." He walked toward the door.

"Don't hold your breath."

Trevor turned to her and smiled. "I remember having a similar conversation with you about two years ago when you told me not to hold my breath about something else."

Corinthians turned a darker shade of brown when she also remembered that conversation.

"I suggest we not keep your father waiting. And I also suggest that you use that kit in there to find out for certain if you're pregnant. I'd hate to jump the gun and give your parents false information."

Without giving Corinthians a chance to respond, Trevor opened the door and closed it behind him.

Colonel Ashton Sinclair waited for the man to finally show his face. He had known that he was being followed from the time he had left the embassy. He continued to sit in his car in a semidarkened area of the parking garage of his apartment complex, waiting. It shouldn't be long now. He would just wait it out.

Although he didn't see anything, he heard a faint sound of movement. His ears sharpened, his vision keened, he scanned the area, and still he didn't see anything.

Ashton's eyes narrowed. So he wants to play games, does he? he thought, as he reached up and disconnected the light in the ceiling of his car. Then, easing the car door open, he slipped outside.

The hunted was about to become the hunter.

Crouching down, he made his way around his car and several others parked nearby. His Indian instincts, those of a fierce hunter, alerted him his prey was nearby, waiting for Ashton just like Ashton was waiting for him.

The standoff had begun. But Ashton was not in the mood. He had missed lunch and his stomach was growling. Deciding that he no longer wanted to play games, he stood to his full height of six feet three inches and looked around, still not seeing anything. He leaned against the vehicle he was standing next to.

"All right, Sir Drake. Playtime is over. I'm hungry."

A mellow chuckle filled the air just moments before Drake Warren materialized like a beam of light in front of him.

"You're getting rusty, my friend."

Ashton frowned. "Sticks and stones may break my bones, but *your* words will never faze me." He smiled when he heard Drake's laughter. He knew his friend had very little to laugh about these days. Drake Carswell Warren was the best weapons and explosives expert around. He knew it, the military knew it and, most important, the United States government knew it. It was also a known fact that he could be a walking piece of dynamite when he chose to be, highly explosive. A special mission three years ago had changed

Drake's life. With all his knowledge, know-how and expertise, he had not been able to save the woman he loved.

"I got your message, Ash. What's up?"

"Does the name Santini mean anything to you?"

"No. It's a fairly common last name in South America.
Why?"

Ashton gave Drake the details of what had gone down
with Trevor.

"Is Trev okay?" Drake asked. There would always be
feelings of brotherhood among the men who served in the
Force Recon.

"Yeah, other than a woman problem, he's fine."

Drake nodded. "I'll find out what I can. I'll do a few
profile searches to see if I can get any type of link to Armond
Thetas. But I doubt that I will. While hanging around Thetas
I got to know the people in his inner circle pretty well, and
the name Santini doesn't ring a bell. But I'll check it out."
He turned to walk away.

"Drake, wait! When will we make contact again?"

Drake gave his friend a cool smile. "When I think you're
ready to play another game. *Adios, amigo.*"

He then disappeared as quickly as he had materialized.

The smile vanished from Trevor's lips the moment he
stepped in the study and gazed into Reverend Nathan Avery's
face. It was evident the man saw no amusement in having discovered him in bed with his daughter. He gave Trevor a look
that clearly said he had a lot of explaining to do.

"Come in, Mr. Grant and take a seat. Where's Corinthians?"

"I think she wanted to use the bathroom first, sir," he said,
taking one of the chairs that sat across from the huge desk in
the room. He suddenly felt very uncomfortable.

He was glad when Corinthians walked into the room.
Without looking at him or her father, she took the chair next

to Trevor. She then looked up at her father, waiting. Evidently she had been party to one of these "study talks" before.

The Reverend Nathan Avery took his place behind the huge desk and settled into what he considered a comfortable position. He then gazed thoughtfully at the young man and woman sitting across from him. He decided not to make things easy on them. From the little bit he could gather, they had some heavy-duty problems between them, problems they definitely needed to work out. He would do whatever he could to help set them on the right course.

"Now then," he began in his most imposing oratorical voice. "Do you mind telling me what the two of you were doing in bed together…in my house?"

Before Corinthians could open her mouth, Trevor began speaking. "Yes, sir, I'll be glad to explain things. Corinthians was not feeling well and when she went into her bedroom to lie down, I followed her to comfort her by lying down beside her. I guess we both fell asleep."

Reverend Avery gave Trevor a look that said his story sounded too pat. "That's the truth, sir."

"That's right, Dad," Corinthians added quickly in an attempt to validate Trevor's story.

The Reverend leaned back in his chair and crossed his arms over his chest. The look on his face indicated he still wasn't buying it. He turned his full attention to his daughter. "What does he mean you weren't feeling well? You seemed fine when I left this morning. Did you suddenly become ill? If you did, you certainly look fine now. Just what kind of sickness was this that lasted a few hours and caused Mr. Grant so much concern that he had to lie down with you in bed?"

Now they were down to the meat of the meal, Trevor though, slanting a glance in Corinthians's direction. He wondered how she would answer her father's question. He saw her hands tighten into fists in her lap. She quickly darted a nervous look at him. He knew from the gesture that she had taken the pregnancy test before coming into the room. And the uneasy look in her eyes and the way she nervously nibbled on her bottom lip immediately told him the results. She was having his baby.

"Corinthians, I asked you a question."

Corinthians clasped her hands together and took a long, deep breath before answering. She met her father's gaze. "Morning sickness. I'm pregnant, Daddy."

Chapter 23

Reverend Avery leaned across the desk toward his daughter, certain he had misunderstood what she'd said. "Did you just say you're pregnant?"

Corinthians drew in another deep breath and dropped her gaze to her lap. During her thirty years, she had never done anything to hurt or disappoint her parents. A depression settled over her in realizing that now she had. She was pregnant with the child of a man who didn't love her.

"Corinthians, I asked you a question."

Trevor glanced from Corinthians to her father. A part of him wanted to draw her into his arms and spare her this, to protect her. It was his fault she was in this predicament. The least he could do was verbally acknowledge that to Reverend Avery.

"She's pregnant with my child and I take full responsibility for it. I forced her into a situation she didn't want to be in."

Corinthians twisted around to look at Trevor, too numb to

speak. Why was he trying to take full blame for her condition? The one thing he had not done was force her. Drawing herself up straight in her chair, she stared at him coldly. "You did not force me to do anything, and I don't need you to take responsibility for my actions in this," she snapped.

"That's tough because I *will* take responsibility."

"No, you won't."

"Watch me."

"I'll watch you try," Corinthians said, tossing her head haughtily.

Reverend Avery frowned, barely holding himself in check as he sat listening to Corinthians and Trevor snap back and forth at each other. He wondered how they had stopped bickering long enough to conceive a child. He had never seen his daughter behave in such an uncivil manner with anyone. Not even in her confrontations with Joshua. She'd always remained an even-tempered, genteel person.

He rose slowly to his feet. "If the two of you don't mind, I have a question I'd like answered."

Corinthians's and Trevor's gazes swung to Reverend Avery regarding him in a way that indicated they had momentarily forgotten he was in the room.

"What is your question, sir?" Trevor asked.

"When will the wedding take place?"

Corinthians could not believe her father would ask such a thing. Her expression said as much. "There isn't going to be a wedding," she answered gruffly, glaring at Trevor.

Reverend Avery looked at his daughter. "Then forgive me, I must have misunderstood. I could have sworn you just told me you and Mr. Grant had made a baby together."

Corinthians felt the color in her cheeks deepen. "No, you didn't misunderstand. I am pregnant, but Trevor and I will not be getting married."

"And why not?"

Corinthians knew exactly why not, especially in her situation. Trevor did not love her, and her pride would not let her admit that to her father in front of him. "A baby is not a good enough reason for two people to marry."

Reverend Avery's frown deepened. "It's not?"

"No, it's not."

He looked pointedly at his daughter. "If that's not a good enough reason, I'd like to know what is." He then turned his full attention to Trevor. "And just how do you feel about this?"

Trevor met Reverend Avery's gaze directly. "I asked Corinthians to marry me and she turned me down," he said, his own anger and frustration escalating. If Corinthians thought for one minute he would let his child be born out of wedlock, she had another thought coming. In the past, he'd always been careful whenever he made love for that very reason. There were too many single mothers raising kids alone because the men responsible did not feel duty-bound beyond obtaining their pleasure in the bedroom. His parents had raised him to be accountable for his actions, and he fully intended to do just that. No matter what their feelings were for each other, he and Corinthians needed to put them aside and think about what would be best for their child. No kid of his would ever doubt that he wanted him.

"Why did you turn down Mr. Grant's proposal? And don't you dare tell me a baby is not a good enough reason. Think of the child you're carrying."

Corinthians sighed wearily. Entering into a marriage without love would only be a mistake. One day Trevor would resent the situation he'd been placed in. When that happened, both she and her child would be the ones to suffer.

She cleared her throat, hoping the reason she was about to give her father was sufficient and he would leave it at that. "My child will be taken care of, Daddy. I don't need a husband for that. If Trevor wants to contribute to the baby's welfare, that's fine. I have nothing against that."

Seeing the frown on her father's face deepen, Corinthians tried to make him understand her position. "Times have changed, Daddy. People don't get married because of a baby anymore. There has to be more to hold a relationship together than a baby," she said quietly.

Reverend Avery came to stand in front of his daughter's chair. "Then you should have thought of that before you gave yourself to this man. You should have considered all the consequences. If he was good enough for you to sleep with, and take the risk of him fathering a child by you, then there should be no question in your mind about him being husband material. By your own words you've admitted that he did not force you to do anything you didn't want to."

"Dad, you don't understand."

"You're right. I don't understand. All I know is that the both of you owe it to your child to give it the best future possible while living with both parents."

Corinthians shook her head. "You want us to enter into a loveless marriage? Just for the sake of our child? What kind of life would he or she have under those conditions?"

Reverend Avery frowned thoughtfully. According to his wife, Corinthians had all but admitted to being in love with Trevor Grant. And no one could convince him that Mr. Grant was not in love with his daughter. That night when the plane had arrived from South America, and Trevor had carried Corinthians off the plane in his arms, then handed her over to him, the expression on his face was like he was giving up something he loved and cherished. How could two people who were undoubtedly in love with each other not know how the other felt? There was definitely a big communication problem between them; one he decided to end rather quickly.

"A loveless marriage? Does that mean the two of you care nothing for each other?" he asked them.

At that moment, Corinthians's heart felt heavier than it had been in the past three weeks. She could not, she would not, say the words that she cared nothing for Trevor when she loved him deeply. "I care for Trevor, Daddy," she said quietly.

Oh, now we're getting somewhere, Reverend Avery thought before shifting his gaze to Trevor who was sitting next to his daughter tight-lipped.

"And what about you, Mr. Grant? Do you not care anything for my daughter?"

Corinthians lowered her head and closed her eyes, having anticipated what Trevor's answer would be. She balled her hands into fists at her side, preparing for the pain she knew would come with his words.

"I love your daughter, Reverend Avery. I love her very much."

Corinthians opened her eyes and turned and looked straight into a pair of unblinking dark ones. Trevor had said the words with so much sincerity, longing and truth. She didn't want to believe them. She couldn't believe them. "You don't love me. You can't."

The look in his eyes was starkly intense. "I do and I can."

Corinthians's mind began whirling. "But you never told me," she whispered softly.

He had told her twice, Trevor started to say. The first time in Portuguese when they'd made love, and the second time while she'd slept in his arms on the plane. But instead of telling her that, he said, "What good would it have done? You're in love with someone else."

"I'm not in love with anyone but you, Trevor. I love you, no one else."

Trevor's eyes widened. He gave her a sidelong glance of utter disbelief. "You don't love me. You can't."

"I do and I can," she said, throwing his words back at him. "But what about Dex?"

Corinthians sighed. She knew she had to clear up the issue of Dex once and for all. Her insides were still glowing with Trevor's admission that he loved her. "I haven't thought of Dex in that way since the night I met you. I feel nothing for

Dex but friendship. I realize now that what I felt for him was nothing more than an oversize crush. I fell in love with you the night I slipped into your hotel room looking for Dex."

"What hotel room?"

Her father's question reminded them they were not alone, something she planned to remedy right away. "Dad, can Trevor and I have some time alone, please?"

Reverend Avery shrugged. "I guess so. There really isn't any more trouble the two of you can get into together, is there? However, our talk is far from over." He walked over to the door, opened it and walked out, closing it behind him.

As soon as the door closed shut behind her father, Corinthians swept out of her chair to stand in front of Trevor. "That night I thought I loved Dex, but since then I've only been thinking of you, Trevor. I had convinced myself that I disliked you because of the way you were making me feel whenever I saw you. I didn't understand the reason for it. When we were in South America together, I came to terms with what I was feeling."

Trevor slowly stood to face her. "I hurt you when we made love. I took something from you that you had intended to give the man you loved."

Corinthians smiled. "And that man was you. Even before we made love, I knew I loved you. So you didn't take anything from me. I gave myself to you. I gave myself to the man I love, Trevor. The physical lovemaking I shared with you did not hurt me. It was special."

She looked up at him and their gazes locked. She wanted him to see the truth in her eyes. She wanted to finally remove any doubt he had of whom she truly loved.

He reached out and placed his hand on her stomach. For a time they stood in emotion-filled silence. Finally, Trevor spoke. "The baby is not the only reason I want to marry you, Corinthians. I want to marry you because I love you. The baby is an added bonus. I knew that before coming here today. Believe that."

Tears welled in her eyes. "I do now. You don't know how much it means to me to hear you say that."

Trevor reached out for her, pulled her into his arms and kissed her. He slid his hand up to cradle the back of her head to hold her in place so their mouths could mate with all the fire and desire that was theirs. His tongue tasted the sweetness he had missed, stroking, savoring and delivering the passion that always came to life with them.

It was a kiss that shook them both of them to the core. It was a kiss that wiped away any lingering doubts.

When breathing became a necessity, their mouths separated to draw in air.

"My life's been so empty these past three weeks," Trevor said softly, brushing light kisses over her cheeks. "The hardest thing I ever had to do was to turn you over to your father in Key West. Afterward, I felt I'd given away my heart. But never again. I'll never give you up again."

Corinthians parted her lips to say something, but Trevor's tongue shot into her mouth with uncontrolled passion. He pulled her closer into his arms. At that moment, he didn't care that her parents were just beyond the study's door. The only thing he could think of was that the woman he loved had admitted to loving him in return.

"Will you marry me, for all the right reasons?" he whispered against her lips. "I know there's a lot we have to work out with our individual jobs and the issue of where we'll live, but I want you in my life, Corinthians, for always. Will you become my wife?"

At first, Corinthians's throat was too tight for her to respond. She expelled a pent-up breath. "Yes."

The muscles in Trevor's chest constricted. His heart swelled. "I promise to make you happy."

Corinthians smiled brightly as tears misted her eyes. "You already have. I love you, Trevor. I love you so much. These past three weeks have been hard on me thinking you didn't want me."

Trevor nodded, knowing they had both suffered needlessly over the past three weeks. There had been so much dislike, misunderstanding, miscommunication and mistrust between them from the very beginning. Now that their true feelings were out in the open, they needed time alone. "Come to Houston with me. I want you to meet my family."

He wanted Corinthians to come to Houston for more than meeting his family. He wanted the complete privacy of spending time with her and making love to her the way he should have in the beginning. "Will you come?"

Corinthians saw the darkened look in Trevor's eyes. "When?"

"Today."

She nodded. "Yes, but Dad will want to finish his talk with us. He'll want to be certain we've gotten things straightened out. We can leave after lunch. Is that okay?"

Trevor pulled her into his arms and gave her his answer in a kiss.

Chapter 24

It was close to midnight when Trevor and Corinthians entered his apartment in Houston. The Reverend Nathan Avery would not be rushed in what ended up being more like a sermon instead of a talk. They had recessed for lunch only to be herded back into his study for yet another sermon, which had lasted until dinnertime.

Trevor was glad he'd been able to reach Gina during one of the infrequent bathroom breaks he'd been allowed during Reverend Avery's lectures. He had given her explicit instructions on what he wanted done. She had promised to have everything ready when he arrived home.

When he walked into his apartment with Corinthians, he knew his sister had come through when he saw the numerous scented candles that were lit around the room and heard the soft music playing on his stereo system.

He watched as surprise, then pleasure lit up Corinthians's face as she glanced around. "Oh, Trevor, how did you manage this?"

Rubbing the back of her neck tenderly, he brought her closer to him. Other than the short time they had spent straightening things out between them in her father's study, this was the only time they had been completely alone. Reverend Avery had made absolutely sure of that. If he didn't know better, Trevor thought, he'd suspect Corinthians's father had gained immense pleasure in keeping them separated until he'd been absolutely sure they had worked out their differences and that there would be a wedding in the very near future. Plans had been made for him and Corinthians to get married in four weeks.

"I called my sister, Gina, and asked her to take care of it for me. I told her exactly how I wanted things."

He leaned down and closed his mouth over hers. The kiss that began gentle and tender became hungry and heated. Three weeks of wanting and longing had intensified their desire, yearning and need to have their passions fulfilled.

On a long breath Trevor pulled back, but didn't release her from his arms. This was *his* woman, and soon she would become his wife and the mother of his child. No other woman would he ever love more. No other woman had taken him through the changes he'd gone through for her. Two years of wanting and craving. Two years of trying to convince himself that he didn't even like her. But now, as he stood with her in his arms, he knew it had been worth it.

Corinthians looked up at Trevor and stared directly into his dark eyes. She wondered just how many dreams she'd had of him over the past two years. How many mornings had she awakened with his features so clearly etched in her mind?

She reached up and placed her hands flat on his chest. "Oh, Trevor. When I woke up this morning, I had no idea the day would end up like this and I'd see you again. Last night all I could think about was the possibility that I was pregnant and you didn't want me."

She wrapped her arms around his neck as a shiver of happiness coursed through her. "Tell me I'm not dreaming. Touch me and prove you're real and that I'm here with you."

Giving her what she wanted was easy, Trevor thought as he kissed her. Before dawn broke, there would be no doubt in either of their minds that this was not a dream, but was reality.

When he felt her tremble in his arms, he leaned back. "You're not dreaming, sweetheart."

He leaned down and outlined her lips with the tip of his tongue. When she released a silky moan, he whispered against the tender skin underneath her ear. "Do you like that?"

When she nodded, he smiled. He then kissed her again, deeply, passionately. His hands slid over the slope of her bottom, nestling her to the cradle of his hips, letting her feel the hard strength of his desire for her.

"Feel that?" he asked in a deep, sexy Texas drawl, as he placed butterfly kisses near the corner of her mouth.

"Oh…yes," she said, trying to catch her breath. Desire swept through her entire body.

"Good, because in a little while, the feel of that will become as much a part of you as it is a part of me."

His words sparked Corinthians's fire. They heightened her desire. When the tip of his tongue teased the corner of her mouth, she turned toward it instinctively. Her skin shivered with delight when his lips parted over hers.

"Corinthians." Trevor exhaled a soft groan when she took the initiative and mated her tongue with his. Desire surged through him when he felt how her tongue was swirling around his, holding, sucking.

"I want you, baby." He slipped his hand beneath her legs and swept her into his arms, and headed for his bedroom.

He stood Corinthians on her feet beside his bed and glanced around. His sister had really outdone herself. She had done everything he'd asked her to do and more. Everything in the room, every corner, every nook and every crevice oozed romance. From the candles providing soft lighting in the room, the soft music playing, the bottle of wine chilling in the ice bucket, the red roses and baby's breaths arranged in a number of vases around the room—some even tossed on the bed for good measure—to the linen netting draped across the huge posters of his king-size bed. The mood was set for lovers.

"Oh, Trevor, this room is beautiful. Your sister outdid herself."

Trevor couldn't help but agree. He gazed down at Corinthians. Before leaving her parents' home, she had changed out of her sundress and into a long, flowing skirt and ribbed-knit blouse. His eyes moved over her face then lowered, zeroing in on her breasts that were outlined under her blouse. He remembered how they looked when he'd made love to her in South America, taut and swollen in his hands.

"Why did you have your sister do all of this? You didn't have to, you know," she said softly.

"I wanted tonight to be special. After I'd made love to you in the cave, on the floor, I knew you deserved better. Your first time should have been like this with candles, flowers and soft music. You deserved more than what I was able to give you. I want to make it up to you."

"I enjoyed how we made love the first time, all wild and hot," she confessed.

"But your first time should have been different. You'd never been touched before. I should have handled you with more tenderness and care," he said, brushing a kiss across her lips. "Dance with me."

Trevor's request surprised her. He left her momentarily to change the music on the stereo. "There are three songs I've chosen for tonight. They will tell their own story of my love. And then, when all three have ended, I will make love to you until the early-morning dawn. I will make love to you until our baby knows my presence and my place inside of you. I will make love to you until our bodies become so connected, that even when we're apart, we'll still be one," he whispered huskily.

Trevor's words touched her like an erotic mist, covering each and every part of her body. He pulled her into his arms when the first of the songs he had selected, "When a Man Loves a Woman" by Percy Sledge, softly filtered through the room.

Corinthians thought it felt good being held by him, so close and intimate, as they moved around the room, barely swaying to the music. She felt every hard inch of his body touch hers. Resting his cheek against the top of her head, he lightly hummed along with the song as he held her.

When the song stopped playing, he looked at her. She returned his warm gaze, feeling light-headed from his love. Then the rich, soulful sound of Jerry Butler came to life when "For Your Precious Love" vibrated softly through the room. Trevor pulled her closer into his arms. She gasped softly when she felt his fingertips glide across her bottom before cupping her in his hands, bringing her closer into the hard fit of him.

He crooned the words of the song in her ear before taking her mouth in his, kissing her with a passion that was all-consuming, all-devouring.

Corinthians's breath caught. Trevor was romancing her in his own special way. It was a way that had the ability to touch everything feminine about her. It went straight to the very heart of what being romanced was all about. It cut to the chase and delivered love at its finest. The songs he had chosen were all classics with meaning. They conveyed each and every thing a woman held dear—the knowledge that her man loved her, and the knowledge that her love was precious to him.

"Now for the finale," he whispered against her lips. She smiled when the song "Fire and Desire" by Rick James and Tina Marie softly began playing. He picked her up and carried her over to the bed. Moving the soft netting aside and brushing the flowers out of the way, he laid her down on the satin sheets, then sat on the edge of the bed, gazing down at her, while the soft, sensuous music floated around them.

Corinthians drew shallow breaths as Trevor continued to look at her. His dark gaze gently glided over every detail of her. Then she watched when he stood and slowly began removing his shirt.

Her breathing quickened when he tossed his shirt aside. She couldn't help but savor the maleness of him, the solidness of his hairy chest and hard muscles. Her lips parted slightly when he began to slowly unzip his pants and remove them. Emotional tears nearly filled her eyes when she thought of just how much she loved him. And when she gazed upon that strong, masculine part of him that had placed their child inside of her, she became hot all over, burning.

"Fire," she whispered when he walked naked back to the bed and her. "You're my fire, Trevor."

"And you're my desire," he whispered huskily. He reached out and began removing her blouse. Tossing it and her bra aside, his palms closed over her breasts. He gently massaged them, noting the difference in them from the last time, and knew the changes were the result of her pregnancy. They were fuller and rounder, he thought, fitting their shape in his hands.

He wrapped his arms around her and began to remove her skirt. His fingers gently stroked her smooth, bare legs. Caressing each one, his fingers kneaded every muscle.

The music had ended. They both knew that now, the passion was about to begin when he had removed all her clothing. "I want you so much," he rasped as he joined her in bed, moving his body over hers. His hands came up to join with hers, lacing their fingers together, binding them. He leaned down and kissed her in a passion that was all hers.

"I love everything about you, Corinthians. And for the rest of my life, I will cherish you and the love we share. And when our children are born, I'll let them know just how much their mother means to me," he said. He then repeated the words to her in Portuguese just as he had done the first time they'd made love.

"Those words, what do they mean? You said them to me before, when we made love the last time," Corinthians said. Her voice was no more than a mere whisper.

"I'm saying I love you in Portuguese, and yes, I said them before. I also told you I loved you in English while you slept in my arms on the plane."

She reached out and cupped his face in her hands. "So, I really hadn't dreamed it after all. Oh, Trevor, I love you so much."

He kissed her again. The kiss made a hot shiver of need consume them. Trevor eased into her slowly, savoring her heat, feeling it, wanting it and needing it. His desire for her overwhelmed him and when she lifted her hips to receive him, he gave up and gave in to the passion consuming him.

Trevor's body made love to his woman as they both soared to the stars and beyond. They made their own music, set their own beat and established their very own rhythm. Their moans became the lyrics that made the melody complete. When they reached the ultimate pitch, their bodies exploded in spasms of passionate waves of pleasure that touched each and every nerve of their bodies. Powerful shudders tore through them as candlelight flickered softly over them. They exploded into the realms of rapture, earth-shattering fulfillment where only love was truly the driving force behind their fire and desire.

Minutes, maybe five, possibly ten, passed before Trevor could summon enough strength to move. Corinthians tightened her legs around him, holding him inside her. She didn't want this moment with him to end just yet.

"I'm too heavy for you, sweetheart," he whispered close to her ear.

Relaxed and depleted, she smiled at him, basking in the

feverish afterglow of their lovemaking. "No, you're not. I'm not ready for you to leave me. I like the feel of you inside me."

"I'm glad to hear that," Trevor said upon feeling his need for her renew itself. "You feel it?"

Corinthians felt his deep, throbbing hardness take shape again within her. A slow grin started at the corners of her mouth. "Yeah, I feel it…and I like it." Arching her body upward, she could feel his need, wanting him to feel hers, as desire reawakened within her.

"Trevor." An urgency consumed her and her mouth sought his. Once again they became caught up in total possession of each other, eager to share in the essence of their love.

Chapter 25

Traffic on Houston's interstate was heavy for noontime, Trevor thought as he maneuvered his Pathfinder from lane to lane. He glanced over at Corinthians as she lifted the can of ginger ale to her mouth. She had awakened feeling nauseated and had been eating saltines and sipping the cool drink ever since.

"Are you sure you're up to visiting my mother, sweetheart?"

Corinthians took another swallow of her drink before answering him. "Yeah, I'm fine now. The sickness usually passes by lunchtime."

He nodded. All this was new to him although Dex swore to this day that he'd been the one who suffered with morning sickness instead of Caitlin while she'd been carrying Ashley. "How long will it last?"

Corinthians smiled at him. "Mom said to expect it to last for at least three months. I guess I'll be getting used to it shortly."

When the vehicle came to a stop at a traffic light, Trevor glanced at his watch and saw it was a little past noon. He couldn't help but wonder where everyone was. He had tried calling Gina and had gotten her answering machine instead. No one answered at his father's house and he couldn't reach his mother, either. He had called the bookstore only to be told his mother wasn't expected in today. Trevor had never known his mother to miss a day in her store.

"I hope your mom likes me."

Corinthians's statement invaded Trevor's thoughts. He smiled over at her. "She'll love you as much as I do. Trust me," he said as he pulled his vehicle into the driveway, bringing it to a stop next to his mother's car. He was glad he had found her home.

He leaned over and kissed Corinthians before getting out of the vehicle. He walked around to open the door for her, and helped her out. Taking her hand in his, they strolled up the brick walkway toward the door.

Corinthians raised a brow when Trevor dug into his pocket and pulled out a door key. "Aren't you going to knock or ring the doorbell first before we go inside?" she asked as he began inserting the key inside the lock.

He looked at her and smiled. "No, why would I?"

Corinthians shrugged. "On the off chance she has company or she isn't dressed for visitors."

Trevor grinned. "Mom's always ready for visitors and she seldom has company. If you're worried that she might be entertaining a male friend, you have nothing to worry about. My mom hasn't dated at all during the years she and my dad have been separated."

He opened the door and went inside. She followed him.

As soon as they entered the foyer, they heard conversation, the voices of a male and female. Trevor frowned. "Sounds like she has company after all. It's probably just a salesman."

When they walked into the living room, they didn't see anyone. It was apparent the voices were coming from the back of the house, where the bedrooms were. And from the sound of the conversation it was a friendly one with occasional laughter.

Corinthians watched as Trevor's mouth tightened. She stopped him before he headed to where the voices were coming from. "It might be better if you stayed right here, Trevor," she said, feeling the tension and anger radiating in him. "I think it will be a good idea to let your mother know we're here. Then we'll sit and wait for her to come out." She leaned up and kissed his lips to calm him. "All right?"

He reluctantly nodded. Turning, he walked backed to the door, opened it then slammed it shut as hard as he could, rocking it on its hinges. "Mom!" he called out at the top of his voice.

Corinthians couldn't help but grin. Trevor definitely wanted to make his presence known. Whoever the man was in the back with his mother was in serious trouble. He would have to face the wrath of her overprotective son.

A few minutes later, an attractive older woman who she assumed was Trevor's mother came out of the back wearing a bathrobe. The first thing Corinthians noticed was that it was evident she and Trevor had interrupted something. Having been made love to practically all night herself, Corinthians immediately recognized that "thoroughly made love to" look the woman wore. Chances were Trevor recognized it, too.

The second thing Corinthians noticed was the huge, radiant smile on the woman's face. She didn't have the look of a person who should be embarrassed at the possibility that her son had walked in on her liaison with a man.

"Trevor, I didn't know you were back." She walked over to them smiling brightly. She ignored the scowl on her son's face and said, "You brought a friend with you. Aren't you going to introduce us?"

Trevor's frown deepened. "Just as soon as you introduce *your* friend. Who is he, Mom?"

Stella Grant smiled innocently up at her son. "Who's who?"

"I heard voices coming from the back. One of them belonged to a man."

Stella shrugged. "Yes, that's right. I have company." She then turned to Corinthians and extended her hand. "Since my son won't introduce us, I guess we'll just have to introduce ourselves. I'm Stella Grant."

Corinthians took the hand offered to her. "And I'm Corinthians Avery."

She raised a dark brow upon recognizing Corinthians's name. "You're the young lady who was with Trevor in South America. I'm so glad you—"

"I want to see him, Mom." Trevor said, cutting into his mother's sentence. There was a sharp edge in his voice.

"See who, Trevor?"

"The man you're entertaining in your bedroom. Either he comes out here or I'm going in there."

Mother and son stared at each other and Corinthians couldn't help but wonder who would be the one to give in. It was obvious Trevor was having a problem dealing with the fact that his mother was entertaining a man in her bedroom.

"I think you've forgotten, young man, that I am your mother, and not your sister. I'm a grown woman, Trevor Maurice Grant. I don't need your permission to have company in my home," Stella Grant said sweetly, but forcefully.

"What's going on out here? Is there a problem?"

Corinthians looked up when a very good-looking older man walked into the room from the back. Like Trevor's mother, he was wearing a bathrobe—a matching one at that. She watched as shock, then disbelief covered Trevor's face when his head snapped around at the sound of the deep, masculine voice. His steady gaze was on the man who was boldly walking toward them.

Corinthians braced herself for what might come next when the man came to a stop in front of them. "I asked if there was a problem."

Trevor shook his head as if to clear it. He then looked at the man again. "Dad, what are you doing here?"

* * *

Trevor pulled Corinthians into his arms. Their bodies were still damp with perspiration from their recent lovemaking. "I can't believe my parents are getting back together after all these years," he said, his voice filled with wonder.

Corinthians turned in his arms and smiled. "I happen to think it's wonderful. They looked so happy together."

Trevor grinned. "Yeah, they did, didn't they. I think we made them even happier when we announced our wedding plans and then the news that they would be grandparents." He chuckled. "I could wring Gina's neck for not telling me about the folks. I don't care that she wanted to surprise me. I could have hurt somebody today if any man, other than Dad, walked out of that bedroom."

Corinthians laughed. "I'm sure you could have. The look on your face was priceless."

"So you think it's funny, huh?" he asked, hooking an arm around her waist and placing her atop him.

"Yes," she said, leaning down and nibbling kisses over his face. "I think it's funny."

Trevor reached out and moved a strand of hair from her face. "I hate you're leaving tomorrow. I have a good mind not to let you go. I'm going to miss you."

Corinthians placed a kiss on his lips. "I'm going to miss you, too. But I have to return to work sometime. Besides, I need to know how I'm going to handle living in Houston but work in Austin after we're married. I need to talk to Adam Flynn about the possibility of me working out of our field office here."

She drew a long, deep breath as she fought back a yawn. Today had been a full day. Besides meeting Trevor's parents, she had gotten to meet his sister, Gina, when she'd shown up at her mother's house later. The two of them had hit it off immediately.

Later, Trevor had taken her to Dex's and Caitlin's house for a visit. Clayton and Syneda had dropped by. It had been good seeing the newlyweds again. Justin had called while they were there, reminding everyone that Lorren's belated birthday party was in two weeks.

Corinthians didn't know who was more surprised with the news of her and Trevor's pending marriage, Dex or Clayton. However, it seemed that Caitlin and Syneda hadn't been the least surprised. On the other hand, Dex and Clayton had not been surprised with the announcement that she was pregnant.

"Are you still coming to Austin this weekend?" she asked Trevor as she cuddled into his chest.

"Even sooner if I can get away," he said, kissing her forehead.

"Good. I'm going to look forward to your visit."

"Are you?" he asked, encircling her with his arms.

She grinned down at him. "You bet. Me and your baby both are."

Corinthians lowered her head and kissed the man she loved.

Chapter 26

The workday should have ended for Corinthians around four o'clock that evening. But time was pushing toward eight and she was still at it. She stared at her desk. There were still a number of reports to go over, some large and complex, others small and simple. Regardless, all of them needed her attention. Having been out of the office for four weeks had set her back big-time.

In the distance, she could hear the fax machine humming as it spit out some document or another. Tossing the papers she was working on aside, she stood, wondering who besides her hadn't had the good sense to leave at closing time. She knew it wasn't Darcy, the personal secretary to Adam Flynn, her boss. The older woman had left the building hours ago.

Corinthians was about to walk out of her office when the ringing telephone stopped her. She noticed it was her private line. Suddenly, all the tension of that day seeped out of her as a breathless sigh escaped her lips. Almost immediately, she felt her breasts tighten, her mouth starting to get warm and her fingertips tingling. Her mind, as well as her body, knew who the caller was.

At that moment, every sensuous detail of the two days she had spent with Trevor in Houston came floating back. She had enjoyed every minute of their time together. It had been so hard getting on the plane to fly home to Austin. She'd been back for three days and already she was missing him something fierce.

In all her life, she had never been so acutely aware of how important and meaningful memories were. In just two days, she and Trevor had made love enough to last a lifetime. He had made love to her with an intensity that had been all-consuming. His kisses, his touch and his lovemaking had nearly driven her insane, and had made her wild with desire. The both of them had been desperate, hungry, hot. He had felt her need and her urgency to be a part of him in the most intimate way, and had obliged her.

She picked up the phone. "This is Corinthians."

"And this, sweetheart, is the man who loves you," the masculine voice said in a deep, Texas drawl. The sound of it was husky, sexy and seductive.

Corinthians sat down and let her body relax in the cushion of the leather chair. It had been a gift from the president of the company, one of many, after she had helped Remington Oil make history with that oil find a year and half ago.

"And I don't think anyone can love me better," she whispered into the phone as she kicked her shoes off and leaned back in the chair. The sound of Trevor's voice always had a stimulating effect on her. Normally, he would call her at night, timing it just right so she would have gotten home, eaten and showered. His pillow talks had been just that. She looked forward to them each night before going to sleep.

"I'm glad you think so," he said in a husky whisper. The sound sent a shiver across her heated skin. "I just called to ask you to do me a favor."

Corinthians smiled. "Anything, I'm easy."

She heard his soft chuckle. "And I'm hard."

The corners of her mouth twitched. "Well, if you were here with me I'd be able to do something about that."

"That's what I'm counting on. I'm on my way."

His words surprised Corinthians. She wondered if she had missed part of the conversation along the way. "You're on your way where?"

"To see you. I managed to work things out here so I wouldn't have to wait until the weekend."

Corinthians sat up straight in her chair. Her body became heated, sensitive, ready. "You're coming here? To Austin?"

"Yes, I'm on my way to the airport now."

She slipped back into her shoes and quickly began shoving the papers on her desk aside. She stood up and put on her jacket. If Trevor was on his way, she wanted things perfect when he got there. She had so much to do.

"Corinthians?"

"Yes?"

"I don't want you to knock yourself out doing anything. The only thing I want when I get there is you."

She felt a warm glow flow through her. "I want you, too, Trevor."

"That's what I'm counting on, which leads me back to that favor I asked you about earlier."

"Which is?"

"Show me," he demanded throatily, in a low, deep, seductive voice. "Tonight, when I get there, I want you to show me just how much you want me."

Her smile creased into an arresting grin. "Like I said earlier, that's easy."

"And like I said earlier, I'm hard. I'll see you in a little while, baby."

Before Corinthians could say anything else, the connection between them had ended.

* * *

Drake Warren tapped his pen lightly against his knee. It was a nervous habit of his, one he had thought about working on and then had decided why bother. Besides, his superiors at the CIA would think working off nervous energy that way was far less dangerous than other ways he could come up with.

He sighed as he looked at the computer screen in front of him. He'd been sitting in the same spot for the past four hours. And he had consumed at least four pots of coffee. He smiled. A pot an hour wasn't so bad. At least he was improving his intake. Who knows? His kidneys might thank him one day if the caffeine didn't do him in first.

He blinked when the lines of data on the computer screen displayed another search. For Pete's sake! There were more South Americans with the last name of Santini that he had thought. So for good measure, he threw other factors into the mix. Were any of them associated with the oil industry? Had any of their incomes increased lately? Had any of them been in the news recently?

He flipped to another screen and brought up one of the pictures he had scanned in earlier. He had contacted an official at McDonald's in São Paulo. He had confirmed that because of the increase in crime against tourists, they had installed a hidden camera on the premises. After checking with Ashton, he had pinpointed the date and time someone had tried to hit on Corinthians Avery. Then using his agency connections, he had obtained various copies of the photographs they had.

He smiled as he rubbed his jaw. Not a bad shot of Miss Avery, he thought as he focused on the photo of her entering the eating establishment. No wonder Trevor was interested. The woman was a looker.

Drake then browsed through the photos of others who had entered McDonald's that day. His smile widened when Trevor's features came up. The expression he wore indicated he'd been a man with purpose that day. No doubt he'd been in hot pursuit of Miss Avery, since it had been documented he had entered McDonald's approximately seven minutes after she had.

Scanning backward, Drake's gaze sharpened on two men who had walked in together a few seconds after Miss Avery had entered. He frowned, wondering why their faces looked familiar. He printed a copy of their likenesses from the computer before going to another screen and pulling up past newspaper clippings on various Santinis.

An hour or so later and *bingo!* He had made a connection. Those two men, the same two that just happened to be in McDonald's that day, were part of Argentina's Ambassador Manuel Santini's entourage. And even more specifically, they were the ambassador's son, Raul Santini's, personal security men.

Drake relaxed in his chair as he punched in the name of Raul Santini, and watched as a wealth of information on the screen came to life. Now, he thought, he was getting somewhere.

A cheerful and excited Corinthians entered her condominium less than thirty minutes after her conversation with Trevor. She went immediately into the bathroom and began running water for her shower. She had just turned to go into the kitchen when she saw a movement out of the corner of her eye. Before she could react, a hand snaked out and grabbed her, placing another over her mouth to silence any sound she was about to make. The hold on her tightened with each struggle she made.

"Listen up," a deep, hard voice whispered close to her ear. "It won't do you any good to fight me. I've been paid too much money to deliver you in one piece. But if you don't stop fighting me, I'll give you something that'll knock you out."

Corinthians immediately stopped struggling when she thought about the baby. She couldn't let him give her anything that may harm the child.

"Now that's more like it. Just do what you're told and you won't get hurt. We need to make your disappearance look like you wanted to get away for a while and left willingly. So you're going to leave a note for anyone who cares."

Ashton Sinclair looked up when the young South American civilian entered his office. The United States government had begun using locals as undercover informants, to keep them abreast of possible terrorists' activities as part of their antiterrorism policy. After the increase of embassy bombings last year, the government wanted to be aware of any possible threats.

"What is it, Carlos?"

"You told me to inform you of any unusual activity involving Armond Thetas."

Ashton stood. He was immediately interested. "What do you know?"

"He left the country last night, *senhor.* In his private plane."

Ashton felt his skin prickle. "Do you have any idea where he's headed?"

"To your country, *senhor.* To North America."

Trevor entered Corinthians's condo using the key she had given to him when they'd been together in Houston. This was the first time he had been to the place she considered home. He glanced around, liking what he saw. The place was huge and roomy. It looked comfortable and was decorated in soft shades of earth-tone colors.

Calling her name, he walked toward the back, wondering where she was since she was expecting him. He didn't see her. He placed his overnight bag on the floor beside her bed. He headed for the kitchen, thinking that perhaps she'd been detained at work. He was just about to open the refrigerator to see if she had anything cool and refreshing to drink when the note taped to the refrigerator door stopped him. He pulled it off and read it. *I've decided that I need to get away for a while. So much has happened lately and I need time to think. Don't worry, I'm okay. For once I need to think only of myself, no one else. Corinthians.*

Trevor felt a knot taking shape in his stomach. His chest felt heavy, constricted. He reread the note then closed his eyes to remember the conversation they'd had earlier that night. He recalled every little detail. The more he thought about it, the more he was convinced something wasn't right. He read the note a third time.

He quickly walked back into her bedroom and opened her closet, wondering where her luggage was kept. He could not tell if any of her clothes were missing. With the eyes of a hawk, he glanced around the room, becoming angry. He felt useless because he could not tell if anything was out of place. But the one thing he did know was that the note he held in his hand was a fake. She may have written it, but he didn't believe one word of it. There was no way anyone could convince him that Corinthians just up and left, leaving just a note as an explanation of her departure.

He picked up the telephone next to her bed to call the police.

Drake reached for the telephone just seconds before it rang. "Yeah?"

"Drake, it's Ashton. We might have a problem."

Drake frowned. "I was just about to call to tell you that very same thing. You go first. What sort of a problem do you think we have?"

"I've just been informed that Armond Thetas left for the United States last night."

Drake forced his attention from the computer screen, shaking his head. "Man, the problem I've uncovered may be even bigger. Do you know how to reach Trev?"

"I tried, but he's not in. I got his answering machine so I called his father. He said Trevor went to Austin to visit Miss Avery for a few days."

"So he went to Austin, huh?" Drake asked as he reached over to retrieve a blank disc. He needed to make a copy of everything he had uncovered.

"Yeah, why?"

"Because that's where we're going. It's my guess Trevor may need us."

That was all that needed to be said. If there was a possibility Trevor needed them, then they were going.

"Let's meet up at the airport in Austin. I'm depending on you to come up with Miss Avery's address," Drake was saying. "I'll fill you in on everything when I see you."

Dex walked into the room, returning after having put his daughters to bed. Caitlin had just sat down at the computer to begin entering data into it. He appreciated her dedication at keeping his employees' work records in order, but at the moment his mind was on something else.

He pulled out the chair next to her, turned it around and straddled it before reaching over and turning off the computer.

Caitlin blinked, stunned. "Dex! What do you think you're doing?"

"Getting your attention."

Every fiber in Caitlin's body reacted to the dark charcoal-gray eyes looking at her. A serious smile touched her lips. "You always have my attention, Dex. Even when you fail to notice that you do. Like earlier today for instance."

She leaned over and whispered in his ear, revealing to him the exact moment that day when he'd had her full attention. He had been swimming in the pool with the girls and had brought them inside to change for dinner. She had seen him in his swim trunks and had nearly lost it.

"You don't know how close you came to being seduced in front of your daughters, Dex. Right in the middle of my kitchen."

Caitlin could feel the sexual magnetism radiating between them and wondered if it would always be this way. Every time he looked at her with those eyes of his, the only thing she could think of was making love. He was so disturbing to her in every way and she loved him tremendously.

"I like being seduced by you, sweetheart," he whispered, slowly leaning toward her, his mouth aiming dead center for hers.

It was at that precise moment that the phone rang.

"Damn," Dex muttered, grabbing for it. "Whoever you are, you're a disturbance, so this had better be good," he barked into the telephone.

All traces of annoyance and irritation left his face. Instead, Caitlin noticed his features became one of shock, disbelief, then anger. Sharp, steel-edged anger.

"Just keep calm, man," he was saying to the caller. "I'll contact Clayton and Justin. We're on our way." He slammed the telephone down and quickly stood up.

"Dex, what is it? What's wrong?"

"That was Trevor calling from Austin. Corinthians is missing."

Chapter 27

Lieutenant Richard Medina looked around at the people assembled in the spacious kitchen. There was a battle line drawn with Senator Joshua Avery on one side; the fiancé, Trevor Grant, on the other; and the parents, Reverend and Mrs. Avery, in the middle.

The preacher and his wife were trying their best to keep peace and ward off any bloodshed, since the look on Grant's face indicated he was ready to kill somebody. Lieutenant Medina suppressed a sigh. Why him? How did he get to be the lucky one assigned to this case? He'd rather be investigating a double murder instead of dealing with this group, especially since the senator was trying his hardest to entice Trevor Grant to kill him. Even a fool could see that Grant was a man on the verge of doing something destructive…like breaking every bone in the senator's body if he didn't get smart and shut up.

Lieutenant Medina shook his head. As an officer of the law, he had an obligation to curtail any possible violence. It was time he stepped in and intervened, since it didn't look like the senator was going to get smart anytime soon.

"All right, all right, let's settle down and go over everything one more time," he finally said, raising his voice over that of Senator Avery's.

"Really, Lieutenant, is that necessary?" Senator Avery was asking. "I think the note my sister left speaks for itself. She needed to get away for a while and took off. I personally resent Mr. Grant calling my parents and upsetting them with the notion that something has happened to Corinthians."

Trevor gave Joshua a hard look. "Something *has* happened to her, Avery. If you know your sister, then you'd know she would never just up and leave like this."

Joshua raised his eyes to the ceiling. "I do know my sister, Grant. I think I happen to know her a lot better than you do. I admit her unexpected and abrupt departure isn't normal behavior for her, but considering the circumstance of the situation, I completely understand why she left."

Lieutenant Medina leaned back against the kitchen wall. He crossed his arms over his chest. Like any politician, Avery was a smooth talker, a true glibber if ever there was one. "Then how about enlightening me of the circumstances of the situation, Senator."

Joshua gave the lieutenant his politician smile. "Why certainly. Corinthians was nearly kidnapped by terrorists last month while in South America. I'm sure you read about it in the papers."

The lieutenant nodded, indicating that he had.

"Well, she was able to get away from the terrorists," Joshua said, conveniently omitting mentioning how Trevor had been instrumental in making that possible. "She and Mr. Grant spent some time together and when she was rescued, she had this insane notion that she had fallen in love with him. I only found out since coming here tonight that she has agreed to marry him."

Joshua took a sip of coffee before continuing. "After reading her note, it looks to me like she's having second thoughts about that decision and went away to think things through. Mr. Grant is definitely not her type, and I'm not completely convinced that she loves him."

"That's enough, Joshua!" Reverend Nathan Avery's voice boomed so loudly, the lieutenant was certain the floor shook. "There is no doubt in my mind of Corinthians's feelings for Trevor. There's a lot you don't know."

The lieutenant looked thoughtfully at Corinthians's father. It was time he brought the preacher out of his neutral zone. "What about you, sir? You know your daughter. Do you think there has been foul play, as Mr. Grant seems to think? Or do you agree with your son and believe she just went away for a while to think?"

Reverend Avery frowned in serious concentration. He glanced at Joshua and then at Trevor. He released a long, deep sigh before finally answering the lieutenant's question. "I agree with Trevor." Ignoring the stunned look on his son's face, he continued, "I believe something bad has happened to my daughter. I'm almost certain of it."

"And why is that, sir?"

"Because her note hints at that fact."

Lieutenant Medina looked down at the note he held in his hand and reread it. He didn't find anything amiss. He glanced back up at Reverend Avery. "What are the hints, sir?"

"The part where she says for once she needed to think only of herself and no one else. I know my daughter, and there is one other person that she would think about right now, no matter what."

The lieutenant's brows rose. "And who is that?"

"The baby."

"What baby?" Joshua demanded to know.

"The baby she and Trevor made together."

Lieutenant Medina could have sworn he saw steam coming

from the young senator's ears with his father's statement. The look he gave Trevor Grant was murderous.

"You got my sister pregnant?" Joshua screamed out the question. The lieutenant was certain the floor actually shook that time.

"Joshua, lower your voice," Reverend Avery demanded harshly. "Corinthians got herself pregnant. By her own admission, Trevor did not hold a gun to her head and force her to do anything. She has a mind of her own and is accountable for her own actions and whatever decisions she makes."

"And you accept this?" Joshua asked in disbelief.

"You and Corinthians both know my position on moral issues. And recently, Trevor and I had a long talk, and he also knows. He and Corinthians were counseled."

Joshua was livid. "Counseled! They were counseled! What about me?" he stormed.

"What about you, Joshua?" Reverend Avery asked his son calmly. "Do you need counseling, as well?"

"No, I don't need counseling," an angry Joshua Avery replied, almost ready to lose it. "I want to know what about me and my political career once the media gets wind that my sister is pregnant and not married?"

"We're getting married," Trevor said in a firm voice with a definite edge to it. "Corinthians is missing and all you can think about is your political career?"

The lieutenant cleared his throat. He thought it was time to get his line of questioning back on track. "I can find nothing to indicate Miss Avery did not leave willingly. There is no sign of forced entry into this condo, and Mrs. Avery, you indicated her luggage is missing, as well as some items of clothing. From the looks of things, she did go away on a short trip."

Maudlin Avery nodded. However, she agreed with her husband and Trevor that Corinthians would not have left without contacting someone first. "Yes, sir, that is correct, but I have a gut feeling she didn't leave willingly."

"Is there anything other than hints and gut feelings that can provide substantial evidence of any foul play?"

When the occupants in the room shook their heads negatively, Lieutenant Medina sighed. "I'll question the other occupants of this building to see if they may have seen anyone or noticed anything unusual. This is a pretty ritzy area of town. Anyone who doesn't fit in will probably stick out like a sore thumb."

"Officer, since there is no sign of forced entry, do you think whoever took my daughter could have been someone she knew, and she let them in?" Maudlin Avery asked.

"That's a good possibility. I'd appreciate it if you'll write down the names and addresses of any friends she has who visit frequently, including any former boyfriends."

"Corinthians didn't date much, so there aren't any former boyfriends," Maudlin Avery said quietly. "She preferred keeping busy by working."

Lieutenant Medina shrugged. He'd obtained a picture of Corinthians Avery from her parents earlier. She was a good-looking woman. He couldn't imagine her not ever having a close male friend. "Mr. Grant, you and Miss Avery got engaged recently, is that correct?" he asked Trevor.

"Yes, just last week," Trevor answered. In fact, he had her engagement ring in his pocket. He had planned to surprise her with it tonight.

"Any arguments since then?"

Trevor's gaze narrowed at the officer. "No. Last weekend we spent some time together in Houston when she met my family. I put her back on the plane Sunday afternoon and had not planned to see her again until this coming weekend. I was able to shorten my work schedule and decided to come earlier."

"Was she expecting you?"

Trevor wondered where the officer's questions were leading. "Yes. I called her on my cellular phone when I was on my way to the airport and told her I was coming."

Lieutenant Medina nodded. "And how did she feel about that?"

Trevor remembered his and Corinthians's last conversation. It had been short, but packed with meaning. Pain settled deep within him at the thought that someone had taken her away from him.

"She was glad we would be together again," he said softly. He turned and walked over to the window and looked out. The night was pitch-black, and the woman he loved was somewhere out there. Why? Why would anyone take Corinthians? It didn't make sense. Did it have anything to do with what went down in South America?

Trevor shook his head. He didn't have any answers. He turned back around to face the group of people. "Lieutenant, unless you have any other questions for me, I want to be alone for a while."

"No, that's all I have for now."

Trevor nodded. He then met Reverend and Mrs. Avery's troubled gazes. "I'm going to get her back," he said with deadly calm and absolute determination. "And whoever had the nerve to take her away is going to pay dearly." He then turned and walked out of the room, going into Corinthians's bedroom and closing the door behind him.

A chill swept through Lieutenant Medina's body. For some reason, he believed every word Trevor Grant had spoken. If Corinthians Avery had been taken against her will, he felt sorry for the person who'd been stupid enough to do it.

Corinthians willed her body to stay calm. She refused to be afraid. She had to believe Trevor would find her. She had to believe that somehow and some way he would know that she had not left on her own and would come for her. She had to believe it. She had to have hope.

She wondered who the men were who had brought her to this place awaiting further orders. She had been placed on a bed. Her hand were tied behind her back, and a blindfold covered her eyes. She strained her ears when she heard two male voices. They had boasted of how one of them had easily slipped into her home past Lenora, her cleaning lady, and had waited for her to come home. From their clipped English, she knew they weren't from this country, but she didn't have a clue where they were from or what they wanted with her. One of them had said something to the other about leaving for the airstrip shortly. She wondered if they had plans to fly her out of Austin. She hoped not. Trevor would never find her if they did. He would spend his time searching Austin for her.

A feeling of fear resurfaced again. She took a deep breath to calm her ragged nerves, willing her body to believe the man she loved would find her.

She bowed her head and softly spoke to the one person she knew she could depend on. She prayed. "Father, please let him come."

Trevor felt like he was ready to explode. While the detective was wasting time gathering information to determine if Corinthians had been taken against her will, the people who had taken her were gaining an advantage in time. He wished there was something he could do. He felt so helpless. He balled his hands into fists at his side as both fear and anger roiled within him. If anything happened to her, he didn't know what he would do. He closed his eyes and silently prayed…for help, for direction and for strength.

Kicking off his shoes, he lay down on her bed. The faintest wisp of her scent clung to the bedcovers. He closed his eyes, wishing he had mental telepathy and she could tell him where she was. He tried to think of any reason why someone would force Corinthians from her home and make it seem like she'd left willingly. The only reason he could think of was that the person didn't want anyone looking for her, at least not for a while. That would give them time…but time to do what?

Trevor sat up when he heard a knock on the door. "Come in."

Moments later, Maudlin Avery walked in. Concern was etched on her face. "Are you okay, Trevor?"

He stood and slipped back into his shoes. *No,* he wanted desperately to say. *He wasn't okay and he wouldn't be okay until he got Corinthians back.* Instead, he said, "Yes, I'm fine. Is Lieutenant Medina still here?"

"No, he left, but indicated he would be back later. He wanted to check out a few things."

Another knock sounded on the door and Reverend Avery stuck his head in. "Trevor, there're two gentlemen here to see you."

Trevor nodded, thinking it was probably two of the Madaris brothers. He had called Dex who said he would call Justin and Clayton to tell them what had happened. When trouble hit, he could always depend on his friends being there for him. "Thanks, I'm coming."

He walked out of the room and stopped short. Drake Warren and Ashton Sinclair were standing in the doorway.

Trevor released a long, deep sigh. His prayers had been answered. He'd been sent the help and direction he'd asked for. The strength would come in knowing he wasn't alone. He shook his head and tried to swallow the golf-ball-size lump forming in his throat. "You don't know how glad I am to see you guys," he said honestly, easily and sincerely.

Rasheed stood at the window of his apartment building, looking out. His mind was heavy, deep in thought. Returning home to Mowaiti for a short visit had been what he'd needed. His people had been glad to see him and had rejoiced in his return with celebrations of feasts and dancing. It had reminded him of just how much his people meant to him, and just how much he was concerned for their welfare.

He was troubled by the way his father had been acting

ately. He had spoken with his mother and had been surprised to learn his father had only contacted her once since he had been in America. Rasheed found that strange. Something was going on and he didn't know what. What had changed his father so drastically over the past months?

Rasheed folded his thoughts when he heard Swalar enter the room. He turned around. "Yes, Swalar, what is it?"

"Mr. Santini is here to see you."

Rasheed inwardly smiled at the slight grunt he heard in Swalar's voice. He knew his trusted valet did not approve of his friendship with Raul. Years ago as teenagers, when Raul had come home with him during one of their school breaks, the two of them had kept Swalar busy keeping them out of trouble. Of course, Swalar blamed Raul for all their mischief, since in Swalar's eyes his young prince could do no wrong.

"Send him in, Swalar."

Rasheed knew something was wrong the moment Santini walked through the door. The back of his neck prickled. "What is it, my friend? What's wrong?"

Santini hesitated a moment, as if regretting the words he was about to say. "I love my country as much as you do yours, Monty. I couldn't have the North Americans thinking that South Americans are evil and villainous. What happened with the terrorists has put my country in a negative light. I organized a special team of men to dig up anything they could find out on the terrorist attack at the hotel in Rio. And I ordered them to search the entire countryside for Araque and to bring him back to me alive."

Rasheed nodded, but didn't say anything. He decided to let Raul finish what he was saying.

"They found him hiding out in the mountains near Argentina. He was in a bad way. He'd been shot, probably from when the Navy SEALs raided his camp to rescue the American hostages. In exchange for a promise that we would not harm his young teenage son, who was found with him, before Araque died he gave us the name of the man who mas-terminded everything."

"And?"

Santini took a deep breath. "It's all here in the report, Rasheed," he said, handing a folder to his friend. "This is the report I'll be giving to the State Department to clear my country of any wrongdoings. I think you need to read it."

Rasheed nodded and, taking the chair behind his desk, he began reading.

Corinthians came awake, wondering how she had managed to sleep for the little while that she had. Her position on the bed wasn't a comfortable one. A blindfold still covered her eyes and her hands were still tied. At least they had not gagged her. They had warned her not to make a sound or they would give her something to knock her out. In the distance, she could still hear the men's voices. She wished there was some-thing she could do to try to escape, but the blindfold and her tied hands limited her capabilities. She forced herself to roll her body to the side when she felt a bout of nausea forming in her stomach. Now was not the time for her to get sick.

She closed her eyes, pretending sleep when she heard the room door open.

"Wake up," a male voice demanded, calling out to her. "The plane is here and we're ready to go."

Rasheed closed the folder. His entire body was consumed in anger. A part of him didn't want to believe any of the things he had read, but the more he thought about it, the more it made sense. His father had been acting strange lately—now he knew why.

He looked up and met Santini's gaze. "Will you trust me to take care of it and to make things right for both of our coun-tries?" he asked his friend. He knew he was asking a lot. He had read the report in its entirety. He knew how damaging it would be if the truth were known. The lives of six Americans had been put in danger because of a man's lust for one woman.

"It may be too late, Monty. I've had your father's residence watched for the past couple of weeks, even more closely after you left to return to Mowaiti. I didn't want to say anything to you until I was sure of the facts."

Santini leaned forward in his chair. In a controlled voice he said, "He's desperate, Monty. He wants Miss Avery in a bad way. He's arranged for her to be abducted from her home in Austin and to be brought here. His plans are to hide her away somewhere until he can get her out of the country. And according to my contacts, he's already set his plans in motion."

Rasheed rose quickly to his feet. "I have to stop him, Santini, but I'm going to need your help. Please say that you will help me."

Santini nodded. He knew if their positions were reversed, Rasheed would help him. "What do you want me to do?"

"Post some of your men at the private airfield that's been designated for international dignitaries to use. If anyone is bringing Corinthians Avery into this city, they will have to arrive there. Tell your men not to intercept them. I just want to know where they take her. I'll handle it from there," Rasheed said, putting on his jacket.

"Where are you going?"

"To see my father."

"Be careful, Monty."

"I will."

Chapter 28

"They're friends of yours, I hope," Joshua Avery muttered under his breath to Trevor as he gazed at the two men. He felt a chill pass through his body that began at the top of his head and quickly went down to his toes.

One of the men Joshua thought he recognized as the Marine colonel who had accompanied the military aircraft that had brought Corinthians to Key West. However, tonight without the military garb, he wasn't too sure. For some reason, he looked rough and rugged, and nothing like a schooled, disciplined, high-ranking military officer. Dressed in jeans and a pullover shirt, he looked primed and ready for trouble of any kind, even that of his own making.

Joshua thought the other man had a look about him that was lethal, deadly, almost barbaric. He gave the appearance of a man who could possibly end another's life without thinking twice about it.

"They are friends of yours, aren't they?" Joshua asked Trevor again. The slight tremble in his voice was apparent.

Trevor found a reason to smile for the first time since he had arrived at Corinthians's home and found her missing. As usual, Sir Drake had put the fear of God into someone. Trevor took great pleasure in knowing *that* person was Joshua Avery.

"Yes, they're friends of mine. Drake Warren and Ashton Sinclair." He introduced his friends to the others in the room. He then gazed at Ashton and Drake thoughtfully. For them to have come, they had to know something. "How did you know Corinthians is missing?"

Drake muttered a curse before saying, "We were hoping to get here before anything could happen."

"What do you mean? Are you saying you know something about my daughter's disappearance?" Reverend Avery asked Drake desperately. Like his son, he remembered Ashton from that night in Key West. Also, like Joshua, he could detect something destructive and dangerous about the man called Drake Warren. However, the look Drake gave him was respectful when he responded to his question.

"Yes, sir," Drake answered politely. "We know something."

"Now wait just a minute," Joshua said heatedly, forgetting for the moment his decision not to rattle either of the two men. He still was not convinced Corinthians was missing and not somewhere rethinking her future. "Who are you and why should we believe you know so much?"

The look Drake turned on Joshua was hard and deadly. "Is he for real?" he asked Trevor without taking his eyes off Joshua.

"I'm afraid so," was Trevor's terse reply.

"I'll let it pass since he's a future relative of yours," Drake said with a sharp edge in his voice.

"Don't do me any favors," was Trevor's reply.

"You sure?"

"Positive."

Drake nodded before slowly walking over to Joshua Avery,

who had the good sense to take a step back. "Keep up the negativity, Senator, and I just might be your worst nightmare. And the reason I know so much is because for the last fifteen hours, I've been sitting in front of a computer reviewing highly classified data. Someone has been trying for the past month or so to get their hands on your sister. Since she's now missing, I can only assume the person has succeeded."

"What do you mean you've been reviewing highly classified data? That's against the law. How did you get access to them?"

"CIA."

Joshua was stunned. "You're with the CIA?"

"Every day." Drake instantaneously dismissed Joshua and turned to Trevor. "I have an idea where they've taken her Trev. Come on, we don't have time to waste. We're going to D.C. I'll update you on the plane."

Trevor looked at Drake and Ashton clearly surprised "What do you mean Armond Thetas had nothing to do with that terrorists' attack in Rio?"

"Oh, don't get me wrong," Drake answered smoothly "He's far from being a choirboy, but he's innocent of any terrorists' activities. He's been too busy planning the assassination of Argentina's chief of police. That's why he's here in this country now. He thinks he's meeting with a hit man. Unfortunately for him, the person he'll be talking with is an undercover agent for the FBI. Hopefully, we'll have Thetas behind bars before the night is over."

Trevor shook his head, trying to clear it. "Well, if he wasn' the person behind it, who was? Why would they want Corinthians now? And why was she taken to Washington?"

Drake knew he had to choose his next words carefully "There have been two men trying to kidnap Corinthians for different reasons. One for the help she could provide to his country and the other because he wants her."

Trevor frowned. "What do you mean because he wants her?"

Ashton looked pointedly at Trevor. "Drake means just what he says. He *wants* her."

Trevor's eyes became hard and cold. The gaze that held Drake and Ashton within their scope was fiery, penetrating. "Who are these two men?"

Drake provided Trevor the names of the two men.

"Do you know which one of them has her?"

"No, but we'll soon find out. So buckle up. It's time for takeoff."

Corinthians couldn't help it—she was sick. The plane flight had shaken her up quite a bit and her stomach was reacting violently to it.

"Do you think it was the plane ride that made her ill?" one of the men asked the other with concern in his voice.

"How would I know? All I know is that he's going to be angry if he thinks we didn't take proper care of her. He gave us specific instructions."

Corinthians frowned. She was still in the dark as to who "he" was. She didn't know who the person was who had ordered her kidnapping or what he wanted with her. The two men weren't saying any names. They had removed her blindfold earlier and she didn't recognize either of them. But from her travels abroad, she knew they were both from the Middle East.

"I am an American citizen, and I demand that you let me go."

They looked at her as if her words meant nothing to them. After mumbling a few more sentences to themselves, this time in their native tongue, they left her in the small, cramped room, locking the door behind them.

Where am I? she wondered to herself. Because of the plane ride, she knew she was no longer in Austin. So where was she? She yawned, feeling tired. She had to believe that no matter where she was, Trevor would eventually come for her. She closed her eyes, drifting off to sleep with that very thought in her mind and that belief in her heart.

* * *

Rasheed looked around the darkened lot before slipping unnoticed through the chain-link fence. He had not been able to locate his father, so he had given Santini explicit instructions to find him.

He removed his shoes so that he would not make a sound as he walked on the gravel. When he heard voices, he lowered his body behind a row of crates. When it was quiet again, he stood and began making his way across the yard once more.

Santini's men had told him that Corinthians had been taken to this empty warehouse. He intended to get her out.

He paused when he came to the room where he knew Corinthians was being held. A key was hanging just above the door. Looking around, he made his way toward the room and using the key, he unlocked the door, slid back the handle and eased inside. It was dark and he couldn't see a thing.

He was about to call out softly to Corinthians when suddenly the door swung open and before he had time to react, a sharp pain went through him and he fell to the floor.

"What do you mean Trevor isn't here?"

Joshua stared at the three men who stood in the doorway, none of whom he recognized. All three wore serious expressions on their faces. The man who had asked the question appeared somewhat intimidating. Well, as far as Joshua was concerned, he'd had enough intimidation for one night and didn't intend to put up with any more. His father was in the study using the phone, and his mother was in the shower. He'd been in the kitchen about to make a sandwich when these three had shown up.

"I meant just what I said. Trevor Grant isn't here," Joshua replied curtly.

The frown on Dex Madaris's face deepened. "Doesn't Corinthians Avery live here?"

"Yes."

"So where's Trevor?"

"You like asking a lot of questions don't you?" Joshua asked smartly, then realized his mistake when the man took a step toward him.

"Dex, stop!" Justin Madaris's sharp voice cut through the air.

Clayton Madaris chuckled as he leaned against the doorjamb. "I don't know, Justin. Maybe it'll be a good idea if he went ahead. I have a feeling Trevor would probably appreciate it."

Justin shot his youngest brother a warning stare before turning his attention back to the man at the door. "We apologize for arriving so late, Senator, but we thought Trevor was here."

Clayton and Dex raised their eyes to the ceiling. Justin was way too nice at times.

"I'm Justin Madaris, and these are my brothers, Clayton and Dex."

Joshua recognized the Madaris name immediately. He had spoken to Dex Madaris on the telephone when he'd gotten the news that Corinthians had managed to escape into the South American jungle with Trevor. Dex Madaris had been rude to him then, but Joshua had dismissed his rudeness. After all, he was Jake Madaris's nephew. And any politician from Texas knew not to get on Jake Madaris's bad side. That could be political suicide.

To save face, he bestowed upon them his biggest politician smile. "Madaris? Oh, why didn't you say so? Come right on in," Joshua said, opening the door wider.

No one moved.

"Just tell us where Trevor is," Dex said with agitation in his voice.

"He's in Washington, D.C."

Clayton straightened his stance, frowning. "Washington? What's he doing in Washington?"

Joshua shrugged. "Two of his military friends showed up and convinced him Corinthians has been taken to Washington."

Justin lifted a dark brow. "I take it you don't believe it."

"Trust me, you don't want to know what I believe."

"You're right," Dex said coldly. "We don't want to know."

Without saying anything else, the three brothers turned and walked away. Joshua had a funny feeling he had not made a good first impression.

Two FBI agents met Drake, Ashton and Trevor at the airport when their plane landed.

"Have you been able to locate either of the Valdemons?" Drake asked one of the agents after they had gotten into the car.

"No, but we've brought Raul Santini in for questioning. He's trying to pull that political immunity crap on us. I think he's trying to protect Rasheed Valdemon."

"So you still don't have any idea where they've taken my fiancée?" Trevor asked. His tone reflected his worry.

"No, unfortunately we don't. But for some reason I think by the time we get back to the office, Raul Santini will have talked."

Trevor nodded. He hoped so.

Rasheed slowly came to. The first face he looked into after gaining consciousness was his father's. The second was that of Corinthians Avery. Like him, they were bound in their chairs with their hands tied behind their backs. One look into his father's face and he knew he had been drugged. Corinthians Avery looked frightened, but physically, she appeared all right.

He looked up into the cold eyes of the man who had masterminded everything. "You disappoint me, Yasir."

"Disappointments are a part of life, young prince. You should have learned that by now."

"Why, Yasir? After all your talk of how we should do anything to keep peace with the United States, why this? Father trusted you. He believed in you. Why have you been drugging him for the past three months, setting him up and making me believe he's been the one with the lust-crazed appetite for all those women, when it was you all along?"

Yasir's laughter was blood-chilling. "I got tired of your father getting credit for all I did. Those were my negotiation policies that were presented to OPEC. But because of the circumstances surrounding my birth, I am nothing but someone who has to serve and do his bidding."

Rasheed frowned. "What are you talking about?"

"Oh, didn't your father ever tell you that we are brothers? He thought he was doing me a favor by making me a part of his staff when he discovered I was the illegitimate son of the old sheikh. Amin made sure I was educated and taken care of. But as far as I am concerned, that wasn't enough. He was not able to give me the love that was due me from the man who had sired me. The old sheikh even resented my presence in the palace."

Yasir laughed again, and it was just as blood-chilling as before. "But it doesn't matter now. Unlike your father, who prefers one woman, I prefer many. I knew I wanted Miss Avery the moment I saw her when she attended that dinner party with you a few months ago. I've been planning to have her ever since."

Corinthians felt cold fear move up her spine. There was no doubt in her mind that the man was crazy. While waiting for Rasheed to gain consciousness, Yasir Bedouins had told her how the young prince had tried kidnapping her, too, but for totally different reasons. He had amusingly shared with her how Rasheed had had this silly notion that she could help his people by finding oil on their land. Her talents, Yasir had told her, would be used exclusively to please him. He did not care about the people. They could starve to death for all he cared. She had known then that he was a cruel and heartless man. On the other hand, she knew that although Rasheed had gone about it the wrong way, he was a man who truly loved his country and wanted to help his people. He would be a good sheikh for Mowaiti one day.

"Let her go, Yasir. Don't get yourself in any more trouble than you're already in. Santini knows all about you. It's in the report he's going to give to an official at the State Department. Araque spilled his guts before he died."

Yasir's face hardened at the thought of his old friend dying. Araque had served him well on a number of secret dealings. "You lie, young prince! If Santini knew the truth, I would have been arrested long ago."

"I'm telling the truth. He waited until I returned from Mowaiti to talk to me first. Then it was important to me that my father was safe. When I went to his home earlier today, he wasn't there. Santini had strict orders to turn that report over to the authorities if I had not returned more than an hour ago. Make it easy on yourself and turn yourself in."

The look on Yasir's face became strange, almost deranged. "I will never turn myself in. I'll go somewhere where I can't be found."

He went over to the chair where Corinthians was sitting and began untying her. "You're coming with me," he snarled, pulling her forcibly from the chair.

Corinthians tried to resist him, but his hold was too strong. It was as if he had some sort of superhuman strength.

"Let her go, Yasir. Think of your honor and let her go," Rasheed was yelling at the top of his voice. But his words didn't do any good. The man didn't intend to let Corinthians go. However, he made the mistake of dragging her past Rasheed's chair while making his escape. In one quick movement, Rasheed kicked his leg out, tripping Yasir and making him loosen his hold on Corinthians.

"Run, Corinthians, run!" Rasheed shouted out to her.

Corinthians tried to free herself completely from Yasir's hold, but the man's hand caught hold of the hem of her dress and she felt herself falling with him.

Then suddenly, she heard a deep human snarl, and the next thing she knew she was being pulled from Yasir's grasp by big, strong arms. They were arms she recognized immediately.

Trevor!

After placing her safely out of the way, Trevor turned his fury on the man who'd had the nerve to take his woman. All the anger he'd felt since finding Corinthians missing came back full-force with every punch and every blow he gave Yasir. The man didn't stand a chance against his fury. Somehow, through his rage, he heard Corinthians calling his name, pleading for him to stop. Giving Yasir one last punishing blow, he dropped him to the ground.

He turned around. The federal authorities had arrived. Agents were everywhere. Rasheed Valdemon was being untied and his father, Sheikh Amin Valdemon, was being cared for by a group of paramedics. Trevor didn't give any of them a second thought. His mind was on his woman. He quickly glanced around for her.

"Trevor!"

He turned toward the sound of her voice and caught her in a fierce, crushing embrace when she came racing toward him. He smothered her lips at first with demanding intensity, then slowly his mouth became softer, tender. He showered kisses around her lips and around her jaw, before taking her mouth again. He couldn't get enough of the woman he had come so close to losing. She was his desire, his heart, his love.

Corinthians's body quivered at the sweet tenderness of Trevor's kiss. She devoured his fiery possession. His kiss was fire, burning her mouth and sending pleasure radiating through her body. He was her fire, her hero, the love of her life.

Trevor felt someone tap him on the back. He broke off the kiss long enough to check out the intrusion. Frowning, he turned to look up into Ashton's smiling face. "The two of you are in the way here, Captain. Some of us have work to do."

Trevor laughed. "Anything you say, Colonel." He gathered

Corinthians into his arms and began walking back toward the parked car. He stopped when he thought of someone and turned around.

"Sir Drake," he called out to the man who was helping to put a badly bruised Yasir in the car.

When Drake looked in his direction, Trevor gave him a thumbs-up, wondering when would be the next time he saw his friend again. Drake Warren was a man on the run from a painful past.

Grinning, Drake returned Trevor's thumbs-up before getting into a car with a group of federal agents.

"Trevor?"

Trevor looked down at Corinthians, thinking he had never seen anything so beautiful. He placed her on her feet then pulled her into his arms and held her close to him. He had no intentions of leaving her again or letting her leave him. Trouble seemed to always nip at his woman's heels.

"We're getting married as soon as we get back to Austin and it can be arranged. We're not waiting any longer. We'll make plans to have a huge reception to make up for it. You got that?" Trevor asked her.

Corinthians looked up at him, smiling. Through it all, somehow she had known her man would come for her. "Yes, I got it. Now, how about you getting this." She reached up, pulled his mouth down to hers and fitted her body snugly to his. The kiss she gave him was a kiss for hearts and souls to entwine. All Trevor could do was succumb to the divine ecstasy he felt as she pressed her open lips to his and mated hotly with his mouth.

When Corinthians released his mouth, her lips curved into a sultry smile. "I think I still need to perfect that a little."

Trevor thought if she perfected it any more, he wouldn't be able to live to tell about it. He took her hand in his. "Come on, sweetheart, let's go home. We have a quick wedding to plan."

Corinthians smiled. "Tell me honestly now, when you caught that garter at Clayton's and Syneda's wedding, did you have any idea that you would actually be the next one to be getting married?"

Trevor shook his head, grinning. "No. What about you? When you caught the bridal bouquet, did you actually think you'd be next?"

"No. Marrying anyone was the last thing on my mind, and definitely not getting married to you. We couldn't stand each other, and you used to deliberately annoy me every chance you got."

Trevor gave her a smooth smile, one that was without shame. "Yeah, I enjoyed getting a rise out of you," he admitted.

Corinthians wrapped her arms around his neck and brought her body close to his. She was so close, she could feel his hardness pressed against her middle. Her lips began placing intimate kisses along the curve of his lips. "And I'm going to enjoy getting a *rise* out of you," she whispered lightly against his lips. "But it will be a different kind of rise than the one you got out of me. This is the kind I'm going to enjoy getting out of you," she said, feeling his body harden against her even more. She heard Trevor's sharp intake of breath when she slid her hand down past his stomach and thigh to cup that very heated part of him in her hand.

"Think you'll be able to handle it, Trevor Grant?"

Trevor was glad a number of parked cars shielded them from curious eyes. He swung Corinthians into his arms. He smiled down at her. "I plan to die trying."

Chapter 29

Two weeks later

Trevor Grant stood, leaning a shoulder against the wall, holding a half-filled champagne glass in his hand. As he looked around the crowded ballroom, he felt a moment of déjà vu. The last wedding reception he had attended had been for his friend, Clayton Madaris. Now here he was, less than three months later, attending his own. He smiled, happy for himself.

He and Corinthians had gotten married within days of returning to Austin, just enough time to assemble their families and close friends. Now tonight, two weeks later, both sets of parents had joined forces to host this gala event. After the reception, he and Corinthians would fly out of Houston to begin their honeymoon in the Cayman Islands, compliments of Senator Joshua Avery, who was still wiping egg off his face.

Trevor's gaze swept over the ballroom. His smile deepened

when he saw that Ashton had cornered Netherland Brooms off to the side. He could only imagine what he was saying to her.

His gaze shifted and lit on the Madaris brothers. All three were on the dance floor with their wives in their arms, holding them close as they swayed to the slow tune being played by the live jazz band.

Trevor shook his head when he saw his parents out on that same dance floor. Seeing them together was taking some getting used to. He was happy for them. They would get the chance to spend the rest of their lives together happily.

His gaze continued to sweep over the ballroom. When it rested upon a particular woman, it stopped. Once again he was struck by another moment of déjà vu.

Corinthians was a very beautiful woman. She was everything male fantasies were made of. He of all people should know since he was married to her and had the pleasure of making love to her each and every night before he went to sleep. He had discovered the real thing was better than any dream he'd ever had—and over the past two years, he'd had plenty.

As if sensing his gaze upon her, Corinthians's head lifted. Her gaze met his and Trevor felt his breath swept away. The look she gave him was sultry, hot and filled with unspoken promises.

He gave her his most charming smile then lifted his champagne glass in a silent toast. With his gaze he communicated his thoughts, a silent, unsubtle message. The smile she gave him indicated she had deciphered his message loud and clear.

Trevor's smile widened when he saw her excuse herself from the group she had been talking to and began walking toward him. She looked absolutely gorgeous dressed in a stunning off-white pant suit. He placed his champagne glass aside and began moving in her direction to meet her on the dance floor.

"Hello, Mr. Grant," she said in a soft, sensuous voice.

"Hello, Mrs. Grant," he replied in a husky tone. He glanced down at her stomach. "And hello, Baby Grant."

He took Corinthians in his arms as they joined the others on the dance floor.

"What do you think about Rio?" Corinthians asked him moments later, savoring the feel of being held by her husband.

Trevor smiled at her question. Rio de Janeiro would always provide him with special memories. It was there that they had begun their South American adventure of a lifetime. One he would never forget.

"I like Rio. Why do you ask? Do you want to go back there soon?" he responded silkily.

"No, I want to name our baby Rio, if it's a boy, and Ria if it's a girl. I think that would be fitting, don't you?"

Trevor chuckled. "Definitely."

He pulled Corinthians closer to him, loving the feel of her in his arms. He thought about the bottle of champagne that was on ice in their hotel room, compliments of Sir Drake. He had sent it from Iceland, of all places.

Trevor leaned down and brushed a light kiss across Corinthians's mouth. "I love you," he said softly, quietly.

"And I love you, too, Trevor."

He gathered her closer into his arms, silently thanking God for giving him friends that had been there for him when he had needed them most, and for this very special woman whom he would love forever. She was his woman, his dream, his passion, the root of his fire and the fulfillment of his desire.

Corinthians wrapped her arms around his neck. She gazed up at him, love clearly shining in the depths of her eyes. "I think the music has stopped."

Trevor smiled. "For us the music will never stop, because we will always make our own."

His hands came up and cupped her face. In the presence of family and friends, on a dance floor where they were the only remaining couple, he leaned down and kissed her. It was a kiss that held promises of a future that would be filled with both fire and desire.

Chapter 30

One month later

"We hope your stay at our hotel is a pleasant one, Mr. Grant."

"Thanks, I'm sure it will be," Trevor replied as he took the room key that was handed to him. Although he had tried sounding cheerful to the hotel clerk, in truth, a hotel room in Phoenix was the very last place he wanted to be. He preferred being home with his wife. He missed her already.

Upon reaching his hotel room, Trevor was glad to see that at least he'd been given a room with a nice view, since he would be spending the next five days in it. His meeting with Lowell Petroleum Company had been set up months ago, before his wedding. He had tried talking Corinthians into making the trip with him, but she was working on a special project at Remington Oil and couldn't get away. Her project was a joint venture between Remington Oil and the government of Mowaiti. If because of her research, oil was discovered in Mowaiti, Remington Oil and Mowaiti would have joint rights to it for the first five years. Then all rights would go to the people of Mowaiti. It was the first type of agreement ever drawn between an American-owned oil company and a foreign nation.

Corinthians had approached S. T. Remington with the idea after realizing how far Prince Valdemon would go to help his people. Mr. Remington had even agreed to let her do most of her research out of their field office in Houston. She only had to travel to Austin occasionally. Already, according to Corinthians, the core samples she had analyzed so far had looked promising.

After doing a couple of stretches to work a few kinks out of his body, Trevor went into the bathroom and turned on the shower. He would place a call home later to let Corinthians know he had arrived in Phoenix safely. He had hated leaving her at the airport when she had taken him there to catch his flight.

Undressing, he went into the bathroom to take his shower, closing the door behind him.

"This is Corinthians Grant. Has Trevor Grant checked in yet? Oh, he has? Thanks."

Corinthians hung up the telephone, smiling. Going over to the full-length mirror, she looked at herself. She didn't think it was possible to get any more daring than this. It was a good thing she was already a married woman.

She knew it was time to make her move when she heard the shower going in the connecting room. Tonight, unlike the last time she'd tried this, some things would be different. There would be no robe for her to wear and no condoms to hide in the pockets. However, one thing would be the same—the man.

Unlike before, no uncertainties crept into her head. She was going to give Trevor Grant a night to remember. Before she had been abducted from her home that night, he had asked her for a favor—to show him just how much she wanted him. Well, tonight she had plans to do just that.

A huge smile covered her face as she opened the door and walked into Trevor's room.

Trevor stepped out of the shower and began toweling himself off. He wasn't in the mood to go downstairs to the restaurant so he thought he'd order room service.

He raised a brow, thinking he'd heard something, then shrugged, dismissing the thought. Wrapping the towel around his middle, he walked out of the bathroom and stopped short when he saw Corinthians standing next to his bed. He blinked. At first he thought he was seeing things, that he was missing her so much he was actually imagining her there. But then after shaking his head a few times to clear his muddled mind, he realized she was actually there, in his hotel room, dressed in...nothing?

Visions of that night nearly two years ago came back, and he thought that tonight she looked even more beautiful and even more sensuous. Remembering that night, he repeated the first words he had ever spoken to her.

"Who the hell are you?"

The smile she gave him was irresistibly sexy. "Your wife," she answered matter-of-factly in a hot, seductive voice. "And who the hell are you?" she asked him right back, trying hard to suppress her grin.

"Your husband."

Corinthians nodded, liking the sound of that. And she liked seeing him with the towel wrapped around his waist. However, if she was going to be daring and bare all, so was he. She slowly began walking toward Trevor as a ripple of desire surged through her body.

"I think we can dispense with this," she said, unhooking the towel from around his waist and letting it fall to the floor between them. "We don't have any secrets between us, do we?" she asked, standing on tiptoes and wrapping her arms around his neck.

"None that I know of." He glanced down at their nude bodies. "In fact, right now we have nothing between us."

"Good."

She leaned up and let her tongue trace the soft fullness of his lips, glorying in the sharp breath he took. When he parted his lips, she placed her mouth over his, giving herself freely to the passion and the desire she felt. Since their marriage, he had shown her that she could be as prim and proper as she wanted to be in the boardroom of Remington Oil. But in the privacy of their bedroom, he wanted prim and proper replaced with sexy and seductive.

Trevor returned Corinthians's kiss with an intensity that nearly shattered his world. Their kiss was slow, thoughtful, hungry. He pulled her to him, loving the feel of being skin to skin with her. He tried to throttle the rush of heated desire racing through him and discovered he couldn't. She had ignited the fire within him to full flame, and he wanted her now.

He gathered her into his arms and placed her on the bed and began his attack. Ruthlessly, he tormented her, placing hot, fiery kisses everywhere on her body, searing her flesh wherever he touched. He loved the feel of the fire leaping on her skin, and he felt a driving need to make love to her in a hot and wild way. Just like he had done in the jungles of South America.

Corinthians's body shuddered from the sensations Trevor was making her feel. She ached for the taste of him, the feel of him. She wanted to be lifted higher than she'd ever been lifted before.

And she was.

She ached, crying out his name when his body joined with hers. This was her husband, her soul mate, her hero, her man. He was all she ever wanted, even when she didn't know what she had actually wanted. Her life with him would be one great adventure. He would give her joy, happiness and more babies. She would give him her undying love, respect and the honor that he was due. He was a proud, hardworking man, born of a race that had endured much. He deserved all the adoration his woman could give him.

She melted in his arms as he continued to drive her toward the point of mindless ecstasy. Her hips raised repeatedly to meet his and in this joining, this very special mating, she knew that together they would live the rest of their lives content and happy.

"Corinthians!"

She heard her name whispered from his lips as the power of love shook them both, plunging them into an oceanic wave of fire and desire.

For the longest moments, neither of them had the energy to move. When finally, Trevor was able to life his head, he looked at her, love clearly shining in the depths of his eyes.

"I thought I left you at the airport in Houston," he whispered, touching his lips to hers.

She smiled up at him. "You did."

"But how?"

Corinthians snuggled closer to him. "I caught a straight flight."

Trevor lifted a brow, frowning. "There weren't any straight flights from Houston to Phoenix."

Corinthians's smile widened. "Yes, there were. You weren't supposed to know about them. In order to beat you here, I had to depend on your two-hour layover in Dallas." She grinned. "Pretty sneaky, huh?"

Trevor shook his head smiling. "Yeah, that's pretty sneaky. And I guess you've had this planned for a while."

"Ever since you mentioned you were coming. The baby and I thought we would tag along and keep you company. What do you think of our idea?"

"I love it." Trevor leaned over and placed a kiss on her

stomach where his baby rested inside. "And I love you, Mrs. Grant."

Corinthians's smile became seductive. "Now it's your turn."

He raised a dark brow. "For what?"

"To do me a favor."

"Which is?"

"Show me," she demanded in a soft, sultry voice. "Show me how much you love me."

And he did.

Hours later, wrapped in each other's arms as they watched the beautiful sunset over the desert valley from their hotel room, Trevor and Corinthians decided that when they had another child, boy or girl, it would be named Phoenix.

USA TODAY Bestselling Author

BRENDA
JACKSON

invites you to discover the always sexy and
always satisfying Madaris Men.

Experience where it all started…

Tonight and Forever
December 2007

Whispered Promises
January 2008

Eternally Yours
February 2008

One Special Moment
March 2008

ARABESQUE®

www.kimanipress.com

The Eatons: For generations, the Eaton family has been dedicated to teaching others. Now siblings Belinda, Myles and Chandra are about to get some sexy, surprising lessons in love....

National Bestselling Author

ROCHELLE ALERS

Bittersweet Love

The Eatons

While committed to teaching, Belinda Eaton isn't interested in committing to a man. But sharing custody of her twin goddaughters with Griffin Rice may change that. And Griffin just might have his own agenda: rethinking his bachelor status!

KIMANI ROMANCE™

Coming the first week of January 2009 wherever books are sold.

Summer just got a little hotter!

National Bestselling Author

MELANIE SCHUSTER

A Case for *Romance*

With all her responsibilities, Ayanna Walker
hasn't had time for romance…until now. While
Johnny Phillips wants to share the future with
Ayanna, she's thinking only one thing: hot summer
fling! Can a man planning forever and a woman
planning the moment find the right time for love?

*Coming the first week of January 2009
wherever books are sold.*

KIMANI™
ROMANCE

The next sexy title in
The Black Stockings Society miniseries by

Favorite author

DARA GIRARD

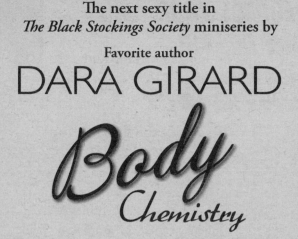

Body

Chemistry

Every good girl deserves to be a little bit wicked....

New Black Stockings Society member Brenda Everton has
excelled in a man's world at the expense of her personal life.
Now, pairing sexy black stockings with a sexy new attitude,
she's meeting with her ex-husband, Dominic Ayers, to find
out whether passion can strike twice....

THE **BLACK**
STOCKINGS
SOCIETY

Four women. One club.
And a secret that will make
all their fantasies come true.

*Coming the first week
of January 2009
wherever books are sold.*

KIMANI™
ROMANCE

REQUEST YOUR FREE BOOKS!

2 FREE NOVELS
PLUS 2 FREE GIFTS!

KIMANI ROMANCE ™

Love's ultimate destination!

KROM08R

THE EDGY SEQUEL TO *SINGLE MAMA DRAMA*

KAYLA PERRIN

This single mama's been through hell—her cheating
(and still married) fiancé is dead, her professional
reputation is in tatters, the man she really loves walked
out of her life and, worst of all, she's about to lose her
fabulous South Beach condo to a conniving witch.

But it ain't over yet....

SINGLE MAMA'S
GOT MORE DRAMA

"A writer that everyone should watch."
—*New York Times* bestselling author
Eric Jerome Dickey

*Available the first week of January 2009
wherever books are sold!*

www.MIRABooks.com

MIRA®

MKP2616

New York Times Bestselling Author

BRENDA JACKSON

invites you to continue your journey with the always sexy and always satisfying Madaris family novels....

FIRE AND DESIRE
January 2009

SECRET LOVE
February 2009

TRUE LOVE
March 2009

SURRENDER
April 2009

ARABESQUE®

www.kimanipress.com
www.myspace.com/kimanipress
